Sentenced to Christmas

MARSHALL THORNTON

KB

KENMORE BOOKS

One

GAGE

I HAD ONE JOB: Keep my mouth shut.

Or, at least, that's what my attorney told me as we were sitting down at the defense table. The courtroom was small and cramped, with low-pile carpeting, maple paneling on the walls, and fluorescent squares placed randomly across the low-slung ceiling. Most of the room was completely obliterated by Christmas decorations. Garlands circled the ceiling, strung with red glass ornaments and silver tinsel. There were bows, stars, mangers, shepherds, strings of flashing lights, carefully wrapped (and presumably empty) gifts, reindeer, many Santas (ranging from slightly husky to morbidly obese), elves and angels. Lots and lots of angels.

Taking it all in, I was relieved that we'd made a plea deal. Any judge who allowed this type of display in his courtroom was not going to look kindly on my case. I felt lucky the district attorney had agreed to restitution and probation.

"Do you know this judge?" I asked my attorney, Lonny Feldman. A nice but frazzled public defender in his mid-forties.

"I've heard things, but I've never appeared before him."

"What kind of things have you heard?"

"You don't want to know."

Just then, Assistant District Attorney Calvin Cutler walked in. He was somewhere in his mid-thirties, with sand-colored hair and gray eyes. Impeccably groomed, wearing a well-tailored charcoal suit that made his eyes stand out. He took an obvious pride in his appearance, which bordered on arrogance.

Setting his briefcase onto the prosecution table, he opened it, and took out a framed, five-by-seven photo of a woman and two small children. She was blonde with rosy cheeks and a gigantic smile. The children, a boy and a girl, looked happy too. The girl, who was nearly in her teens, wore glasses and held a smartphone in one hand—suggesting a negotiation had taken place to get her to stop looking at it long enough for the photo. The boy, who was six or seven, had a book tucked under one arm. Cal carefully positioned the photo to face the judge.

"What is that about?" I asked Lonny.

"I don't know. But I don't like it."

"He's obviously seeking some kind of advantage."

"It's a plea hearing, though. It's all decided. We're just here for a rubber stamp."

Just then, the door to the judge's chambers opened and in came the judge. The bailiff, who was dressed as an elf—a very tall elf—stood up and said, "All rise. The Honorable Dudley Winthrop presiding. Court is now in session."

Judge Dudley Winthrop was an angry-looking, red-faced, old man. His eyes were sharp and aggrieved. He glowered at the courtroom and then sat down. Something like a smile broke out on his face when he noticed Cutler's photograph.

"Ah, Mr. Cutler, your lovely family. Bring that up here."

The assistant DA picked up the photo and brought it to the judge, who took it and studied it closely.

"Tell me your wife's name again."

"Mary Ann."

"Lovely name. I like a woman with a little meat on her bones."

"I'll let her know."

Lonny stood up. "Your honor, this feels very prejudicial."

"This is your first appearance before me, isn't it Mr.—"

"Feldman."

"Do you have children, Mr. Feldman?"

"Three. But I don't see why—"

"Pictures?"

"You want to see pictures of my children?"

Judge Winthrop nodded enthusiastically. Lonny thought about it for a moment, then said, "Yes, of course." What else was he going to do? He took out his phone, and asked, "May I approach?"

"To show me pictures of your children? Absolutely."

Scrolling through the photos on his phone, Lonny walked up to the judge's bench. Finding the right shots, he held out his phone to the judge. The judge inspected the photos closely.

"Lovely family. Your wife's name?"

"Rachel."

"Biblical. Very nice. What kind of jersey is that on the youngest?"

"Soccer."

"Oh. Well. He's young. You'll have time to guide him toward real football."

"Probably not for us. My wife and I are concerned about traumatic brain injury."

"Nonsense. I played football at <u>MSU</u>. I was scouted, I was that good. Probably wouldn't have gone to law school if I hadn't been hit in the head one too many times."

My lawyer smiled weakly at him. Then the judge looked at his large elfin bailiff, and asked, "What is this again?"

"State vs. Gage Hammond, Your Honor. Plea hearing. An agreement has been reached."

"Oh yes, thank you." He began poking through the files in front of him.

Meanwhile, Cutler stood. "Your honor, in exchange for a guilty plea to fifth-degree arson the state has agreed to restitution of seven hundred dollars and two years' probation."

"Seven hundred dollars? What kind of structure is worth only seven hundred dollars?"

"It wasn't exactly a structure," Cutler hedged.

"Then what was it?"

"It was a Christmas tree."

"Young man, you set fire to a Christmas tree?" he asked me.

"It wasn't just a—"

Lonny put a hand on my forearm, then said, "Your Honor, I've advised my client not to speak per his Fifth Amendment right not to incriminate himself."

"He's pleading guilty. I don't see what difference it makes."

"Well, you haven't actually signed off on the deal. Your Honor."

"No, I haven't."

"So, I'm advising my client not to speak."

The judge rolled his eyes and said, "Lawyers." Then he turned to the assistant district attorney and said, "You. I assume there's evidence."

"Yes, of course. On the evening of December 5th, the forty-five-foot-tall Christmas tree in the parking lot of WRWG at 4250 Farm-to-Market Road right outside of Bellflower was set on fire, requiring two fire engines, one from Bellflower and the other from Masons Bay. The fire was quickly extinguished, having been contained to the Christmas tree with no damage to the WRWG building, parking lot or any vehicles present."

"And what evidence do you have against the defendant?"

"He confessed, Your Honor."

The judge raised an eyebrow. "Did he say why he set the Christmas tree on fire? Is this part of the war on Christmas?"

Biting my tongue, I elbowed my attorney who then jumped up and said, "With respect, Your Honor, the war on Christmas is not an actual thing."

"Given that a Christmas tree has been attacked, I beg to differ. Continue Mr. Cutler."

"No, Your Honor, no explanation was given. The defendant did not submit to questioning. He stated that he was responsible for the fire and then asked for an attorney."

The judge frowned deeply. "He confessed, then lawyered up. That seems contradictory. What other evidence do you have?"

"Um, well, none."

"None? No witnesses, security video, fingerprints on gas cans, soot on clothing, online statements of anti-Christian sentiment, known connections to Antifa—nothing?"

"Just the confession. The very brief confession."

Lonny stood up and said, "Your Honor, we've agreed to a plea bargain. None of this is necessary."

"I have to sign off on your agreement so, yes, it is necessary."

Just then, the door to the courtroom opened and in walked an overly polished man whom I recognized from, well, from everywhere. Jeff David Stickney, the main attraction at WRWG had been on radio, television, the internet and in print, decrying what had happened to the WRWG Christmas tree, which he called America's Christmas Tree—often with a salute.

"Is there something else you'd like to know, Your Honor?" Cutler asked. "Or can we move on?"

Ignoring him, the judge said, "Mr. Stickney, welcome to my courtroom. It's an honor—"

"Can I give a victim statement now? The press is waiting outside for me."

Which explained the eerie rumbling coming from the lobby.

"Oh, my," Judge Winthrop said. "Well, yes, I don't see why not. Now, why is the press outside?"

Cutler stood and said, "Judge Trilby barred the press after the arraignment. It was kind of a circus."

"That's ridiculous. I fully support freedom of the press. Well, some of it at least. Not the lying mainstream—"

Lonny stood. "Judge Trilby used the term bully pulpit."

"Your client refuses to speak, how can he be accused of bullying?"

"Not my client. Certain members of the press."

"Are you talking about that awful Leslie Stahl? If she's in my town again I'll have her—"

Cutler interrupted, "Your Honor, we can be done with this in ten minutes, less even. The state does not see a compelling reason to spend any more time on this matter. There are other matters far more pressing."

"Hhhhmmmmpfff," the judge said. "Very well. Give your statement, Mr. Stickney."

"Where should I stand?"

"Right there is fine," Judge Winthrop said. "We would have gotten you a podium if we'd been expecting you."

"That's fine, Your Honor," Stickney said. Then, after taking a deep breath, he bellowed: "What has been perpetrated upon me is domestic terrorism of the worst sort. The war on Christmas, which has been raging, raging I tell you, for *decades*, has reached a new low with this heinous attack! We will NOT stand for it, I tell you, we simply will NOT!"

"Hear, hear..." Judge Winthrop called out.

I cleared my throat loudly, making Lonny stand up, saying, "Your Honor, as I said before, there really is no such thing as a war against..."

The judge's glare made my attorney wilt. I couldn't believe it. This whole thing was getting worse by the minute. The judge looked like he wanted to give me the death penalty.

"And what about the ornaments, Your Honor?" Stickney asked.

"What about them?"

"The seven hundred dollars would reimburse me for the forty-foot tree shipped from Oregon, but there's no compensation offered for the ornaments. Not to mention my pain and suffering."

"Pain and—" Lonny began. "The publicity you've gotten has been priceless. You've been on a press tour for the last two weeks."

"We're not here to talk about what Mr. Stickney does on his own time," said the judge. "Mr. Cutler, what about these ornaments?"

"I'm sorry, but he has no receipts, no inventory, no actual proof that there were any ornaments on the tree. I assume there were, but they could have come from Good Will..."

"Ah-ha! I have a catalog," Stickney announced, waving one in the air. "They did not come from Good Will, they came from Ye Olde Christmas Eagle."

"I'd like to see that catalog, you may approach."

As Stickney made his way to the bench, I glanced over at Cutler. He didn't look any happier than we were. The judge took the catalog from Stickney, saying, "While you're up here —if you wouldn't mind—a few autographs for my grandchildren: Ted, Todd and Mercy. They're toddlers, but it's never too early to start teaching them right from wrong. Bailiff, would you get him something to write on?"

Judge Winthrop began to flip through the catalog. "I see you've marked which ornaments you purchased, very good. Oh my, yes... Santa Claus dressed as a patriot. Wonderful. Could I keep this? I'm already seeing things we'll need for next year."

I glanced at my lawyer; his mouth had fallen open.

"Of course, Your Honor," Stickney said. "You'll notice that twenty percent of each sale goes to my not-for-profit political action group to support the Christmas Warriors Fund."

"Oh my God!" I heard myself blurt. I hadn't known I was about to speak. The words just popped out and kept popping out. "How many times do we have to say this? There is no such thing as a war on Christmas! It's propaganda. It's lies. It's something right wing nut jobs like you talk about to raise money!"

The judge was hammering his gavel. "Mr. Feldman restrain your client! Immediately!"

Forcing me back into my seat, Lonny leaned over, and whispered, "No.1: Shut up. No. 2: Are you willing to raise the amount of restitution?"

I hissed back, "You know he started a GoFundMe and has raised over a hundred and fifty thousand dollars? They're talking about taking his show national. This is probably the best thing that ever happened to him."

"I know all that. But my job is to make sure this is not the worst thing that ever happened to you."

"Fine. Just get me out of here."

Lonny stood up. "Your Honor, my client would like to double the amount of restitution to fifteen hundred dollars."

"These ornaments are awfully expensive, and it was a very large tree," Judge Winthrop said.

"Two thousand dollars."

The judge looked at Stickney, and asked, "In the spirit of Christmas?"

With a grumble, he said, "If I must."

Cutler stood and said, "Great. We have a deal. Two thousand dollars and two years' probation. My office will correct the paperwork and get it over for you to sign, Your Honor."

"No so fast," Judge Winthrop said. Then the courtroom fell completely silent while we waited for the judge to continue. Finally, he said, "I have something to add to this plea deal."

My stomach churned like a cement mixer. My lawyer said, "Oh God," under his breath.

"Obviously, anyone who would burn down a Christmas tree does not understand the true meaning of Christmas. Therefore, I sentence you to spend the holiday with your counsel and his lovely family to learn the meaning—"

"Your Honor," Lonny said. "My family and I don't celebrate Christmas."

"For heaven's sake, why?"

"We're Jewish."

"But I thought... Don't they make those blue ornaments specifically for you people?"

"You people?" Lonny said under his breath and then cleared his throat. "It's true that some Jews celebrate the secular aspects of Christmas. We don't happen—"

"There's nothing secular about Christmas," Judge Winthrop said. "Mr. Stickney, is there any possibility you could—"

"No, Your Honor, absolutely not. You will not further traumatize me by forcing me to spend even a few minutes with this, this, vile—"

"All right, I get your point," Winthrop said. Then, he decreed, "Mr. Hammond, I sentence you to spend Christmas with Mr. Cutler and *his* lovely Christmas-celebrating family."

Cutler was already standing, but I could see his entire body tense. "Your Honor, that's... No. I would need to speak to the DA, and I don't know that it would be fair to my wi—"

"A man is the king of his castle, Mr. Cutler. Be the king of your castle."

"Uh, well... No."

"Uh, well, *yes*. Today is the 21st. In two days, the 23rd, you'll meet Mr. Hammond before noon and bring him to your home to spend the holiday. You'll be back in my courtroom on the 27th. Bailiff, is there room on my docket?"

"Your Honor," Cutler said, "I'm on your docket beginning January fourth and continuing for three months. I'm not sure... I mean, I have to prepare for trial. As you know, I'm prosecuting the Van Husen murder. There are dozens of boxes of discovery. Jury selection begins on January fourth."

"Was I speaking to you, Mr. Cutler?"

"No, Your Honor."

"Then be silent. Bailiff, is there room on the 27th?"

"I can move some things around." Clearly, the elf wanted this to be over. "How about two o'clock?"

"Mr. Hammond, on the 27th at two o'clock, you will return to my courtroom and provide me with a suitable meaning of Christmas. And I do mean suitable. If you're able to do that, I'll sign off on this ridiculous plea arrangement. But if you can't do that, you'll be going to trial. Does everyone understand?"

We grumbled. Then the judge smashed down his gavel.

Lonny looked at me and said, "You should have kept your mouth shut.

CALVIN

"WELL, SAY SOMETHING!" Danny Shepard, district attorney for Wyandot County screamed into the phone. Honestly, I'd been trying to say something for the last ten minutes, but he was too busy screaming at me. "How did you screw this up? I told you to make this go away as quietly as possible, and what have you done? You've made our office, *my* office, national news! Again!"

It was literally only a few hours since I'd left court and Danny had heard what happened all the way out in Colorado where he was skiing with his family. Meanwhile, I was huddled in my car with the engine running so I didn't freeze to death.

I considered defending myself. I mean, I didn't think this was all *my* fault. But I knew from experience, if Danny thought you were in the wrong, then you were in the wrong no matter how right you were.

I could have brought up any of the many ethical issues at play here, but since they didn't matter to Judge Winthrop, they were unlikely to matter to my boss. I said what he wanted to hear. "I'll fix it, Danny. I promise."

"You may have to take this one to trial just to make the judge happy."

"No, no, no, I can't do that. For one thing, there's barely any evidence. And for another, the Van Husen murder trial starts right after New Year's."

The Van Husen murder was the best case I'd been given since I took the job almost ten years ago. Murders in Wyandot County were few and far between. Most of the work I'd done during that decade was prosecuting people in trouble, poor people, people with addictions, people with mental illnesses, veterans with PTSD. People I actually felt sorry for.

But the Van Husen murder was every prosecutor's dream. Rupert Van Husen, a personal trainer and amateur body builder, had shot his much older, much wealthier wife when she tried to divorce him. Now he was claiming to be a victim of spousal abuse and that he shot his abusive wife because he couldn't see any other way out. A form of self-defense. To me, it was the perfect case, Van Husen was pure evil, and I was going to dismantle his defense and send him to prison for life. I couldn't wait.

And then Danny said the words I was dreading, "Look, I'm sorry, but if you can't handle this simple little case I may have to take the Van Husen murder away from you."

"No, no, you can't do that! Don't worry, I'm going to make the judge happy. All of this will be cleared up by end of day on the 27th. I guarantee."

"It had better be," he said, and hung up on me. I put the car in gear and drove half a block down the street.

Snow had fallen the night before, so the house looked like something you'd find on the front of a Christmas card. About a hundred and fifty years old, it was a perfect example of Victorian architecture, two and a half stories with a wrap-around porch. Gingerbread accents, peaked roof, tall windows, all painted in traditional colors: cream, eggplant and

Kelly green. Mary Ann's mother had given it to her a few years back, claiming that it was just too much work. And it probably was.

Still, it was a wonderful house. Located on Second Street in Bellflower, two blocks from the charming shopping district on main street. It had two parlors, a formal dining room, a kitchen with a breakfast nook *and* a butler's pantry. Upstairs were three bedrooms and very few closets, since two had been turned into a bathroom when indoor plumbing became all the rage. The attic had been converted into a bedroom perfect for a teenaged girl.

I pulled into the driveway behind Mary Ann's SUV. Remaining in the car, I took a moment and closed my eyes, trying to concentrate. How was I going to tell her a criminal would be spending the holiday with us? Actually, *tell* was the wrong word. I needed to *ask* if a criminal could spend the holiday with us. And, I needed to ask in such a way she couldn't say no.

I grabbed my briefcase and made my way up the carefully shoveled walkway to the house. In the summer, the porch was lovely: wicker furniture, hanging plants, a card table. Now everything was tucked away while snow drifted into the corners.

The door was unlocked. People in Bellflower don't bother much with locks. I let myself in, calling out, "Honey, I'm home."

"In the kitchen," Mary Ann replied. Christmas music wafted throughout the house. Dean Martin was letting it snow.

Taking off my winter coat, I carefully hung it on a hook by the front door and gave it a quick brush with one hand. Then, I walked through the main parlor, the dining room and into the well-appointed kitchen. I found Mary Ann at the extra-large breakfast nook, surrounded by several textbooks and a scattering of papers. She looked up at me and said, "Don't call me honey. It confuses the kids."

"Where are they?"

"Up in Piper's room."

"In the attic? Well, they didn't hear me up there."

"I wouldn't count on that. Sound carries in this house. The kids used to think I was psychic until they figured it out."

Time to change the subject. I wasn't going to win that argument.

"What *are* you doing?"

"Homework."

"Whose homework? Did you go back to school? You shouldn't be making decisions like that without your best friend's input."

"It's mostly Gus's, and one short essay for Piper."

"Why aren't they doing their own homework?"

"They get bored. It's just easier this way."

"Won't the teachers recognize your handwriting?"

She held up a sheet of paper, a fill-in-the-blank assignment. The answers were written in a childish, near-demented, scrawl. "It's taken years to perfect."

"That's what Gus's handwriting looks like?"

"Of course not. He has perfect penmanship. I let him do his own homework at the beginning of the school year and I got called in for a conference, accused of doing it for him. I have to do Gus' homework to avoid being accused of cheating."

"Why don't you just have your kids bumped up a grade or two?" Something I'd been wondering about for years.

"And lose the social advantages of being with children their own age?"

"Are you saying they have friends?"

"No. I'm saying it could happen. Any day now." She

pushed the homework away and stared me down. "Why are you here?"

"I have an enormous favor to ask. You know how I'm spending the holiday with you?"

"I haven't invited you."

"But you will. You always do."

"Do you want to come for Christmas?"

"Let me check my calendar—of course, I do. You're my best friend."

"Oh God, you want something. You've mentioned our friendship, twice in two minutes."

"Well, since you brought it up, I'm prosecuting this case. The activist who burned down America's Christmas Tree at WRWG."

"I've heard of that, but... I thought you were doing that murder case, the one with the abusive husband?"

"I am. I'm doing both. I almost had the arson case finished this morning. Plea deal, two years' probation, restitution."

"You know that case is all over the news. It's certainly the best thing that ever happened to that radio station."

"Yes, well... Danny gave me the case because he knew I could handle it. And I am; handling it."

"Danny gave you that case so it would blow up in your face and not his. Oh my God! It blew up in your face, didn't it?"

"I wouldn't say that, exactly."

"What happened?"

"As I said, we reached a plea deal and then the judge didn't like it, so he added the stipulation that the defendant learn the meaning of Christmas by spending the holiday with me and my little family."

"Wait. What?"

"The defendant, his name is Gage Hammond, he has to spend the holiday with us."

"No, you said you and *your* little family. How is that us?"

"You remember that portrait of you and the kids you had done last year after you and Douglas separated?"

"You mean, after he left me for a nineteen-year-old waitress from Buffalo Wild Wings? The one with the fake tits that I paid for? And the lovely veneers that I also paid—"

"Yes, that. Thank you for the extra details I already knew."

I had walked every step of her crumbling marriage with her and knew exactly what kind of scum bag Douglas was. Come to think of it, she owed me for that. I might be able to use it. Best to hold it in reserve, though. Don't want to play all my cards.

"Douglas and his little whore are spending the holiday in Aruba."

"Just to be the feminist in the room, it's really not the little whore's fault Douglas is an asshole."

She glared at me. "It's also not *not* her fault."

"Wouldn't the kids be with Douglas for the holiday if he were here? You get to spend Christmas with your kids!" I said, trying to find the bright side.

"I'm not so sure that's a good thing. I could have spent the holiday alone with a nice bottle of pinot."

Time to get back to me. "Anyway, the portrait..."

"Hold on, that disappeared six months ago. It used to be on the table in the front parlor."

"I borrowed it."

"You stole it is probably more accurate."

"You have your version, I have mine. Anyway, Judge Winthrop saw the photo—he compliments you every time he sees it."

"Wait, how does he see it? Isn't his office in one building and yours is in another?"

"Well, I put it on the prosecution table facing him."

"That is fine." He tightened his lips. "If that is all, Clara, I will depart for a bit. Hanging window dressings is quite wearying." He vanished.

I sighed. William's mood always seemed to change whenever I brought up the past. I guess I couldn't blame him. If something awful took place, there was no need to be reminded of it again and again. I spoke from experience. I was happy to forget the eight years I spent being married to Joe. Still, I couldn't help but wonder what that awful thing was that was plaguing William.

Bark!

I looked down at Boy, who was peering up at me through wisps of black-and-white hair on his snout. The blond wig lay squished under his little body.

"You're right. No need to dwell. Onward and upward!"

I placed the framed document on the table and finished bagging up the old shades, placing everything outside with the rest of the trash, which was beginning to pile up. I had no idea when garbage pickup was yet. There was much to learn. And many years of neglect to correct.

"Why, Ms. Clara, how are you today?"

Mr. Wiggins was standing in front of his house, all dressed up in a suit and tie. White strands of hair were neatly combed across the top of his age-spotted head. "Well, don't you look dapper, Mr. Wiggins."

He blushed slightly. "I'm having lunch with my great-grandson. He just started driving, you know. Nothing makes an old man feel older than all the young people around him moving on in years." He chuckled.

"Well, you're younger in spirit than most people I know, Mr. Wiggins."

"You are very kind." He motioned toward my trash. "How is the renovating coming along? A big job for one person."

Well, one person plus a friendly neighborhood ghost. "I don't mind it. It keeps me busy."

Mr. Wiggins nodded. I had always wondered how much he heard of the argument Joe and I had been having that night. He never mentioned it or asked me about him. Which was fine by me. *Rule Number Four: We don't talk about the past.*

A little boy was walking down the street with his parents. I could tell they were tourists because they were holding a map in their hands and checking the street signs.

"Halloween will be here soon," Mr. Wiggins said. "I know most people around here don't like it, but I like the noise and seeing Salem full of life every October."

The little boy's eyes opened wide when he got to the front of my house, and he pointed toward my windows. "Mommy, Mommy, a ghost!"

My insides froze. *He can see William?*

The boy's mom looked up. I was about to come up with some lie about early Halloween decorations when the mom smiled and picked up her son. "You see a ghost in there, sweetie?" She kissed him on the cheek.

A storm cloud passed over her face. "Are you telling me, I'm a beard? You're in the closet at work?"

"You know I hate that term. I'm not in *any* closet. I'm just... selectively discreet."

"That's closeted."

"Why should I give up the privileges afforded to White, Christian, heterosexual, cisgendered males just because I happen not to be *all* of those things?"

"Because it's scummy."

"I think it's radical. I'm taking what I'm entitled to."

"You're taking what we're *all* entitled to. And we're not *all* going to get it unless we're *all* honest about who we are."

"Said the woman doing her children's homework."

She scrunched her face at me and said, "There are antidiscrimination laws in this state. You are protected."

"Where did we meet?"

She knew perfectly well where we met. It was Torts, first year of law school. Like me, Mary Ann had a JD. She just never took the bar. She met Douglas and fell into the yawning pit of motherhood, from which she had yet to escape.

"I'm assuming there's a point to that question," she said.

"Yes. You know what the law is like. Antidiscrimination laws only prevent employers from *telling* you they're firing you because you're Black or a woman or gay or Jewish or old or whatever. They can easily find a pretext to fire you and they do."

"A pretext is still illegal."

"Yes, but very difficult to prove."

"You work for the government; they're not going to fire you for being gay."

"No. But they will fire me for not winning cases. You know perfectly well that half the judges up here are rabid homophobes who'd happily rule against me if they knew I was gay... All I do is let them assume otherwise."

"And by assume you mean you show them a photo of your wife and kiddies." And then something clicked for her. "That's not the first photograph that's gone missing. Oh my God, how long have you been doing this?"

"That's not the important thing. The important thing is that I consider you and the kids my family." I waited. Crickets. Finally, I said, "You're supposed to say it back."

"I might if you weren't trying to involve me in a scheme that means I have to teach my children to lie."

"Your children already know how to lie, trust me."

"I don't like the way you said that."

"You know perfectly well you can't teach children not to lie. All you can do is teach them when to lie and when not to lie. This is a perfect opportunity to teach them that lying for a friend is squarely in the when-to-lie column."

"All right, fine. It's just dinner, I'm sure we can get through that."

"Actually, it's a little more than dinner."

"How much more?"

"The afternoon of the 23rd through the morning of the 26th."

"Four days. FOUR DAYS!"

"Really more like three."

She looked at me as though I might be crazy. "No, absolutely not."

"It's my career on the line."

She shrugged. "You seem to think lying is such a great idea. Can't you lie your way out of this?"

"I suppose I could give you a deadly disease."

"Don't you dare. So this guy is supposed to spend four days with us—

"Really more like three."

"And then what? What's the point?"

"He has to stand up in front of the judge and give him a suitable meaning of Christmas."

"Peace on earth, goodwill toward man. Done."

"There's more to it than that. Judge Winthrop probably wants to hear something along the lines of Christianity being the best religion in the world, Jesus is White, Santa is too, the war on Christmas is real, throw in a dash of American exceptionalism, veiled racism, greed is good and God Bless America the most Christian country in the world."

"See, you know what the judge wants to hear. All you have to do is tell this person what to say and then you don't have to spend any time with him at all."

That might work, I thought. In fact, it was a very good idea. I wish I'd thought of it myself.

"Wow, you should have been a lawyer."

"Screw you, Cal."

It was meant as a compliment.

Three

GAGE

WHAT DO you wear to spend the holiday with your prosecutor? Honestly, I had no idea. And even if I did, I probably didn't own clothes like that. Most of my clothes came from thrift shops and clearance racks. I didn't look like I belonged on the same planet with Calvin Cutler, no less the same room.

My father and I were in the bedroom of my apartment, a mother-in-law's unit over an elderly couple's two-car garage. He stood by the window, peeking out, watching the street. He'd been peeking out windows my whole life, checking to see if he was being followed. I was almost certain he'd never been followed.

"I'm sorry I couldn't be at your trial the other day," he said. "But you know how I am about government buildings."

My dad, also known as Nate Hammond, was still handsome in his mid-sixties. Trim, with a full head of gray hair and dark, often suspicious, eyes. You might also say he had a few screws loose. You'd be right.

"It wasn't a trial," I pointed out. "It was a plea hearing. We reached a plea deal. We were expecting the judge to put a rubber stamp on it, but then he upended the whole thing by adding this ridiculous condition."

"They were talking about it online." And by online he meant the strange hidey-holes where he got information since anything remotely capitalist was deemed instantly evil. "That judge has no right to torture you."

"I wouldn't call it torture. It's just a few days with straight people."

"Mmmm-hmmm," he said, with great doubt.

I packed a couple of nice secondhand sweaters. I had no idea how well their house would be heated. And pajamas—though I rarely wore them at home. If their house caught fire, I didn't want to run around naked. God, I hoped their house didn't catch fire—I'd be blamed for that.

"This is all my fault," my dad said. "I'm sure they're trying to flush me out. Outstanding warrants."

"There are no outstanding warrants. That's why we hired a private detective last year. He did a search and found nothing."

"They got to him. We should have paid him more."

"Dad."

"I know, I know... I sound paranoid. But just because I'm paranoid doesn't mean they aren't out to get me."

That had been his mantra since I was a child.

"You know, there are things that went down in the eighties..."

He never actually said what things. He implied he'd been involved with radical left-wing causes, but that was more sixties than eighties. By the eighties the left had been pushed aside by khakis, deck shoes, pastel Polo shirts and the pleasures of corporate greed.

"I'm sorry you have to go through this," he said very seriously.

"It's just Christmas," I said brightly. "I'm sure I'll survive."

Actually, I knew exactly how I was going to survive. I'd already packed my tablet. I had eBooks, audiobooks, old episodes of *The West Wing*, Netflix and Candy Crush. All I needed was their wi-fi password and I could basically ignore them for the entire holiday.

What I didn't know was what I was going to say on the 27th. Lonny promised to draft a statement he thought the judge might accept and I might actually be able to read—a very narrow window. I was skeptical but knew we were going to have to come up with something. I certainly didn't expect to learn anything new about Christmas from the Cutlers.

"Did you call your mother? Let her know..."

"No. I'll call her on Christmas Day. I'm bringing my phone. And my tablet. I'm sure I'll be given some privacy. Probably lots of privacy. The assistant DA didn't seem any more excited about this than I am."

"What's he like? Good-looking?"

"Don't go there, Dad."

"Just because I am regrettably heterosexual, doesn't mean I can't appreciate a good-looking man. Not to mention, I'm your dad. I want to see you hook up with hot, thirst-trapping studs. As many as you want. As often as you want. Construction workers, cowboys, pizza delivery guys."

"You've been watching gay porn again, haven't you?"

"I still don't get it."

"You don't have to get it. It's okay to be straight."

"It's nice of you to say that. Do you have your toothbrush? Do you know if they've got a guest room? Or will you have to sleep on the couch?"

"I don't know. He's just an assistant prosecutor, they don't make that much, so I'm not expecting anything grand."

"Doesn't seem fair making you sleep on someone's sofa for the holiday. That's hardly the Christmas spirit."

"It's fine. I just need to get through the next few days and this will all be over."

"Except for the probation."

"I think I can manage not to set fire to anything for the next two years." I zipped up my duffle bag and said, "I think I'm ready."

"Okay, let's go."

Outside my apartment, my dad's RV sat waiting. It was older than I was. The front half was a Chevy van, beige, with a replacement door on the passenger side in army green. The back half was basically a travel trailer with a small loft hanging over the driver's compartment.

I climbed in and threw my duffle into the back. The bucket seat could spin around and double as a recliner. I tried not to look at the way my dad lived. The van was messy, nothing was put away. I mentally prepared myself for a very noisy ride. Fortunately, it wasn't far.

We were a few blocks from my apartment, when my dad asked, "Do you want me to get you a new identity, just in case you need to go underground?"

"No thanks."

"I still know a very good document forger."

"I'll keep it in mind."

We hit a pothole and everything behind me shook and clattered.

"Where are you parking this thing?"

"I'd rather not say."

"I should know where you're living. Or parking. Whichever. I promise not to write it down."

"It's better you not know."

"It's actually not better I not know. What if something happened to you?"

"That's what I'm trying to avoid."

I gave up. We'd been having some version of this conversation for years. I never won. It wasn't impossible that some government agency somewhere was keeping an eye on my father. They'd certainly kept track of others equally as innocent.

"I know you're worried about me," he said. "I'm worried about you, too. You do too much for other people, and not enough for yourself."

"Thanks Dad. Is that your Christmas gift?"

It wouldn't be the first time I'd gotten nothing but a bit of advice.

"Whenever you're alone, look for listening devices and hidden cameras. This could all be a ruse to see if they can't catch you doing something much bigger than burning down a Christmas tree."

"I'm not doing anything..."

"That doesn't mean they won't invent something."

I bit my tongue. Despite my upbringing, I've never been a believer in conspiracy theories primarily because people are big blabbermouths. Two or three people might be able to keep a secret. Five at the most. But that's about it. Any conspiracy that would require dozens or more people to keep a secret was just hard for me to believe. One of them was going to blab. It's just human nature.

I didn't say any of that to my dad. I'd said it before. And as much as I wanted to say it all again, I kept my mouth shut. We were almost to the coffee shop, when he said, "This reminds me of dropping you off at summer camp."

"Oh yeah, good old Camp Wannashare."

"Nothing like a progressive liberal arts summer camp to teach a teenager the fallacy of trickle-down-economics."

"Yeah, we did a musical about that."

"Oh, I bet it was good. Sorry I wasn't able to make it. A life of activism has its challenges."

"It's okay." Then I said, "You don't need to park, I'm just going to jump out. I'll see you in four days."

"Fight the good fight."

"Thanks Dad. I love you, too."

Then I jumped out of the RV and onto the sidewalk.

Drip was a local institution that had been there at least twenty-five years. It had gone through several ownership changes and at least five makeovers. Most recently, the storefront had been gutted and painted Tom Sawyer white with black pipes on the ceiling and plastic lawn furniture.

Looking around, I saw that I had gotten there first. I ordered an almond milk latte and took a seat in the back. I took out my phone and watched a short video I'd already seen a half dozen times. Jeff David Stickney outside the courtroom after the sentencing. He was surrounded by a small group of reporters. Wisely, Lonny had gotten the bailiff to take us out the back.

In the video, Stickney was saying, "...I call on Congress to begin an investigation into the war on Christmas. I call on them to allocate funds for us to fight this war. And, I call on them to provide the assistance of the National Guard as needed."

That was the point where I clicked the mute button every time. How did people take this guy seriously? But they did, that was obvious from the comments. Most of which were supportive, though some did ask the obvious question, "Is this a joke?"

I'd been lucky with the publicity so far. There had not been a lot of pictures of me. Really just one. My high school graduation picture. At the time, I'd had a giant mop of hair. In fact, I usually had giant mop of hair. It was kind of my thing. But I'd had to buzz it all off so people didn't recognize me. I looked like I was AWOL from the Marines.

I looked up to see that Cutler had arrived. He saw me,

scowled for a moment, then went to the counter and ordered just a regular coffee. That made me wonder if he was in a hurry to get out of there. I clicked off my phone and waited.

He wore a sleek, tan trench coat over a dark blue suit that flattered him. On his feet, he wore a gorgeous pair of mahogany penny loafers. As he paid for his order, he took off a pair of thin, leather gloves. When his coffee was poured, he walked over, put on a big, fake smile, and said, "Technically, we haven't met. You can call me Cal."

He held out his hand. I shook it. The handshake was warm and comfortable, and seemed to go on for a moment too long—but I was probably being paranoid. That often happened after I spent time with my father.

We sat down and, as instructed by my lawyer, I slid a piece of paper in front of him. "Please sign."

An offended look passed over his face, but then he banished it. He read the document over quickly.

"Hmmmm... Nothing you say over the holiday can be used against you in court. Kudos to Lonny, it's like the opposite of a Miranda warning."

With a bit too much flair, he signed it.

"Thank you," I said. "You can call me Gage."

"Gage. That's a real soap opera name."

"It's my mother's maiden name."

He shrugged, as though that were almost a good excuse for my overly dramatic name. I brushed that aside and said, "I'm curious, why was the plea deal so good? You could have gotten a lot of votes throwing the book at me."

"I'm not the one who needs votes. I'm not an elected official. That's my boss. It's a purple county, so he calculated he'd lose as many votes as he'd gain. Possibly more. He handed me the case and said make it go away."

"You could have dropped the charges, that would have made it go away."

"With a bang, yes. But we want this to go away with a whimper. We want people to forget it ever happened."

"I think the judge made that impossible."

"His ruling has generated some press, I'll grant you that, but it will calm down once there's some actual news to compete with. After Christmas it should fade away completely. I think we've gotten it under control."

"Is that the goal? To keep this under control?"

"Of course. Your goal was to create chaos. My goal is to control that chaos."

"You don't know what my goal was. You don't get to decide what other people think and feel."

"You're very unpleasant, aren't you?"

"Funny, I was about to say the same thing about you."

After a slight pause, he said, "So, cards on the table. You don't like me, I don't like you. The thing is, we don't really need to spend the holiday together. We'll just tell the judge we did. All we really need to do is figure out what the judge wants to hear and then give him that."

"Really? As an officer of the court you're suggesting we lie to the judge?"

"Don't be naïve. We'd hardly be the first. It's not uncommon when an order is this extreme."

"Lonny thought you might suggest that."

"Ah, so you've already thought about it. Great. Why don't we talk through what you might say on the 27th."

"Sorry, we're going to have to follow the judge's order to the letter."

"In case you didn't notice, the judge is, with respect, a whack job."

"Which didn't stop you from trying to gain an advantage. Putting out that picture of your family; you should be ashamed."

"I have every right to be proud of my family."

"That's not what I meant and you know it."

"Look, it will be fine if we don't do this. If something goes wrong, I'll take full responsibility."

Seriously, he wanted me to trust him? I didn't know him from Adam, and what I did know... Well, no. I wasn't going to trust him. "Lonny advised me against the idea and what he had to say made a lot of sense."

"What did he say?"

"If the judge even suspects we didn't follow his order, you might be fined for contempt. I, on the other hand, would probably go immediately to trial. A jury could, and would, send me to prison for five years."

"I could be fined a thousand dollars for contempt."

"Yeah, five years. Five."

"I can almost guarantee you that's not going to happen."

"It's the 'almost' that's a problem."

"What if we cut it back to just dinner?"

"Should I be offended? You really don't want to do this, do you?"

"Please don't take it personally. It's not about you."

"Except it's all about me, isn't it?"

He looked very unhappy for a moment, and then said, "I need a muffin. Can I get you another—"

"Almond milk latte."

"Great."

He got up and went over to the counter. He was stalling; I could tell. He was going to come back and have another go at me. I tried to imagine the argument he'd use. He could tell me his wife didn't want their kids around a criminal. Not a very strong argument; it was doubtful I'd be spending time alone with them. He could decide they suddenly had to leave town for the holiday to see relatives. I'd suggest he call and update the judge, which would likely end up with my going on a road trip with them.

Nope, I was pretty sure he was stuck with me. When he came back, he set my latte in front of me—he'd switched to a coffee drink as well—and said, "If we have to spend the holiday together, I suppose we should get to know each other. Tell me about yourself."

I wasn't expecting that. It was some kind of angle, I was sure. I didn't know what it was, but I wasn't going to fall for it.

"You have a whole file on me. I doubt there's anything you don't already know."

"I'd rather hear it from you."

"Actually, I'd rather hear it from you. Tell me what you already know about me."

"Fine. You're the director of NorthStar, which is a drop-in center for queer and questioning youth. Your salary is barely above poverty-level, you went to U of M—on scholarship—and got a degree in social work with a minor in LGBTQ... whatever, studies. You've had a string of roommates, none of whom lasted more than a year, which suggests they were more than just roommates and that it's romantic relationships you're not good at rather than friendship relationships or relationships in general. Your parents are divorced and have been for a very long time. You have a sister who lives with her husband in Arizona. She's active in the Republican Party, which makes her the black sheep. You don't have an arrest record, but both your parents do."

"Wow, in less than sixty seconds you've managed to sneer at my job, my education, my community, my relationships and my family. Kudos to you."

"That wasn't—" He stopped, tamped down his anger, and thought for a moment. "Your turn. Did you Google me?"

"No. I didn't have the slightest idea who you were until a few weeks ago and I'm looking forward to having no idea who you are in the near future."

"You must at least be curious."

"Not really. I only have to take one look at you. You come from an upper middle-class family, you got a very expensive private school education, if it's Ivy League you went as a legacy. Your grades were always good but never great. Your parents gave you your first car—one they bought new for themselves and gave to you when it was a few years old rather than trade it in. It was very suburban, possibly a minivan. The fact that you happily drove it made you feel like you weren't an elitist snob. You rushed a second-tier fraternity and got in. You met your wife in your sophomore year. You married between undergrad and law school. You went to a so-so law school, which has a lot to do with how you ended up stuck in Wyandot County. That and the fact that straight, White, cisgender men do very well up here."

"None of that is true," he said in a small enough voice that I knew it was right on the money.

"Go ahead," I said.

"Go ahead what?"

"You're going to ask me again to ignore the judge's order. That's why you were fishing around in my personal life. Looking for a wedge. I don't have a boyfriend. Locally there's just my dad and yes, I would like to see him on Christmas Day. And then there are the kids at NorthStar, I would really like to be available to them."

"So, you'll do it? We can just go home?"

"Absolutely not. As I said, we're doing this to the letter."

Clearly angry, he abruptly stood and said, "I need to make a call. To... my wife. I may not have explained things clearly to her."

Then he turned around and walked out of the coffee shop. I could see him through the window with his phone to his ear. He paced as he spoke. He started gesturing a lot.

He was exactly the kind of straight guy I hated. Privilege

hung around him like an aura. Most people couldn't see it, but we all knew it was there. What bothered him most was not that we'd have to spend the holiday together, but that I'd thwarted him. I'd said 'no.' People like Calvin Cutler didn't hear 'no' often.

Finally, he came back into the coffee shop. When he got back to the table he didn't sit down. He seemed to be formulating his thoughts, so I said, "I'm sorry that this is a problem. I wouldn't force myself on you if it weren't keeping me out of prison."

"I get it. It's okay. It's not you. It's me."

"Are you breaking up with me?" I joked.

"What? Why would you say something like that?"

"'It's not you. It's me.' Classic breakup line. Sorry, I was just trying to lighten the mood."

He stared at me for a moment and then burst out laughing, "Right. That's funny. So, do you want me to bring you to your car... or can you leave it..."

"My dad dropped me off."

"Okay, that works... It's, uh, time to pick up the kids. My kids. My two children. Yay."

Four

CALVIN

"MARY ANN, you have to do this for me," I told my friend as I paced outside the coffee shop, phone to my ear.

"No, I don't."

"You owe me. I was there for you when Douglas dumped you." Yes, I played that card. It didn't feel good.

"I—"

I could tell she wanted to counter that. But there was no counter. She did owe me, and she knew it.

She said, "It's really not fair for you to bring that up."

"I know. I feel horrible."

"You were a good friend to me. Now you're being a shitty friend."

"I know. I feel horrible."

"You realize this could seriously damage our friendship."

"I know. I feel horrible."

"If I do this for you, we're even. You can never use the 'I was there for you when you got dumped' card again. Are you sure you want to use it now?"

I took a moment. She had a point; I could save this 'debt' for later. But for what? I led a law-abiding life, that came with my job. I would never need her as an alibi. I would never borrow money from her—that would be too, too humiliating. And it was unlikely that I'd need her to pretend to be my wife again. Well, hopefully not.

"Yes, I want to use it now," I said, resolutely.

I am aware that part of being a good friend is supporting them in a time of crisis and never asking for anything in return. And I wish I could have been that good friend. I knew I was being a bad friend and felt guilty about it—at least until Mary Ann said, "I need you to pick up the kids."

"What? No. I can't do that, they don't know what's going on. You need to explain it to them—"

"No, you can do it. It's fine."

"It's not fine. You pick them up, you explain what they have to do, and then I'll bring this guy over in an hour or two."

"Really? You're my fake husband for less than thirty seconds and you're already refusing to do your share? Typical male."

"You're seriously going to make me do this?"

"Yes, I'm very serious."

"Fine. I'll pick up the kids. Tell me what to say to them so they'll pretend I'm their dad."

"Oh Cal, you can figure that out. Parenting is easy. Or at least everyone who's never done it tells me so."

"That's not fair."

"No, it's not—but then none of this is. See you in an hour." And then she hung up.

I walked back into Drip, back toward Gage Hammond. I wondered what people thought of us sitting together. He didn't look like someone I'd know. His hair was buzzed and looked more like a five o'clock shadow than a hairstyle. Something about it made his eyes seem enormous. They were a velvety brown, so dark they were almost black.

He wore a vintage jacket, from the seventies I think, Levi on the outside and some kind of fake lamb's wool lining. Beneath that he wore a black turtleneck, which he must have ordered online; I hadn't seen one in a store in years. On his feet were a pair of gigantic winter boots—as though he was expecting two to three feet of snow. Possible, but not without warning if you had a decent weather app.

On the lapel of his jacket was a large rainbow pin—the kind with all the extra colors, a vintage ACT UP pin, and a red ribbon (so retro). He was exactly the kind of gay guy I couldn't stand. He wore his gayness on his sleeve like a badge of honor. He made sex political, which in my opinion made sex dull. He was very... in your face.

When I got back to the table, I stood there for a moment wondering if I should simply run. Then he apologized for the situation.

"Don't worry, it's not your fault."

He made some kind of joke that I did not get. Then he tried to explain it, which only made it worse. I laughed, mainly so we could stop talking about it.

"You drove?" I asked.

"No, my dad dropped me off."

"That makes things easier. It's time to pick up my kids."

* * *

Things in Wyandot County are booming. The population is growing, houses are going up left and right—but there's no end in sight to the housing shortage, so the whole thing is kind of its own little gold rush. Weirdly, or perhaps not so weirdly, most of the population growth is people of retirement age— many buying second and even third homes. Which means that even with the population growth the number of children going to Bellflower High School is shrinking.

Bellflower Elementary, Bellflower Middle School and Bell-flower High School are all located in the same sprawling one-story complex. I say sprawling, but in reality the whole thing is smaller than an IKEA. Not that there's an IKEA within three hundred miles. And not that I wouldn't rather be going to IKEA.

Gage and I pulled up in front of the school. The ride had been a bit uncomfortable. We'd chatted a little about my five-year-old Prius—it didn't fit his image of what a prosecutor would drive.

"I can believe in law and order, and still do my part to save the environment."

"If you really wanted to do your part for the environment, you'd have an all-electric vehicle with a home solar charger."

For a moment, I wished my Prius came with the option of an ejector seat. I'd have loved to shoot him through the roof. Unfortunately, that wasn't one of the options. What pissed me off the most was that he was basically right. I'd bought the used Prius primarily because in the long run it would save me a lot on gas, and in a world where gas prices regularly jumped from a couple bucks to five and back again, it mattered. Partic-ularly on my salary.

"I'll be right back," I said, not wanting him to come with me. I needed to talk to the kids alone. Somehow, I had to convince them to call me Dad and go along with this whole crazy mess I'd gotten myself into.

There weren't many kids waiting to be picked up. The school had about ten buses which picked up and delivered kids from the furthest reaches of the district. Mary Ann's house wasn't far from the school, so there was no bus. In point of fact, the kids could walk home if they wanted to. Mary Ann would never allow that. Like most parents of our generation, she'd seen too many episodes of *Dateline* to ever let her chil-dren walk anywhere alone.

I saw them as they came out of the main entrance. Piper was just on the cusp of becoming a woman—though if you asked her, she'd say she was already there. She looked like her dad: tall and angular with nicely proportioned features. She was reading something on her phone while holding her brother's hand.

Gus was around seven, eight, six? I couldn't remember. Small for his age whatever it was, he took after his mother with round cheeks and a tiny little belly. Last year the teacher had wanted him to play Santa Claus in the holiday play. Mary Ann refused, even though it meant the holiday play didn't happen.

Piper looked up and saw me, and as soon as she was near asked, "What are you doing here?"

"I'm here to pick you up."

"Who's the guy in the car?"

"I need to talk to you about him."

"He's not your boyfriend. Mom said you're not the boyfriend type."

"No, he's not my boyfriend, and I'm going to have to have a talk with your mom about that comment... Listen, we're going to play a game of pretend. The judge in the trial I'm prosecuting has asked that I bring home the defendant— the guy in the car—to have Christmas with my family. So we're going to pretend that you're my family, which you kind of are, and that I'm your dad and your mom is my wife."

They looked very confused. I couldn't blame them.

"You mean, lie," Piper said.

"Our dad's in Aruba," Gus said. "You want us to say you're in Aruba?"

"It's okay to lie for a friend. And no, I'm not in Aruba."

"No, it's not okay," Piper said. "There's this girl in my class named Cher. She stole Ricky Pulver's dessert at lunchtime. I thought she might be my friend if I lied and said she didn't do it. But then we both got into trouble. And she's still not my friend."

Wow, she was good.

"Well, okay, your story is really more about stealing than lying, and no, it's not okay to steal." I said a silent prayer that I would not have to ask her to steal in the next four days. "This whole thing is okay with your mom. I talked to her about it and you're not going to get into trouble."

She narrowed her eyes at me. "So, defendant? You mean criminal?"

"He's a criminal?" Gus jumped in.

"He's not a bad criminal, per se. We're talking misdemeanor. Practically a parking ticket."

"What did he do?"

"He burned down a Christmas tree."

"Was it his Christmas tree?" Gus asked.

"Well, no. It's not illegal to burn down your own Christmas tree. Unless you submit an insurance claim. Or you do it in the house and the house burns down and then you submit—If you take your Christmas tree to a well-ventilated, secure area you can legally burn it down."

They seemed thoroughly stymied by what I'd just said. "Look, can you just do this for me, your Uncle Cal—I mean, call me Dad, your Dad."

Piper shrugged.

"Can I call you Uncle Dad?" Gus asked.

"No, that doesn't work. He has to believe I'm your real dad. My job depends on it. My whole world depends on it. And, yes, I can see that this is a perfect example of why you shouldn't tell lies, but I did tell a lie and now we all need to lie to cover it up. Does that make sense?"

Gus was looking at me, slightly frightened. Piper stepped in and said to her brother, "Just call him Dad, okay?"

"Okay."

Nervously, I walked them to the car. This wasn't going to work, this wasn't going to work, oh my God, this wasn't going to work... meanwhile, Gage got out of the car and stood next to it.

"Kids, this is Gage," I said. Oh crap, should I have had them call him Mr. Hammond? Out of respect? No, wait, as Piper pointed out, he was a criminal. He didn't deserve respect.

He told them it was nice to meet them and asked their names. Piper looked up from her phone briefly. Gus asked, "Why did you burn down a Christmas tree?"

"That's a little complicated. Let's just say it seemed like a good idea at the time."

Gus had no idea what to make of that.

"Okay," I said. "Time to go home."

"Uh-no," Piper said.

"What do you mean? No?"

"Uh, *Dad*, we need to go Christmas shopping for Mom. Don't you remember?"

"Of course, I remember—"

"He always forgets," Piper said to Gage.

"Does it have to be today? You and I could slip out tomorrow afternoon."

"I'm not shopping on Christmas eve. I'm old enough to know that's a bad idea."

"Okay," I said, and then we all got into the car. I drove us to the Greater Bellflower Mall which was only a ten-minute drive, most of which was driven in silence—which meant it felt like an hour.

How was I going to do this? I had to convince this guy I was straight, married and a father of two. So what kind of straight guy was I? Was I the kind who said, man and dude and bro all the time? Could I maintain that for four days?

Probably not. Plus, we'd been together for half an hour and I hadn't used any of those words. Probably already too late.

I was definitely the kind of straight guy who liked to dress nice. What did they used to call that? Metro... sexual? I was a metrosexual heterosexual. I was definitely not the kind who liked sports or mowing the lawn or Bruce Willis movies or hitting on girls just because they were there.

Gripping the wheel tightly, I tried to calm myself. The best way to do this was to be myself; and occasionally mention how much I like vaginas. That was it. That would be my entire impersonation of a straight man. It worked at the office. The judges believed I was straight. And my boss, Danny, thought... I don't know what he thought. I didn't use the photo trick with him, but we'd also never talked about anything personal. I mean, I knew he had a wife and kids, they were part of his campaigns. I never mentioned a wife and kids because I didn't have to campaign, and I didn't... Oh God, he knew. He had to know. Why did that never occur to me before?

Finally, finally, finally, I pulled into the mall's parking lot. Like a lot of malls in America, this one was failing, and even at Christmas there was ample parking, short lines to checkout and lots and lots of inventory.

As we walked from the car, the kids were way in front of us. I had to say something. I couldn't keep not talking to this guy. But what should I say? "So, if you weren't with us for the holiday what would you be doing?"

"Attending a Black Mass and then roasting a child for Christmas dinner. Chestnut dressing. Family tradition."

"Ha-ha. I didn't ask what Judge Winthrop thinks you'd normally be doing for the holiday. I asked what *you* would be doing."

"Didn't we kind of talk about this already?"

I guess we had, and not in a very nice way.

"You mentioned being with the kids at NorthStar. Do you do something specific?"

He glanced at me, not trusting me, before saying, "We have an event on Christmas Eve afternoon. A lot of the kids are still with their families, so we do an event so they can connect with their community before facing what is for many of them a challenging holiday."

That was a road I didn't want to go down, so I asked, "And the rest of the holiday?"

"Christmas morning I Facetime my mother, and then I host my annual misfits Christmas dinner for anyone who has nowhere to go. At some point, I see my dad."

"You mean anyone LGBT…" I stumbled. "I know there's more, but I don't know what they are."

"Anyone can come. Any letter. Even H."

"H? What's H?"

"Heterosexual."

"Oh. Well. I'm sorry the judge threw a wrench into your plans."

"Are you? You're not without blame, you know. You could have slow-walked the deal and we'd be doing this in January or… you could have just dropped the charges entirely."

And then, thankfully, we were in the failing anchor store whose name I won't mention out of respect for the nearly dead. The kids were waiting for us at the front, which was jewelry and perfumes. Piper looked up from her phone and said, "Dad, you forgot to give me my allowance this week."

"Your mother didn't give it to you?" Already I was grinding my teeth.

"Oh, no… she forgot."

"So, when I ask her, she'll say she forgot?"

"Probably. Unless she forgot she forgot. You know what she's like."

Grudgingly, I took my wallet out. Of course, I had no idea

how much a twelve-year-old got for an allowance. I tried a twenty, thinking I was being generous. She gave me a disparaging look. I gave her another twenty.

"Gus, did I forget to give you your allowance, too?"

After a glance at his sister, he reluctantly said, "Mom gave it to me."

My heart sank. This would all boil down to a loyalty test for the little fellow and I was already hating that.

"Here, have an extra ten," I said, giving him two fives.

"I think Mom would like some jewelry," Piper said. "You should get her something."

"I've already gotten your mother a gift."

"No, you haven't," she said confidently. Mainly because she was right. While I'd spent the last few Christmases with them I always arrived well after gift giving, so a card and a bottle of wine was always enough. "I think she's expecting something big this year anyway. Like jewelry."

"No, I remember your mom saying specifically that she didn't want jewelry." Totally a lie, but hardly my first of the day.

"That's one of those things moms say but don't mean. You really should get her jewelry."

I was pretty sure I knew where this was coming from. She'd been texting her mother. I didn't think for a minute Mary Ann wanted jewelry from me, but clearly she wanted me to spend a lot of money. She wanted her pound of flesh, or at least her pound of credit card charges at twenty-nine percent interest.

"How about perfume?" she suggested.

"That might work." Given the gleam in her eye, I added, "Nothing too expensive."

"But nothing cheap," she said back to me with a smile. And then she walked away.

Gus was standing next to me. I could tell he wanted to go

with his sister, but he already knew that boys weren't supposed to want to go to the perfume counter.

Gage had heard most of our exchange, so I shouldn't have been surprised when he asked, "Twelve going on thirty?"

I smiled and said, "Kids. Can't live with them, can't sell them on the black market."

He winced and said, "You know, I've heard of people doing exactly that."

So had I for that matter.

"Yes, sorry, bad joke. I must be nervous."

"About what?"

"Having a stranger around. No offense."

"None taken." He watched me a moment, seeming to reassess. Maybe he didn't think I was as big a jerk as he did at the coffee shop. And I wasn't. Normally.

Meanwhile, Gus slipped his hand in mine. I'd almost forgotten he was down there. I looked at him for a moment, and then asked, "What do you want to get your mom?"

"Chocolate."

"Well then, let's go find some chocolate."

We wandered around the store looking for the boxed chocolate. It would be in one of the aisles. Not that I had a lot of experience shopping during the holidays. But I had made the mistake of trying to buy dress shirts in December one year.

"So, how did you and your wife meet?" Gage asked. He had reassessed. Unless... I couldn't tell. Did he have an ulterior motive? Or was he sincerely trying to get to know me?

Stick to the truth as much as possible, I told myself, it's easier. "We met in law school. Mary Ann is from Bellflower. My aunt has a summer home on Lemon Lake, so I was familiar with the area from visits as a kid. My aunt's house is an old chalet my grandfather built on weekends. It's too hot in the summer and too cold in the winter, poorly insulated, drafty, moldy, mice running through the ceiling. Sometimes I wonder how I can stand to live there. But it's cheap."

Gage looked confused. Oh, crap, I'd stuck too close to the truth. I'd slipped into my standard description of where I lived.

"You live there with your family?"

"Well, no. We live there in the summertime for a few weeks. Most of the time we live in Bellflower. We have a house on Second. Are you from the area?"

"You already know the answer to that, remember?"

"I'd still rather hear it from you." Mainly because if he was talking, I wasn't screwing up.

"When I was a kid we bounced around a lot, mostly the UP, sometimes even Canada, although I don't think we were ever legally in Canada. Anyway, college was kind of a shock. I'd never lived anywhere with that many people. Afterward, I was looking for something a little more rural, though not completely empty. Eventually, I ended up here."

"You mentioned your dad. He lives with you?"

"Not exactly. He lives off the grid."

I knew that, of course. So I said, "That must be hard on you."

"Me? No. It's fine. I'm used to it."

"Chocolate!" Gus yelled. He ran a few feet ahead of us to a six-foot tall display of boxed chocolate.

"What kind do you think she'd like?" I asked.

The boy looked a bit overwhelmed. There were so many flavors: milk chocolate, dark chocolate, mint in both milk and dark, sea salt caramel dark chocolate, white chocolate raspberry, dark chocolate raspberry and a sampler box.

I was about to suggest the sampler when Piper had caught up to us. "I need your credit card."

"No, you don't. I gave you forty dollars."

"Not for me. I'm getting some perfume for Mom, from you. It's Fucking Fabulous."

"Um, you need to watch your mouth, young lady," I said reflexively. It did bring me up short, though. I'd been a parent for less than fifteen minutes and I already sounded like my father.

"I can say it. That's the name of the perfume. Fucking Fabulous by Tom Ford."

"Oh," I said, with a look to Gage.

"What? You think because I'm gay I know all about women's perfume?"

"No, I didn't... I just... I know who Tom Ford is," I ended defensively. Reluctantly I took out my Visa. I had about six hundred dollars in available credit, so I didn't expect a problem.

"Here," I said to Piper. "Make sure they wrap it."

"This one," Gus said as his sister walked away. The box he was holding was white chocolate raspberry.

"Okay, we have a winner," I said. I really wanted to get out of there, but I wasn't sure if Piper had a gift for her mother. I made an executive decision and grabbed a box of dark chocolate mint to go with Gus' choice.

"Do you see a cashier?" I asked Gage.

"Over that way."

As we walked over, Gage said, "Your kids are great."

"Yes, they are," I said, because what else would a father say. Of course, everyone says kids are great—they have to be throwing tantrums or actively committing felonies to get people to say anything else. And even then...

I put the chocolate on the counter with the last of my cash. While we were being rung up, my phone beeped. I'd gotten a text. When I looked, I saw it was from Visa telling me that my card was over the limit by $24.93. They'd gone ahead and covered the charge but asked that I make a payment as soon as possible.

"Fucking Fabulous," I said under my breath.

Five

GAGE

I DID MEAN it when I said his kids were great. And why shouldn't they be? They come from a middle-class home with two actively engaged parents. Most of the kids I saw at the drop-in center were nowhere near as privileged. Many of them had housing issues, educational issues, food insecurity—and a bunch of other problems. Which didn't mean they weren't great. It just meant they had to fight a lot harder to achieve it, and they had a lot of trouble seeing it for themselves.

We left the mall and drove the short distance to Second Street where the Cutler house was. So, yeah, it was a surprise. Their house is an older, grand home on probably the best street in Bellflower. Cal could not have afforded it on his salary. There had to be family money. Oh, and he mentioned they had access to a vacation home. Yup, definitely family money.

The kids ran ahead while we got my bag out of the trunk. Also in the trunk were four... bankers boxes, I think they're called. Cal took out a collapsible dolly, stretched it open, then set three of the boxes onto it.

"Do you need help?" I asked.

"I got it."

"What is all that?"

"My next case. I'm going to need to spend some time prepping."

"I don't suppose you can talk about it."

"Not really."

Something told me he *could* talk about it; he just wasn't going to with me. Tilting the hand truck, he shut the trunk and we walked up the driveway.

"What about your parents?" I asked. "Will they be here for Christmas dinner?"

"Oh. I lost my parents years ago."

That was an odd turn of phrase. When people use it, I'm always tempted to blurt out, 'Did you look under the sofa?' But seriously, he was talking about his parents dying. What kind of asshole would make a joke, you know? I did the normal, unhelpful thing, and said, "I'm sorry to hear that."

The front door stood open and the woman I'd seen in Cal's photo stood there hugging a cardigan tightly around her. She smiled at us, a broad friendly smile.

The kids had already disappeared into the house.

"Mary Ann, this is Gage Hammond. Gage this is my... Mary Ann."

I said what felt like the first thing I should say was: "I'm sorry to intrude on your holiday. It wasn't my idea."

"It wasn't mine either," Cal added defensively.

"How about we just make the best of it?" Mary Ann said. "It's almost dinner time. Let me show you to the guest room so you can make yourself comfortable."

I followed her up the wide stairs to the second floor. Cal left his boxes in the foyer and followed close at heel.

"Your house is lovely, Mrs. Cutler."

"Oh, I'm not Mrs. Cutler. I did not take his name. But please just call me Mary Ann."

"Okay. You have a lovely home, Mary Ann."

"Thank you. My mother gave it to me."

"That was nice of her."

"Not really. It was a tax dodge cooked up by her accountant. Plus, she spends roughly the same amount of time here that she always did—which in the last ten years has not been a lot. Plus, I have to pay all the upkeep."

"We," Cal said behind me. "We have to pay all the upkeep."

"Yes, of course. Sorry to leave you out. Honey."

I sensed tension between them. Which didn't mean anything, lots of couples thrived on tension. Not to mention it was likely to disappear as soon as she opened the probably very expensive perfume he'd just bought her for Christmas.

We walked down a hallway on the second floor. "This is the bathroom right here," Mary Ann said, pointing it out. "And here's the guest room."

The room was small, but it had a dormer window. A full-size bed was pushed up against the wall, a couple of nesting tables floated nearby with a lamp sitting on them. There was a dresser and a small flip-down desk. It certainly seemed that I'd be comfortable over the holiday.

"I hope I'm not putting anyone out."

Mary Ann shook her head. "Not at all. Why don't we leave you alone for a few minutes. Go ahead and unpack, there are couple of empty drawers in the dresser and hangers in the closet. Dinner is in an hour and afterward we're going to walk over to see the mayor light the city's Christmas tree. You can come with us, or not. It's up to you."

"Really you don't have to," Cal said, wearing that annoying fake smile.

"I'm sure the judge would want me to come," I pointed out.

"Then it's settled," Mary Ann said. "See you in an hour."

They slipped out of the guest room and closed the door behind them. Almost as soon as they left, I heard them arguing in low voices. The house was old and drafty and sound carried. Something was said about the house, and someone named Douglas. My guess was that they were arguing about a contractor.

I didn't want to listen though, so I quickly put in my AirPods and turned the music way up. I could still hear the rumble of them arguing, but I couldn't hear what they were saying.

Then, I checked the room for cameras and listening devices. There weren't any. Well, I am my father's son, after all. When I was done with that, I took out the AirPods and called Neo, who was my number one volunteer and taking over most of my duties for the holiday.

The hallway outside my room had gone quiet, Cal and Mary Ann had stopped fighting. That was good. I hoped they'd stopped for the whole holiday.

"How is it? Is it awful?" Neo asked.

"It's weird. We're having dinner and then going to a Christmas tree lighting."

"Not your kind of Christmas tree lighting, I hope?"

"No, the regular kind."

"I guess that will be anticlimactic," they said. I could hear them smirking.

I decided to ignore that. I'd been the butt of fire jokes on three different late night shows for almost the entire month. My skin was now as thick as it could possibly get.

"Uh-huh. Listen, thank you for covering the pre-Christmas Eve party. I'm sure the kids will appreciate it."

"No problem."

"There are some presents in my office. If you'd pass them out, I'd appreciate it. They're clearly labeled."

"Got it."

"Now, if for some reason anyone is suddenly homeless—it happened two years ago—if someone doesn't have a place to stay, you can put them up at my place."

"Yeah, that's probably not going to work."

"What do you mean?"

"There was a reporter nosing around the drop-in center a couple of hours ago. I moved the pre-Christmas Eve get together to Drip and I'm trying to find a new location for the misfits' dinner."

"You think they know where my apartment is?"

"I don't want to take the chance."

"I'm sorry for this. I know it's a hassle."

"It's okay. That Stickney fellow had it coming. He doesn't do much besides attack queer people on his show. Makes fun of trans kids. Jokes about pronouns. Misgendering people. Drag queens are pedophiles. You know the drill."

"I do."

"You should have burned the station down and left the tree."

I decided to ignore that. I couldn't imagine the amount of trouble I'd be in had I done that.

"There's money in petty cash," I told them. "Take that for the pre-party at Drip. Make sure the kids have a good time. And for the misfits' dinner, spend whatever you need to in order to make it nice, I'll be able to pay you back in a day or two. We've actually been receiving a lot of donations."

"Really? That's great."

"It is, but I haven't wanted to say anything. I don't want anyone to think I did what I did for profit."

I'd gone over to the dormer window and was looking out. The street was like Americana porn. Two rows of dream homes resting under a blanket of snow. I couldn't help thinking about the fact that the people who'd built these homes probably couldn't afford them today.

Downstairs, a door opened and shut. Then, Cal hurried out of the house, down the walkway to his car. He jumped in and pulled out of the driveway. Where was he going? Did Mary Ann need something for dinner? It seemed odd.

"Gage?"

"What?"

"I asked you a question. Why did you do it? I mean, I get that Jeff David Stickney is an asshole and he deserves whatever he gets... but a Christmas tree? That hasn't gone over well with a lot of people."

"It was a rash decision. Um, I need to go now."

I didn't, but I also didn't like the direction the conversation was headed. I didn't want to think about how all this began. I wanted to stay focused on how to make it end.

About an hour later, I freshened up and put on an argyle sweater that had a hole under the arm that one of the kids at NorthStar had darned for me. I checked the weather app on my phone, and it was going down to nearly twenty degrees. I read a bit of *My Lucky Star* by Joe Keenan on my tablet and then went downstairs for dinner.

I hadn't been shown the first floor, but it was easy enough to find my way through the front parlor, the formal dining room and into the kitchen. The room had been redone in the last few years with brand new gleaming appliances, a wide island and a built-in dining booth in front of a large window overlooking the backyard, which was now covered in snow.

The kids were already sitting in the breakfast nook, Piper's nose deep in her phone, Gus reading *A Christmas Carol* by Dickens. That seemed a little old for him; not the story so much but the language, which I recalled from college as being a challenge. Then, I noticed that the cover also said "Kid's Classic" so maybe it wasn't that far out of range for the little guy.

Mary Ann was pulling a bubbling mac and cheese out of

the oven. Cal was nowhere to be seen, but his bankers boxes had found their way next to the nook.

"Hello," I said. "Looks like I'm right on time."

"You are. Did you want a glass of wine?"

"Um, sure. Can I help myself? You look kind of busy."

"Thank you. It's in the wine fridge, whites at the bottom, reds on top. Glasses are in the cupboard right above."

The wine fridge wasn't hard to find, and a moment or two later I was pouring myself a glass of white that I chose for its screw top. "Can I get you something?" I asked.

"Sure, I'll have what you're having." As I was pouring the glass, she asked, "Do you have a boyfriend?"

"Not at the moment, no."

"I'll have to tell Cal."

"He already asked," I said, wondering why she thought she should tell him? I handed her the wine.

"You're what, twenty-five, twenty-six?"

"Twenty-seven."

"Have you ever had a boyfriend?"

"In college. It was kind of a disaster."

"Yeah, college romances are always doomed."

"I thought you met Cal in college."

"Oh, well, law school. I suppose that's different. Under-grad romances are always doomed. Perhaps that's what I meant."

Just then, Cal walked in. He'd changed out of his suit and wore a pair of carefully pressed khakis and a thin, light-yellow sweater, probably cashmere, with a crisp dress shirt under-neath. He was dressed more for casual Friday at the office than dinner with his family.

"I just opened a bottle of white, did you want a glass?"

"No, thank you. I need a clear head. I have work to do later tonight."

"Oh, Cal," Mary Ann said.

"After the kids go to bed." He stood there awkwardly, and that was strange. It was his kitchen after all. Why did he look so out of place? Mary Ann had stacked five plates on the island.

"Honey, why don't you set the table."

Yeah, there was still tension between them. The way she said the word 'honey' was not exactly an endearment. The fight in the hallway had not settled things. If anything, it looked to have made things worse. I hoped they'd make up soon. The holiday would be challenging enough without two angry married people.

Cal was setting the dishes on the table. Mary Ann put out napkins, flatware, glasses on the island for him. It made me wonder if he knew where things were. Was he that kind of husband? Yuck.

"Does your family go all out for Christmas?" Mary Ann asked me.

"Not really. My parents split when I was a teenager, and before that we were kind of nomads. Actually, my father's still a nomad."

"Really? No traditions at all?"

"I guess we'd go to a movie on Christmas Day—if we could find one my parents didn't think was too right wing. We'd always have take-out, usually Chinese. So, you guys met in law school, how long ago was that?"

"Ten years," Cal said, as he picked up the napkins and flatware.

"Thirteen, honey. Remember, Piper is twelve."

"The years have just flown by. It feels like ten."

"Why do they say men are good at math when they're so obviously not?" Mary Ann asked me, as though I might have a good answer.

I shrugged and said, "Who knows where stereotypes come from. Probably wishful thinking."

Cal picked up the glasses as I asked, "Did you have a big wedding?"

Cal was shaking his head as Mary Ann said, "Gigantic." Quickly, Cal began nodding.

"If you met my mother, you'd understand why the wedding was gigantic. She invited almost every single person she'd ever met and almost none that I had. Worst day of my life. If I ever get married again, I'm eloping."

"If you ever get married again?" Cal said. "Honey, don't say things like that. Not in front of the kids."

"I said 'if' not 'when.'"

Cal looked at his kids and said, "Don't worry, I'm not going anywhere."

They didn't look worried.

"Why don't we sit down," Mary Ann suggested.

We took our places around the table, and I said, "Your mac and cheese looks amazing."

"Thank you," she said.

We passed the food around. I took a bite of the mac and cheese first. Oh my God, it was so much better than it looked —and it looked really good. Thick, creamy, cheesy, and the breadcrumbs soaked in butter. Wow. This might end up being a very pleasant holiday. At least, food-wise.

There wasn't a lot to say as we dug into the dinner.

Abruptly, Gus asked, "How come we never have Christmas goose?" It took a moment to figure out where that question came from, but then I remembered he was reading *A Christmas Carol*.

"I don't know where to get them," Mary Ann said. "And I don't know how to cook them. Those would be two reasons."

Piper was already furiously typing into her phone.

"And I don't think they're very big, that would be three."

"Geese are very big," Gus said with authority.

"Canadian Geese are very big," Cal said. "But I don't think they sell those in the store."

"They're not very nice," Gus said.

"No, they're not," I said. Most of us in Wyandot County were experienced with Canadian Geese. We lived on the migratory path for Canadian Geese, which meant that they stopped in our yards in the spring and the fall, and took big green craps everywhere.

"Do you want to eat one for Christmas?" Cal asked.

Gus nodded his head furiously, while Mary Ann glared at her husband.

"You have to order them online," Piper said.

"Ah, maybe next year," Mary Ann said.

In addition to the mac and cheese, there was a simple salad with dried cherries, walnuts and blue cheese, topped with a balsamic vinaigrette dressing. There was also a warm loaf of French bread.

"This is wonderful," I said. I didn't cook much. My yearly misfits' dinner was a potluck. I've managed the turkey each year but hadn't gone much further into cooking than that. I've mastered the aluminum foil tent method, which is not exactly complicated.

I was shoveling salad into my mouth when Piper put her phone down, and asked me, "So, why are you here again?"

"Piper!" her mother said.

"It's all right," I said. "Basically, the judge sentenced me to Christmas with your family."

"He's meant to learn the meaning of Christmas," Cal added.

"From us? Good luck with that."

"Piper," Mary Ann said. "Where did that attitude come from? We have lots of Christmas spirit. We have Christmas spirit to spare."

The girl shrugged and said, "Christ wasn't even born on

the twenty-fifth. He was born like in January. And a Christmas tree doesn't have anything to do with Christianity. It's a pagan symbol of the Winter Solstice—which actually *is* in December. Do we have Winter Solstice spirit?"

"She likes to show off," Mary Ann said. Then, in an obvious attempt to change the subject, she asked, "Have you been to the tree lighting before?"

"No, there's always something else going on."

"It's not that interesting, but it's basically three blocks away so it feels un-neighborly not to go. And it's nice to get out and see people. Adult people."

"Things don't have to be exciting to make good family traditions," Cal said. He tried to put his hand over Mary Ann's, but she yanked hers away.

In college, I'd taken a lit class where we had to read a famous Russian novel. I don't remember which one, I've blocked it from my memory. I do remember that it was so dull I could not finish it. What I remember most about it, though, was the first page. It made the claim that all happy families are all the same and that all unhappy families are unique. I did not believe that one bit.

In fact, I think it's the reverse. The happy families I'd known had all been very different. Some were sporty, some were bookish, some were rich, some poor. Unhappy families, though. They *were* always the same. There was tension in the air, a lack of physical affection, a palpable distance, they forgot to say *we* instead of *I*, they told obvious lies, they neglected to include each other in talk of the future. Cal and Mary Ann Cutler's family was clearly unhappy. And not in an original way.

Six

CALVIN

AFTER SHOWING Gage to the guest room, Mary Ann and I had a little spat. I suppose it was my fault. The situation we were in was my fault, so I was going to be responsible for anything that did not go well over the next few days. It was all going to be my fault. I was not happy about that.

"You need to get him out of the house tomorrow. It's Christmas Eve and Douglas will want to Zoom with the kids."

"Can't he do that some other time?"

"He's their father. He gets to talk to them on Christmas Eve."

"Wasn't this his Christmas, though? Wasn't he supposed to be with his kids and not his girlfriend?"

"That has nothing to do with this."

"He doesn't seem particularly concerned with spending time with his kids, that's all I'm saying."

"All right. Look, Douglas was an awful husband, but he's a good dad and the kids love him so just don't go there, all right?"

I shut my mouth. I had the feeling she didn't really believe Douglas was a good dad but was just holding onto the idea because then she didn't seem like a complete idiot having been married to him for thirteen years.

"Do you know what time he wants to talk to them?"

"He's not very specific."

"Could he *get* more specific?"

"I'm working on that."

"Okay, let me know when he's going to call, and I'll think of something. "

"I hate this, you know."

"Yes, you've made that abundantly clear."

"This is a terrible position you've put me in."

"This is a terrible position you're helping me out of. You're a great friend."

"Fuck you."

Before dinner, I had time to sneak out and go home to pick up some clothes for the next few days. On the way, I decided not to give Gage Hammond a single thought. I had a murder case to prepare for.

Spousal abuse, that was what Van Husen was claiming. Self-defense. It was a hard defense to prove. So, yes, I fully expected to win the case. The thing was, I wanted to win it as first-degree murder and I hadn't even charged that yet.

The defense had already come to me and tried to plea bargain for voluntary manslaughter, which would have been a sentence of less than fifteen years and a small fine. The wife was wealthy and the money was willed to Van Husen. A voluntary manslaughter plea would mean he'd be out of prison in a few years with a large lump of cash all to himself.

No, I wanted to find something that indicated he planned the murder, which would mean a first-degree charge resulting in life in prison and no inheritance. If I could somehow prove he'd been planning the spousal abuse defense, that would get me where I wanted to go. But I just hadn't found the right piece of evidence.

Getting back to Mary Ann's, I handled dinner brilliantly. She and I played the perfect couple. I wondered if she'd taken any acting classes when she was an undergrad. I had. Just one. I thought it might help my presentation when I became an attorney. I'd gotten an A. Something that was showing during dinner. Mostly we talked about the kids, which was perfect. That was most of what straight people talked about, anyway. I'm sure we bored Gage to death. Which was perfect. Absolutely perfect.

After dinner, we cleaned up and then it was time to go downtown and watch them light the tree. Mary Ann made sure the kids were bundled up. At twelve, Piper wouldn't have tolerated it, except she was, as always, nose-deep in her phone. Sometimes I wasn't sure she even knew where she was.

"Did you know that it was Prince Albert who popularized Christmas trees and that there wasn't a Christmas tree in the Whitehouse until Franklin Pierce in 1856?"

"No, we did not, Piper. But thank you for the lesson," I said. "Can we not talk about Christmas trees? It's kind of a sore subject for some of us."

"I'm fine," Gage said. But honestly, he looked pained every time the subject came up.

"Cal, we're going to a Christmas tree lighting," Mary Ann said, as she put on her giant puffer coat. "I don't think it's realistic to *not* talk about Christmas trees."

"One hundred-and-sixty Christmas trees catch fire every year."

"All right Piper, that's really pushing it," Mary Ann said.

"If he'd been a little more patient, it might have caught fire on its own."

"I said, enough. Do you want me to take that phone away from you?"

Piper grew quiet. It always surprised me that worked. 'Do you want me to take your phone away,' was the modern equivalent of 'Do you want me to get the belt?' Somehow it carried the same weight. Yes, I couldn't remember a time when people didn't have cell phones, but none of the kids I knew had them when I was growing up. I was fourteen when the iPhone came out—Lindsey Lohan had one of the first. If I'd asked for one, it would have caused my father to go and get the belt. I knew better and didn't ask.

We walked the two blocks to Main Street where there were a lot of shops and where they put up a giant Christmas tree in a patch of park on the corner of Lakeshore and Main. Fortunately, the sidewalks were always well shoveled and salted, so it was unusual for anyone to take a fall. The weather was chilly but dry. I decided to forego my galoshes. It would be fine.

When we got there, we found a small crowd gathering. The gigantic tree was decorated and also waiting. Next to it was a platform, where a few local dignitaries were already seated.

Mary Ann said, "The kids and I are going to slip into the fudge shop, we'll be right back."

That left Gage and me alone. We stood awkwardly, not knowing what to say. I glanced around to see if there was anyone I knew. There rarely was. I didn't know a lot of people in the area other than the people I worked with, Mary Ann and my aunt—who lived most of the year in New Mexico.

I had all the gay apps on my phone, but I knew better than to use a face pic. Torso only. I also rarely felt comfortable enough to hook-up. Every few months, I'd go for a weekend in Grand Rapids or Detroit or even Chicago, and that was enough.

"How does your boss feel about the judge's order?" Gage asked.

"Oh, he's fine. He knows I can handle it."

Well, I wasn't going to tell this guy my boss had been

screaming at me about it two days ago. I was sure he'd calmed down by now. He probably *was* fine with it.

"And by handle it, you mean what exactly?"

"On the 27th, you're going to make a suitable statement about the meaning of Christmas and then this whole thing will be over."

"What if he doesn't accept my statement?"

"Let's cross that bridge when we come to it."

Of course, I knew exactly what would happen We'd be going to trial. Which, honestly, would be a whole lot worse for me than it would be for Gage. All we had was his confession. The only witness I could put on the stand was the officer who took his statement. His very brief statement.

The mayor of Bellflower, Toni Marston Weller, got up in front of the microphone. She flicked it a few times with her fingers to make sure it was on.

"Good evening, ladies and gentlemen, and welcome to the annual Bellflower Christmas tree lighting."

The small crowd applauded. The mayor held a few large white cards in her hand, occasionally referring to them.

"First, I want to tell you about our tree, which was donated to the city by Donaldson Lumber in Masons Bay. It's a white spruce, thirty-eight feet six inches tall, and nearly fifty feet at the base. There are nearly a thousand feet of electric lights given to us by Lakeside Electric. Jerry Drinkwater—you all know Jerry, he's right here down in front. Give the crowd a wave, Jerry."

A hand popped up down front and waved at us all.

"Mass-produced Christmas tree lights first went on sale in 1890," Piper read off the internet. I hadn't realized she was back.

"That was fast," I said.

"I can't stand fudge."

As her dad I should know that, so I looked at Gage and said, "Kids, you learn something new about them every day."

The mayor had begun to thank those local businesses who had donated ornaments. It was a very long list.

"...and last, but not least, I'd like to thank the Bellflower 4-H club for stringing an astonishing seven hundred feet of cranberry and popcorn garlands. Let's give them a round of applause."

The crowd did.

"And remind them they're coming back on January third to sweep up the mess... Anyway, now I'd like to bring up Martha Waznakowski to play 'Ave Maria' for us on her accordion."

We applauded again as a woman in her mid-fifties climbed onto the platform. She wore a green dirndl dress and carried a very large instrument. As soon as she hit center stage she began. Fortunately, it wasn't horrible.

Mary Ann and Gus got back just then. She carried a bag of fudge; he was already halfway through a large paper-wrapped chunk.

Mary Ann gave me a sweet smile, which immediately put me on my guard. Then she whispered—just loud enough for Gage to hear—

"Gus can't see. You should pick him up, honey."

"Oh no, he can see just fine."

"He's three-foot-ten. Pick him up."

Now, if I really were Mary Ann's husband, I'd have insisted she hold his piece of fudge before I picked him up. But I was only pretending to be her husband, which meant I picked him up.

I couldn't take my eyes off the fudge for fear it was about to land all over my Burberry coat.

"Oh, sweetheart, you're such a good dad," she said with all the venom of a black widow spider.

"Ave Maria" ended and we applauded. Well everyone else did. I was still carefully watching Gus and his chocolate. He was doing well with it though. There was none on his face and none on me. He'd even pulled the paper back to expose more of the fudge.

On stage, Martha did her best to bow while holding an accordion. Before the applause completely ended, she said into the microphone, "Make sure to join us in Turtlehead for Polkapalooza the third Friday of every month at Kaminski's Tap Room."

The mayor was ready to push her off the stage. When Martha finally ran off, the mayor said into the microphone, "Well, that was rousing. Okay, now, each year we invite someone special to turn the lights on for us, someone whose life captures the spirit of the holiday.

My eyes remained on Gus the whole time as he carefully and fastidiously ate his fudge. While the mayor continued, "In the past we've had champion athletes... like the golf team from Masons Bay and the middle-grade tennis team from Turtlehead. We had that girl who won the essay contest for the entire state, it was about nature or something, and that boy who beat cancer."

Behind her, a young man cleared his throat loudly. The mayor turned and looked at him. He mouthed something.

"Oh my, that is sad. Anyway, this year, as our honorary turner-on-er—" She turned back to the young man and hissed, "We need to work on that." Then back to the audience with a big phony smile, "This year we have, from radio station WRWG, noted journalist Jeff David Stickney!"

And then he was on the stage, camera-ready with too much make-up, an overly white smile, and a helmet of sprayed hair. He looked mean and fake, which would only get worse when he opened his mouth.

I looked at Gage and quickly said, "I'm sorry, I had no idea he was coming."

"We didn't, honestly," Mary Ann added.

Someone behind me decided they needed to get closer to see their hero, jostling me in the process—shoving me might be more accurate. I fell into the older woman in front of me. Pulling back, I whispered, "I'm so sorry."

She gave me a look that suggested I might be a serial killer. I looked down and saw that Gus' fudge had been smeared across the collar of my coat. He looked horrified. His mother was smirking next to me.

I put Gus back on the ground, managing not to cringe too much as his now chocolate-covered hands wiped across my cashmere sweater and the collar of my Armani shirt. I decided I'd be giving Mary Ann my dry-cleaning bill—which I'm sure she'd give right back to me. Leaving my only option small claims court, and there was no way I was explaining any of this to a judge.

"We should get out of here."

"It's okay," said Gage. "I don't want to ruin your tradition."

Well, that made me feel like crap. This was hardly a tradition, or if it was, it was one that hadn't ever included me.

On stage Jeff David Stickney was pontificating, "...And, of course, I want to thank Mayor Weller for her strong support during the War on Christmas. Now it may surprise some of you to hear that I'm sometimes sneered at when I talk about the War on Christmas. There are those who'd like you to believe that it's not a real war, that no one is trying to take Christmas away from us. Well, I'm sure they've changed their minds after this year's terrorist attack on Christmas. As you know, America's Christmas Tree, which stood in front of WRWG, was destroyed by fire just a few short weeks ago. And the heinous villain who committed that crime, do you know what happened to him?" He paused dramatically, too dramatically. "Nothing. A slap on the wrist. Probation. Probation! For an attack on Christmas! The most important holiday on the Christian calendar. He gets a slap on the wrist. Do you think they'd treat Jews like that? Would they treat Muslims that way? No, they wouldn't. Mark my words, first they come for your holidays, then they come for you!"

Prodded by her assistant, the mayor came over holding the cords for Stickney to plug in.

"Oh, yes, of course, I got carried..." he mumbled as he took the cords from her. He was about to plug in the lights when he looked out at the audience and saw... me. Then he looked at Gage next to me. *Oh God*, I thought, *this is going to be bad*.

Stickney dropped both cords and pointed, "Him! He's the one who burned down America's Christmas Tree!"

Everyone near us turned and stared at Gage. He smiled tentatively at them then, under his breath, he said "Mary Ann, get the kids out of here."

Which, honestly, should have been my line. Without a word, Mary Ann began pulling the kids away. As Gage drifted in the other direction.

"You should go too," he said to me.

"You're my legal responsibility..."

"I really doubt that."

"I'm not going back into court and explain that you were devoured by an angry mob while I ran in the opposite direction."

"I really don't think Judge Winthrop—" Then someone in the crowd began to move, and he yelled, "Run!"

We spun around and bolted. Behind us the crowd was thinner, so it wasn't too hard to slip through. That is, until we got to the very back, when this guy, who must have been six-foot-a-lot, deliberately stepped in front of us like a wall. Gage went in one direction and I went in the other. The wall made a grab for both of us but missed. We dashed down the sidewalk.

I glanced behind us and saw that we were being chased by more than a dozen guys, all of them White, all of them young, all of them scary. We ran by the little shops, many of which were just closing. In front of us was a bar between an antique shop and a bakery that was called Mr. Chips. At one time, Mr. Chips was a gay bar, but now you'd call it more of a 'welcoming' bar. Most importantly, though, it had a back door.

Grabbing Gage by the coat, I pulled him into Mr. Chips. I rushed him through the skinny bar and out the back door. We were in a wide alley that opened onto the river that ran through Bellflower. The alley had some parking, a few dumpsters, and many piles of crusty snow—most of which we managed to run through. When we were a half a block down from Mr. Chips, I knew that the men chasing us soon would be popping out into the alley. I grabbed Gage and pulled him into a pizza place (well, not *a* pizza place, *the* pizza place, the *only* pizza place) and then directly into the men's room. The not very clean men's room. I flicked the light off so we stood there in the dark.

"How did you know Mr. Chips had a back door?" Gage asked me.

"A lot of these businesses do," I said. Then, realizing that probably wasn't sufficient, added, "I met a witness there a couple of times. He always came in the back entrance. Be quiet."

Someone smashed through the back door. I pressed Gage up against the space next to the door, we were nose to nose, chest to chest, hip to hip. The door flung open. We were behind the door, I couldn't see who was looking in, but I knew that what they saw was a dark, empty bathroom. I prayed they wouldn't turn on the light, wouldn't step inside.

After a very intense few seconds, the door closed, and we heard whoever it was run out the back door.

I stayed there; body pressed up against Gage for a long, far too pleasurable, moment. Finally, he said, "They're gone."

"Yes, of course." I stood back and cleared my throat.

"You're very good at being chased," Gage said.

"It's hardly a skill."

"Have you been chased a lot in your life?"

I took a deep breath, the gay-me would answer "unfortunately, yes," because that happened to be true. But I wasn't the gay-me, I was the straight-me, and I couldn't think of any reason—

"No, of course not."

"You're just naturally gifted that way."

I had to change the subject, so I said, "We'd better get home. Mary Ann will be worried."

We left the men's room and snuck out the back door of the pizza place. Behind the building there was no one to be seen. I looked around and said, "I think we should go down that way a couple of blocks and then cut down to second. It's the long way, but we won't get near any of the street traffic."

"I do know my way around, you know."

"Yes, of course, you do. How long have you been in the area?"

"Five years. But you know that, remember?"

"I remember some of your file, but not all of it. I'm not one of those creepy savants with a photographic memory."

"Oh, I actually happen to be..."

"Oh, shit."

"No, I'm not. I'm kidding."

Why did he think that was funny? Well, he probably didn't think that was funny—he thought the sour look it produced on my face was funny. I tried to smile in hopes of ruining his fun, but I don't think it came off.

Even though we went the long way, it wasn't what you'd call long. Three blocks east, two blocks south and then four blocks west. Easy. And it was. We didn't encounter any scary guys running around trying to protect Christmas. In fact, we barely saw anyone. Halfway back, I realized that my feet were wet. Which meant my shoes were ruined.

Bruno Magli slip-on loafers, four-hundred dollars a pair, that I'd gotten at twenty-five percent off but still very expensive, and I'd only worn them four or five times. It was an absolute tragedy and I wanted to cry. But I couldn't. A heterosexual man with two children would not cry over a pair of Italian shoes.

"Did you like U of M?" I asked Gage.

"I did, very much. Where did you go to school?"

"I started at a community college down near Detroit and finished my BA at Wayne State."

"In?"

"American History. Always good prep for law."

"So you wanted to be a lawyer right from the start?"

"For a long time, yes. I went to Mercy for law school."

"Ah, you went to state schools the whole way. And I said you were probably a private school brat. Sorry about that."

"That's all right. I've always aspired to be a private school brat."

We were nearly back to Mary Ann's when Gage noticed the squishing sound coming from my shoes.

"Oh my God, you ruined your shoes."

"I did," I said, keeping my voice even.

"You ruined your shoes for me. That's so... romantic."

"Uh, yes. Let's go in the house."

Seven

GAGE

ROMANTIC? Really? Why did that pop out of my mouth? I could have said kind or generous or self-sacrificing. But romantic? Was I starting to vibe on this guy? That would be such a mistake. I mean, his wife, his kids. Not to mention the humiliation of being one of those gay guys who crushed on a straight guy.

Yeah, it was a little weird that he knew Mr. Chips had a back door, but it was not a gay bar, exactly. And it's been there for thirty-some years, so maybe he went there before he and Mary Ann got together. Or maybe the story he told about meeting a witness there was true. Who knows?

But then, the bathroom. Dude was pressed up against me... well, not like a straight guy. I mean, yeah, we would have gotten the shit beat out of us if we were caught. Which did make for a good reason to press up against, crush me against the wall, his lips almost brushing against mine. It felt—okay it felt amazing. On my side. I have no idea what he felt. For all I know he might have been thinking, 'Oh yeah, this is why I don't like guys.'

Mary Ann opened the front door before we got there. "There you are. Are you okay?"

"His shoes have been mortally wounded," I said.

"I'm sorry for your loss," she said to her husband. "Did they chase you for a long time?"

"A few blocks," I said quickly. Cal scowled at me. I think he might have wanted to work it. But really, it was only a few blocks.

"That must have been terrifying."

Of course, it was terrifying. Being chased was always terrifying. It wasn't the first time I'd been chased. Once when we were living in the UP, I took a short cut through a wooded area and ended up getting chased by a group of high school kids in a chopped-up VW bug. I could have told that story, but it wasn't always the kind of thing straight people wanted to hear.

I said, "It wasn't horrible, and it was over quickly."

"That Stickney guy is something else. I've never listened to his show and now I never will. The kids are watching *Finding Nemo*." She lowered her voice and said to both of us, "How about I open a bottle of wine?"

"God yes," Cal said, taking the words right out of my mouth.

The sound of the movie was coming from my left, behind a closed door, which meant there was a TV room or family room right there opposite the more formal parlor. We went through the parlor and dining room back into the kitchen. We could still hear the movie in the background.

"I have a Late Riesling," Mary Ann said. "It's local, one of my favorites."

"Whatever," I said. I hadn't paid any attention to the wine I'd opened for dinner. Seriously, my favorite wines were cheap and cheaper. Which meant I didn't spend much time tasting local wines.

This time Mary Ann did the honors and poured us each a glass. We sat down at the breakfast nook, in amongst the boxes of Cal's upcoming case.

"I think Jeff David Stickney should be arrested for inciting a riot," Mary Ann said, giving Cal a sharp glance.

"I don't arrest people."

"Yes, but you can call the sheriff."

"Who would give Stickney a medal. You do read the newspaper, right?"

Our sheriff had a long history of refusing to enforce any law he didn't agree with. Something which frequently put him at odds with the governor and the attorney general.

"I really didn't mean to put your family in danger," I said.

"Of course, you didn't," Mary Ann said, then she elbowed her husband.

"Yes, definitely not your fault," he said. "You can stop apologizing."

Other than continuing to apologize, I didn't know what to say to these people. I had, certainly not on purpose, disrupted their lives. It was nice of them not to blame me.

"I hope it's okay to talk about this," Mary Ann said. "Do you know what you're going to say to the judge when you're back in court?"

"I'm not going to say I was chased by a group of right-wing wackos."

"Yes, probably not a good idea," Cal chimed in.

"To be more serious, I'm trying to find an overlap between what I'd be comfortable saying and what I think the judge wants to hear. Like a Venn diagram."

"That's a very small overlap, I imagine," Mary Ann said. Then she carefully asked, "So can you tell me why you did it?"

This would be hard to explain, and I knew it. I glanced at Cal, who just said, "This won't be used against you. The document you made me sign is binding."

"Well, it's not that I'm against Christianity—though it does have its issues. And I'm certainly not against patriotism, as long as it's real patriotism."

"What is real patriotism to you?" Mary Ann asked, sipping her wine.

"Real patriotism is a belief in our Constitution, our laws, our form of government, rather than adherence to symbols—or worse, individuals."

"The problem for you was the combination?" Cal suggested. "You don't believe that the flag should be strewn all over a Christian symbol?"

"Christmas trees are actually a pagan symbol," Mary Ann said. Then added, "Sorry, too much time with Piper."

"I do believe in the separation of church and state. Not that it applies to a Christmas tree. But, if you think about it, conflating Christmas and patriotism is offensive in a lot of ways. For one, not every Christian is an American. For another, not every American is a Christian. Claiming that these ideas go together appeals to one group while othering the remaining groups."

"Stickney does have freedom of speech," Mary Ann pointed out.

"True, but radio waves are owned by all of us. WRWG is only leasing them. That's why there are certain words you can't use. For instance, you can't say asshole on the radio even though you can be one."

"Unfortunately, that's exactly right," Cal said.

"Didn't it occur to you that someone like Stickney would just use this to raise money and increase his profile?" Mary Ann asked.

"It was a rash decision. I sort of just jumped in."

Mary Ann sipped her wine and considered for a moment. "Let's see, you can say something positive about Christianity to the judge, and then something positive about patriotism."

"I'm supposed to be learning the meaning of Christmas from you."

"Oh God, you're sunk," Mary Ann said. "Oh God, that sounded like Piper, too. I'm becoming my twelve-year-old."

"Your family is not as bad as you think. Christmas is about kindness. You've kindly taken me into your home, fed me, protected me from a mob, and one of you sacrificed a pair of shoes."

"Don't use the word sacrifice in court, Winthrop will think you're talking about ritual animal sacrifice," Cal said.

"You know, I'm a little tired to be thinking about this. Do you mind if I turn in early?"

"Of course, not," Mary Ann said. "If you need anything, just let us know."

I said good night and left the kitchen. Upstairs, I lay on the bed for a while reading *My Lucky Star*. The book is a little farcical, though after the evening we had it seemed a bit more realistic than it had earlier in the day.

I was getting drowsy when my phone rang. Flipping it over, I saw that the call was coming from an unknown number. I wished that I might have the luxury of not answering unknown calls, but I couldn't *not* answer them. It might be one of the kids who uses the drop-in center. They could be in trouble. I couldn't just ignore them. I picked up. It was my father.

"Dad, where are you calling me from?"

"It's a burner phone. I'm only going to keep it for a week."

"Everything's fine. You don't have anything to worry about."

"I read about the riot downtown on a Substack. It said you started it. I'm so proud—"

"There was no riot. And I did *not* start it. We were just chased a few blocks by some rednecks. That's all."

"I'm still proud of you. And, and… I want to thank you. Again."

"It's okay, Dad. We don't need to talk about this."

"Yes, we do. Thank you. You're taking the blame for something I did."

"It's almost over."

"But I'm the one who should be there, not you—well, I wouldn't be there, would I? If the government got their hands on me, I'd be in Guantanamo or some other black site lickety-split."

"Dad, I'm not even sure those places exist. And if they do exist they're for people who are a threat to the United States, not people who use phrases like 'lickety-split.'"

"Are you saying I'm not a threat to the United States?"

There was hurt in his voice. Clearly, I'd bruised his ego.

"Dad, you are definitely a left-wing radical, but that does not automatically make you a threat to the United States. You have no plans to blow up any buildings—"

"I'm trying to change the world, not start a war."

"Exactly. And you're not going to assassinate anyone."

"I'm a terrible aim. And I'm against guns."

"And you're not going to try and overthrow democracy."

"Who do you think I am? Rudy Giuliani?"

"All you have are opinions and no one is going to try to put you away for having opinions."

"Oh, you are such a sweet, naïve boy."

Eight

CALVIN

AFTER GAGE WENT TO BED, we had to tuck Gus in. A normal seven-year-old would have stories read to him at bedtime. However, Gus' reading level was so advanced that reading him Dr. Seuss made no sense. What Mary Ann did instead was ask him to tell her the story of whatever he was reading.

That night we were treated to the story of Ebenezer Scrooge. After the first ghost appeared, Gus asked, "Why are people like that? Why do they have to have ghosts show up in order to make them nice people? Why can't they just be nice people because it's more fun to be a nice person?"

"Well, sometimes that does happen," Mary Ann said. "Sometimes people think about what's happened in their lives and they decide to be better."

For some reason she was looking at me when she said that.

Gus went on, "So, maybe we could write a story about Mr. Scrooge where he just goes to bed one night and realizes it's bad to be greedy and selfish and that you have to help the poor and be nice to people and if you do that everybody will like you."

"You could write it that way, yes," Mary Ann said.

"But it's better with the ghosts, isn't it? Even if ghosts aren't real."

"Yeah, I think it's better with the ghosts."

She kissed him on the forehead and said, "Good night. I love you."

"Night Mommy."

Standing behind her, I said, "Good night, buddy."

"Mmm-hmm," he said, rolling over to drift off.

Out in the hallway, we stopped at the door that led to the attic stairs. Mary Ann called up them, "Night Piper! We love you."

"Yeah, okay."

We continued down the hallway until we got to Mary Ann's bedroom door. She opened it and we went inside.

Kicking off her shoes, she quietly said, "You know, you should just tell Gage the truth."

Even though the bedroom was the largest in the house it wasn't what you'd call large. The queen-sized bed took up most of the available space. A hundred and fifty years ago people didn't do as many things in their bedrooms, so the rooms were small... and had very few electrical outlets.

I decided to pretend I hadn't heard her, and asked, "Where can I plug in my phone?"

"Did you hear what I said? You should tell him the truth." She'd opened a dresser drawer and was looking for a nightgown.

"I heard you, it's just very important that I plug in my phone."

"Why, why is that important?"

"Um, because it is."

It wasn't. It was just a habit. And honestly, if anyone called me I probably wouldn't even answer. She turned around and was staring at me, waiting.

"You want me to tell him we're not married?"

"He seems like a nice guy. It would make this all much easier."

"You're not thinking it through, Mary Ann, he could blackmail me."

"He's not going to blackmail you. You're being melodramatic."

"He's already mentioned my dropping the charges a couple of times. If he knew we weren't really married, he could force me to drop the charges and God knows what Judge Winthrop would do then."

"Turn around, I want to put my nightgown on."

My bag, which I'd snuck out and driven to my house to get, sat on a chair in the corner. I pulled out a pair of pajamas and began to change myself. Folding my clothes neatly on a chair and setting my phone on top. I still hadn't found an outlet.

"What could the judge do to you if you did drop the charges?"

"Let's see, he could hold me in contempt, fine me, put me in jail, not to mention there would be publicity. I'd be the assistant district attorney who let the man who burned down America's Christmas Tree go without so much as a slap on the wrist. I'd never work again. Anywhere."

"I doubt that's true," she said. "You can turn around now, I'm dressed."

I wasn't, I was still buttoning my pajama top, but I turned around anyway. "Even if you're right, even if only some of the bad things I think might happen did happen, they're happening to me, not you."

Mary Ann squirted some moisturizer into her palm and then began to rub it on her arms and elbows.

"Well, I like him," she said. "He wouldn't blackmail you. He's not the type."

"He's not the type to commit arson, either. But he did."

"He's very cute. When this is over you should ask him out."

"I doubt he dates married men."

"You are going to have to tell him the truth someday."

"Uh, no, that's not a good idea. When this is over, he might not suffer any consequences, but I still could."

"God, you're so paranoid."

"I'm a lawyer, that is literally the definition of my job."

"So, you're just going to be in the closet forever?" she asked, as she moved on to moisturizing her legs.

"It won't be that bad."

"As your fake wife, I disagree with that statement. Also, this is the last time I'm pretending to be your wife."

"Yeah, I think you said that already."

"It bears repeating."

"Look, it means a lot to me that you're doing this. I know it's difficult and annoying. You really are my best friend."

"Oh my God, you're going to try to get me to do this in the future, aren't you? Well, the answer is no. Never, ever, again."

"I was not—" I stopped because of course I might need her to do this again and expressing gratitude might make that possible. I grabbed my travel bag, which held my toothbrush, toothpaste, floss, shaving things (for the morning) and my moisturizer, which I was certainly not putting on in front of her.

"I'm going to brush my teeth," I started to say but then my cell phone rang. I picked it up.

"Hello, Danny."

"A riot? Really? How did you let this Hammond guy out of your sight?"

"I didn't let him out of my sight. I was with him."

"You were with him while he started a riot?"

"Okay, calm down. It wasn't a riot. It was just a bunch of random rednecks chasing us through town screaming obscenities and threatening violence. Is that *really* a riot?"

"Yes! It is!"

"Okay. Well. All we did was go to the Christmas tree lighting. Jeff David Stickney was there—"

"What?!"

"We didn't know he was going to be there. Anyway, he saw us and started pointing and yelling. Actually, if you truly do believe there was a riot, Stickney incited it. Should we call Sheriff Watkins?"

"Are you insane? Sheriff Watkins is not going to arrest Jeff David Stickney for anything, ever. He wants to arrest Hammond."

"You spoke to him?"

"Of course, I spoke to him. He wants me to convene a grand jury and indict Hammond."

"All we did was run for our lives."

"Well, obviously I'm not calling you as a witness."

Mary Ann cleared her throat. I turned and she pushed her phone in my face. On it was video of Gage and I being chased down Main Street.

"Oh wow," I said. Then, "Danny there's video online of Hammond and I getting chased. You need to find it and send it to the sheriff. If he doesn't want to prosecute the guys chasing us that's fine, but he's not going to arrest Hammond. Understood?"

"You're walking a fine line, Cal. I told you before if you can't handle this case—"

"I am handling it. And I will keep handling it and it will be over in three days."

"Watch your step."

And then he hung up. I took a few deep breaths to calm myself.

"That sounded intense," Mary Ann said.

"It was. I think everything's okay though. I'm going to brush my teeth."

"One more thing—"

"Really? Now?"

"Tomorrow you're going to get the Christmas tree."

"Okay. Are we all going?"

"No, I got a text from Douglas. He said he'll call around lunchtime, so you need to get Gage out of the house by ten."

"Seriously? Out of the house is not such a great idea."

"You can't be here when Douglas calls."

"How long do we have to be gone?"

"I'm not sure. All he said was lunchtime. Aruba is two hours ahead, so I'm thinking you need to be out of here by ten, nine-thirty would be better. And then I'll text you and let you know when you can come back."

"That could be noon or one o'clock. It won't take three hours to get a Christmas tree."

"I'm sure we'll be finished well before one o'clock, that's three o'clock in Aruba. No one has lunch at three o'clock."

"They do if they're on vacation. They're going to sleep late and have breakfast at ten or eleven, which definitely puts lunch at three."

"Stop thinking like a lawyer. Douglas is not a lawyer. When he says around lunchtime he means around noon, okay?"

"But does he mean our noon or his noon?"

"Our noon, okay?!"

We weren't getting anywhere, and she was close to staring daggers at me—well maybe not close, maybe she was looking at me with her best serial killer eyes.

"Okay, then. I'm going to the bathroom." And I walked out of the bedroom.

When this was over, I knew I would owe Mary Ann a lot. I

was going to have to make a gesture. Roses? A nice dinner out? A free spa day? They all seemed so lame. This was a lot. A whole lot. To make it up to her I might need to murder her soon-to-be ex-husband. She wouldn't want that, but I should at least offer.

Just as I got to the bathroom, Gage came out. He wore a tiny pair of gym shorts—and nothing else. He held a travel bag in one hand, very much like the one I was holding. He had muscles, just not the kind that made it look like that was all he thought about. His shoulders were wide, his waist narrow, his chest sculpted... I suddenly realized my mouth might have fallen open.

"So you play sports?" I asked.

"No. I'm not a team kind of person."

"Work out?"

"Not much really..." He looked puzzled, then, "Oh, the shorts. Yeah, at home I don't wear anything to bed. I thought I should probably wear something here. I have a pair of pajamas if you'd prefer—"

"Whatever. I don't have a preference. And, ah, yes, good idea. Wear something. In case of fire—oh, I didn't mean..." My God, I couldn't think, not with him standing there wearing basically only a few tiny inches of fabric.

"Don't worry. You can't eliminate the word fire from your vocabulary."

"I could probably try harder, though. Well, I should—"

I slipped around him so I could get to the bathroom.

As I closed the door he said, "Good night."

"Good night."

I wasn't entirely sure I'd taken a breath in the last two minutes. I couldn't believe he looked like that. And he said he didn't work out? How was that possible? I went to the gym five times a week, worked with a trainer two of those times, and I did not look like that.

I brushed my teeth, then flossed, then moisturized—wait, did I floss? I couldn't remember. I was too busy remembering being in the men's room at the pizza restaurant, pushing myself up against Gage, and that's what he looked like under his clothes. No wonder he felt—

Oh God, now I had an issue. I couldn't go back into Mary Ann's bedroom like this. I ran the cold water tap and put my wrist underneath it. Didn't exactly work. Then I did, what I often do, I answered the first essay question I was asked in law school.

What is habeas corpus? Literally meaning 'show me the body,' habeas corpus provides that a prisoner must be brought before a judge and told the charges against them. It guards against unlawful imprisonment. A writ of habeas corpus compels...

Okay, better. Crisis fading. I flossed again. Just to be sure. Then I walked back down to Mary Ann's bedroom.

When I walked in, she was in bed reading the latest in the *Lincoln Lawyer* series. I walked around the bed, put my travel bag on the nightstand and started to get into bed.

"Um, what are you doing?"

"Getting into bed."

"Yeah, no. You're sleeping on the floor."

"You have a queen-sized bed."

"I sleep diagonally."

"Could you possibly sleep perpendicularly for one night—well, three, but still..."

"Nope not going to happen. There's an extra blanket in the closet. You can take this pillow," she said, pushing one of hers off the bed.

"Mary Ann, you know nothing is going to happen between us. I'm fully, one hundred percent, nothing but gay."

"All the more reason for you to sleep on the floor. If there was even a hint of sexual tension between us, I might let you into the bed. But there's not, so I don't even get the pleasure of a fantasy."

"But—"

"No buts."

It was probably a good idea not to fight this, so I went over to the closet and pulled out the blanket. This was going to be painful; I could tell already. Mary Ann turned the light off.

I got on the floor and tried to make myself comfortable. It was not possible. Ten or fifteen minutes later Mary Ann asked in the dark, "Do you really think he's buying this? It feels like he can see right through us."

"If he can see right through us then there's no reason to tell him the truth, is there?"

"You're such a lawyer."

Nine

❧

GAGE

DO I PLAY SPORTS? Are you kidding me? Straight guys are all alike. Sports and tits, that's all they ever talk about. I mean, he could have asked if I was comfortable, or did I need anything? But, no, he asked, "Do I play sports?" Wow.

I can't say I slept well. The bed was nice and the bedding especially cozy, but it was weird not being in my own space. Not that my own space is all that great—in fact, the bed in the Cutler's guest room was much more comfortable than my lumpy, thrift store mattress. And maybe that was the problem, I was too comfortable.

Of course, there was lots to think about. I was convinced that Cal and Mary Ann's marriage was in trouble. It took me a little while to realize, but when we met in the hallway, he was carrying a travel bag just like I was. Which he would only do if he didn't live here. Right?

I got up around one in the morning and went down the hallway to the bathroom. I turned the light on and took a good look around. There was a cup for toothbrushes on the sink. Three. Just three toothbrushes—one of which was a Transformers toothbrush, which I assumed belonged to Gus.

I opened the medicine cabinet and scanned it. No shaving cream, no razor blades—well, the pink kind women use on their legs—no body spray, no aftershave, no cologne in black bottles... nothing remotely male.

Cal didn't live here anymore. They were pretending. Why? Okay, that was an easy one. They were pretending for Judge Winthrop—and by extension, me. Cal didn't want him to find out his little routine with his family photo was a sham. Not to mention, Winthrop was probably enough of a wacko to think divorce was some progressive plot to nuke the nuclear family.

Back in bed, I told myself I only had to be there three more days. Seventy-two hours. Less than seventy-two probably. Really it was just a few hours and I'd be going home. Yeah, I didn't really buy that. It was going to be forever. I was going to be there in the middle of Cal and Mary Ann's bad marriage forever.

I didn't really notice that I fell asleep, so it was a bit of a surprise when I woke up around eight-thirty. I hated sleeping that late when it still meant I hadn't gotten enough sleep. I got up and took a shower.

The house was quiet. I wasn't even sure anyone else was there. I got dressed in a pair of jeans and an actual Christmas sweater I bought in August for four dollars, and made my way downstairs. I was almost through the dining room, about to push open the kitchen door, when I heard Cal say, "My back is killing me."

"It's your own fault you're sleeping on the floor," his wife replied.

Yeah, that made it all very clear. They *were* separated. Definitely. I took a few steps backward and then clomped my way over to the door so they could hear me coming.

"Good morning," I said as I opened the door.

"Oh, hello," Mary Ann said. "How did you sleep?"

"Great. Thanks." Okay, yeah, that was a lie. But the thing

about lying is that it's contagious, like a bad flu. To be more truthful I added, "It's a lovely room."

"Thank you. Help yourself to coffee."

On the island in front of Mary Ann were all the ingredients for holiday cookies. In fact, the air smelled of sugar and spice. Cal sat at the dining table with a cup of coffee in front of him. He did not look so hot. He was surrounded by stacks of paper. His big case.

I grabbed a cup of coffee, then went and stood by the breakfast nook. "How is that going?"

"I can't talk about it."

"Have you read about this case, Gage?" Mary Ann asked. "The personal trainer who shot his wife and is now trying to claim that he was an abused spouse?"

"I think I saw something about it."

"Cal's looking for some proof of premeditation so that he can prove first-degree murder."

"I said I can't talk about it."

"You're not talking about it, I am," Mary Ann said.

"What proof does he have that he was abused?"

Mary Ann said, "Bruising, selfies of the bruises, medical records, a gym friend he talked to about the abuse."

Cal glowered at her.

"Well, he didn't tell his doctor and his doctor didn't suspect anything. If a medical professional is aware of abuse they're required to report it to the police."

"How do you know that?" Mary Ann asked.

"He has a B.A. in social work. A doctor is a mandated reporter, as is a social worker," Cal said.

"That he told his friend seems odd," I said. "Statistically, men are less likely to report abuse. In the broadest terms they feel shame, while abused women feel they deserve the abuse. A man is unlikely to question the shame, while many women eventually question whether it's their fault and that's when they kind of verify that with a friend."

Mary Ann put a tray of cookies into the oven. Cal remained quiet. I wondered if I'd offended him. Was he really so thin-skinned that my having an idea about his case bothered him? Jesus, what an ego. I decided to change the subject and asked, "Where are the kids?"

"Delivering cookies to the neighbors. This is my sixth batch. I was up kind of early."

"That's definitely Christmas-y."

"I like to do what I can to make the neighborhood just a little bit fatter." Then she asked, "How about breakfast? You can have cereal, oatmeal... or milk and cookies for breakfast."

"Cookies and coffee?"

"Certainly." Mary Ann quickly made up a plate of six cookies for me. They were your basic vanilla cookies cut into different shapes and iced in a number of colors. Two of them were Christmas trees, iced in green with pink and white ornaments. Thankfully, neither tree was on fire.

"After you've had your breakfast, you and Cal are going to go and get a Christmas tree for us." Mary Ann said, taking another batch of cookies out of the oven. "It's our yearly tradition. He insists on picking out the tree every year. And cutting it down himself."

"Cutting it—?" he said, as though this were a very new idea. Maybe this wasn't a tradition at all.

"Gage, have you been to the tree farm out in Turtlehead?" Mary Ann asked.

"No, I haven't. I think I've driven by it."

"Wilson Family Farm. It's quite the experience. You'll really enjoy it."

"You and the kids don't come along?"

"No, it's more a guy thing. We'll all be together this evening. Our Christmas Eve tradition is to get takeout and trim the tree. Then before bed, the kids get to open one present each."

"This won't make you feel weird, will it?" Cal asked. "I mean, the whole Christmas tree thing?"

"I don't hate Christmas trees, honest."

"Cal, you should take Gage to lunch afterward. He's not going to be able to go all day on a few cookies."

"Such a good mom," Cal said, and not in a nice way.

We left right before ten. As we put our coats on, I noticed that Cal's coat was still stained with chocolate at the collar. He saw where I was looking and said, "Not much I can do about it. It goes to the dry cleaner the day after Christmas.

As it turned out, it was a wonderful winter day. The clear sky was a remarkable cornflower blue. The snow wasn't old enough to have gotten ugly. Everything was white and blue and Christmas green. We didn't say a whole lot on the drive out.

"You seemed kind of angry when we were talking about your case," I said.

"Not at you, exactly. Look, having you in my home is kind of unethical. It was mandated by a judge, so I have leeway. As long as it only affects your case it shouldn't be a big deal. But if it starts to bleed over into my other cases, that could be a problem."

"Got it."

"What you said was good, though. I'm going to dig up a psychologist and get more background. Possibly put them on the stand if I need to."

There wasn't much to say since I'd basically been told to shut up in a very polite way. Changing directions, I asked, "What's your favorite Christmas memory?"

"This is supposed to be about you."

"Yeah, I know. I'm just being interested in another human being. Which usually seems like a good thing."

"Why don't you tell me *your* favorite Christmas memory."

"Actually, most of my childhood Christmases kind of blur together. Wherever we were, we'd spend Christmas day volunteering at a food pantry handing out holiday dinners. People were nice. It was always kind of fun. But, different."

Cal didn't say anything for a bit. Then he said, "I was seven, maybe eight, I don't remember. My mom got me a Tickle-Me-Elmo. They were very hard to get so I wasn't expecting it. I was so excited. It was exactly what I wanted. My dad took it away by the end of the day. He said I was too old for dolls. I probably was."

Since he was opening up to me, I went ahead and asked, "So, not that it's any of my business, but how are things between you and Mary Ann?"

"Why would you ask a question like that?"

"I'm sorry, I probably shouldn't have said anything. I just noticed a few things that suggest things might not be going well in your marriage. And if you needed someone to talk to... I'm kind of stuck here."

"Mary Ann and I are fine. We're deeply in love."

"Well, just so you know, people who are deeply in love sometimes have problems."

"We're deeply in love and we don't have problems."

"Okay. No worries."

Oh yeah, they had problems. No one got that defensive unless they had problems. Serious problems. We didn't say much after that.

The Wilson Family Farm sprawled across thirty or forty acres. Near the road there was a stereotypical white, two-story farmhouse. Surrounding it, a barn, a fruit stand that was only open in the summer, and acre after acre of different kinds of pine trees of various heights. In the parking area in front there were more than a dozen cars. The place was crawling with people.

"I've driven by here, but I've never stopped," I said, right as a young college-aged woman in a red Christmas sweater and an elf's hat came over and said, "Hi! I'm Farmer Wendy Wilson. I bet you're here to cut down your own Christmas tree!"

"We are," I said. Cal just looked shocked by her exuberance.

"That's great! Normally, we have pre-cut trees for sale, but we sold out about an hour ago. The early bird catches the pre-cut Christmas tree!"

She spent far too long chuckling at her own joke.

"I love your sweater," she said to me. It was almost exactly like hers.

"Okay. So, what do we need to do?" Cal asked.

"Did you watch our video on YouTube? It tells you everything you need to bring with you."

"We did not."

"Bummer," she said, giving the kind of look a first-grade teacher reserved for an unruly class. "I bet that means you don't have a tarp or a saw or gloves or even bungee cords?"

"We do not," Cal said.

"We have kits available for rent. Well, not the bungee cords. They go home with you. You don't need to bring them back. I mean, you should bring them back. Next year."

"How much is the kit?"

"It's an extra forty-nine-ninety-nine."

"I guess we don't have a choice," Cal said.

"You do not," Farmer Wendy replied. "So, what kind of a tree do you think you want?"

"Tall."

"Most of the trees are tall. We've got balsam fir, grand fir, noble fir, Douglas—"

"Not Douglas."

"Okay, white pine, scotch pine, Virginia pine...white spruce, blue spruce..."

"Honestly, I don't know which is which... um, what I want is very dense, very green, very fragrant. I don't want any branches that kind of wander off this way and that."

"It sounds like you want a Douglas fir. About fifty percent of all Christmas trees are Douglas firs."

"I don't want a Douglas fir. Unless it has another name."

"Some people call it an Oregon pine. But they mostly live in Oregon."

"That's it, that's what we want. We want an Oregon pine."

"All right then," Farmer Wendy said. "I'm going to go get your cutting kit, and while I'm gone I recommend you watch our YouTube channel. There's a video on there that explains how to cut down a Christmas tree."

I took out my phone, unlocked it, and hopped onto YouTube. As I did, I asked Cal, "What's the problem with Douglas?"

"Uh, before she met me Mary Ann went out with this guy named Douglas. Real douche bag. So she hates the name. She can't even watch a Michael Douglas movie, it's that bad."

"Oregon pine it is."

Then I found the video and started it, holding out the phone so that Cal could watch it with me. Farmer Wyatt Wilson came on, standing out in a field in front of a very tall pine, saying, "Now, I'm going to teach you how to cut down your own Christmas tree. First, you want to put down the tarp you hopefully brought with you."

"They're really harping on that," Cal said.

"Next, take your saw, or ours if you didn't bring one—oh and by the way we do not allow chainsaws or any other kind of motorized saw. It really ruins our holiday when our customers cut their limbs off."

"He did not just say that," Cal said.

"He did."

I paused the video, "You've never been here before, have you?"

He sighed heavily. "No, I haven't. I usually get a tree at a lot in Bellflower and then finish up my Christmas shopping. Mary Ann thinks I come all the way out here."

"You should probably tell her the truth. It would be good for your marriage," I said, though honestly, I had no idea if it was true. Maybe it would be horrible for their marriage. Some people were actually happier lying to each other.

"Look, about earlier, I'm sorry I got so touchy," Cal said. "And you're right, Mary Ann and I are having trouble. I think... she's not ready to deal with it, so don't say anything, but, I think my wife is a lesbian. Our relationship, well it's never been what you'd call passionate. Really, it's like we've been friends all these years. I think there's a part of her that she needs to explore."

"Wow, you're taking it really well."

"Trust me, I'm not."

And then Farmer Wendy was back, dragging a tarp and a burlap bag of tools. "Okay, so, you've watched the video and you know what you're doing. The Doug—um, Oregon pines are seven rows down that way. Pick out your tree, cut it down, then drag it back here on the tarp, we'll measure it to deter-mine the price, wrap it tight for you, put it on top of your car, strap it down, and off you go. Simple."

If only it had been.

Ten

CALVIN

OH MY GOD, how would I keep all my lies straight? I'd just told Gage that my wife, Mary Ann, was a lesbian. She was going to hate that. Not that she had anything against lesbians, it's just—well, who wants to be labeled something they're not? Particularly when it's by a friend who's pretending to be something he's not... oh God.

As we walked down the rows to the Oregon pines, which was probably a total of seven or eight acres, dragging the tarp and tools behind us, I attempted to decide what I should do next. Part of me wanted to retract the whole Mary Ann is a lesbian thing. But honestly it did seem to have led Gage off the trail.

I'm sure Mary Ann was wrong; he didn't see right through us. I mean, yeah, he had suspicions, but I was doing a pretty good job of deflecting his concerns. As soon as we got back home, I was going to have to tell Mary Ann all about our troubled marriage and her confused sexuality. She deserved to know.

"Do you know how tall a tree you want?" Gage asked.

"About six feet," I guessed.

"Six feet?" he said. "You have twelve-foot ceilings, it will look tiny in your parlor."

"So, like nine?" I guessed.

"Nine would be better," Gage said. "Ten would probably be best."

They had a pretty impressive sound system that was spread all over the farm. Christmas music spewed out of speakers hung on posts. They looked like the kind you'd find at a drive-in movie. A lot of old music: Wham, Whitney, and Mariah.

Walking in the snow wasn't hard. It had been tamped down in the last few days. Fortunately, it hadn't turned to mud. I did have enough sense to wear a pair of boots. I wasn't going to ruin another pair of Italian shoes.

We arrived at the row that was marked Douglas fir and started walking down it, looking for a tree that was the right size. Most of the trees we passed were obviously too short. We were a few hundred feet down the row, I was beginning to get tired of dragging the tarp around, when the row just north of us fell off into a gully. The farm was hilly—which might have played into why they started growing Christmas trees in the first place. Most crops do better if they have a flat surface to grow on.

At first, we were walking by saplings. That made sense, I guess. The first trees in any row to reach heights appealing to customers would get cut down. The ones that were ten feet tall were pretty far down the row.

Since we weren't saying much, I decided to text Mary Ann and see if Douglas had called yet. It was about twenty after eleven, which would have been well after one in Aruba. Definitely lunchtime. She must have been near her phone because she texted back a NO very quickly.

Looking up from my phone, I saw a tree that might do. I pointed at it, saying, "What about that one?"

"Too short. It's about eight feet."

"How do you know?"

"I just do."

"Is there a tape measure in the sack?" I asked.

Gage poked around in the very large burlap bag we'd rented and finally said, "I don't see one."

"How are we going to know what ten feet is?"

"Well, I'm almost six feet tall."

"Okay, so four feet taller than you."

He shot his arm up into the air. "I think this adds about a foot and a half, so I can stand next to the tree, and we'll know where seven and a half feet is."

Keeping his arm in the air, he walked over to the tree in question. His fingers were a few inches below the very top of the tree. "See? Eight feet."

It was annoying that he could do that. I looked down the row for a taller tree. "What about that one down there?"

"Yeah, it looks about right."

"Why do I feel like Goldilocks?"

"Because you're indecisive?" he asked. It was a joke. I could tell it was a joke, but I still bristled. I was not indecisive.

We were standing in front of the tree I'd pointed out, so I said, "Yes, this one."

"I'll saw and you hold," Gage said.

"I can saw, you hold."

"Okay, I was just trying to be nice."

We spread the tarp out on the ground next to the tree.

"You know, it's kind of on a hill. It might be easier if we cut it on the other side."

I walked around to look down the hill. It was pretty steep. It was only about thirty feet to the bottom of the gully, but still.

"No, I think I want to do it on this side."

But then, as soon as I got down onto the tarp, I saw how he might have had a better idea. There was only about eight inches of room between the lowest branch and the snow-covered ground. Squeezing under there would very likely destroy my Burberry coat.

Stubbornly, I did not move around the tree. Instead, I stood back up, took off the coat, folded it carefully onto the tarp, then did the same with the sweater I was wearing.

"Do you always undress to cut down Christmas trees?"

"I don't cut down—" Oh, it was a joke. He was teasing me. Why did he keep teasing me?

Grabbing the saw, I got back down onto the tarp and slid under the bottom branches. The trunk was only about five inches across. This was going to be a piece of cake.

Trying to stay on the tarp, I slid under the tree with the saw. It was tight, but I managed to get the saw into position. The saw was a hack saw—maybe, I'm not sure. It had a long blade with thick teeth and a bent bar that made the whole thing a triangle.

I pushed it across the trunk to make a groove and then stuck to that groove, back and forth, and back and forth. When I was a little more than halfway through, the weight of the tree began to bear down on the blade, and I couldn't get it to move.

"I'm stuck."

"Stuck how?"

"I can't move the saw anymore. The weight of the tree is pressing down on it."

"Maybe if I pull on the tree," Gage said, and as he did the trunk lifted off the blade. Great. Except, well, I kept sawing, and he kept pulling and then snap, the tree broke away. It was almost instantly gone, sliding down the hill.

As I stood, I wondered... *Where is Gage?* I couldn't see

him anywhere. Oh my God, he was under the tree. I ran, slid, hopped, bounced down the hill. As I did that, he dragged himself out from under the tree just in time for me to trip and fall on top of him.

We lay there, noses touching, he smelled amazing, felt amazing. I could feel his breath on my lips. Then he asked, "Are we going to be doing this a lot?"

"No. We only need one tree."

"I meant this thing where you end up pressed against me."

"Believe me, it's not deliberate."

"I didn't say it was deliberate. I said it keeps happening."

"Twice. Twice is not 'it keeps happening.'"

"Twice in less than twenty-four hours."

"Okay, you've made your point."

"Do you think you could get off me now?"

"With pleasure." Okay, maybe that wasn't exactly the right response. "I mean, okay, sure. No problem."

I got off him—perhaps a little reluctantly. When I stood up, I reached out a hand to help him up. He ignored it and scrambled to his feet.

"How are we going to drag this tree uphill?"

"Um, well, I say we get the tarp and drag it through this gully until we get back to the main row."

He shrugged agreement and we trudged up the steep hill, slipping a few times. At the top, we were breathing heavily.

"I think it's safe to put your sweater and coat on again. You must be freezing."

"I'm sure I would be, if I wasn't sweating so much."

He picked up the sack and threw it down the hill. It didn't hit the ground until it was at the very bottom.

"Not bad."

"Grab the tarp," I said, picking up my sweater and coat. Then I started back down the hill, trying very hard not to fall on my ass.

As we walked back, dragging the tree—which by the way was now absolutely exhausting—I insisted we stop so I could text Mary Ann. HAS HE CALLED YET? Moments later: NO.

It was eleven thirty. It would take another twenty to thirty minutes before we were all checked out and had the tree on the roof. Then an hour home. That gave Douglas plenty of time to call. But I've met Douglas, it was entirely possible he wouldn't call anywhere near on time, or even call at all. That meant I should find something else to do with Gage.

"You had an event this afternoon, didn't you?"

"Yes, a pre-Christmas Eve get together. It's going to be at Drip, starting I think at one."

"Well, we'll just be able to make that on time."

"You want to do *my* Christmas?"

"I do."

Okay, I really didn't, but it was the only idea I could come up with that made any sense. I could say, 'hey let's go have lunch'— but why wouldn't we just go home and have lunch? It didn't really make any sense. Doing him a favor and letting him do what he was going to do anyway, that would keep him from wondering why we weren't going home.

Getting the tree wrapped and strapped to the top of my car went well—or at least no one fell down. I paid for the tree and the kit to chop it down with my emergency credit card, hoping that I'd be able to get through the next three days without running this one over the limit.

Driving back, I decided to broach the issue of his statement again. "I think we need to talk a bit more seriously about what you're going to say to the judge. Let's work on an opening sentence. 'Mr. Hammond, what did you learn by spending Christmas with a nice Christian family?'"

"Well, I learned that some Christians are kind and generous people."

"You have to take out the word some."

"Then it's not a true statement. Not *all* Christians are kind and generous. Some Christians are downright evil."

"I know that. You know that. That's not how Judge Winthrop sees the world."

"I can't say all Christians are kind and generous people."

"Can you say that you learned *most* Christians are kind and generous people?"

"But I didn't learn that. I learned that you and your wife are kind and generous people. That's two. Two Christians are not most."

"How about many? Can you say that many Christians are kind and generous people?

"Two is not many."

"What about the kids, can you throw them in? That would make four. Four is many. You've learned that many Christians are kind and generous people. Do you think you could say that?"

"Maybe."

"You will need to say you regret burning down the Christmas tree."

"I do regret that."

"Great!"

"It's turned Jeff David Stickney into a national hero."

"Okay, leave that part off. Stick to how you regret burning down the Christmas tree at WRWG. Now, it might be a good idea to say that you've learned that it's a good idea to love everyone even if you don't agree with them."

"So, you're saying I have to be a better Christian than Jeff David Stickney? He hates anyone who isn't like him."

"Yes, I'm aware of that. And yes, you do have to be a better Christian—wait, are you a Christian?"

"Not exactly, no."

"Definitely don't say that to the judge. And, honestly, just because you're not a Christian doesn't mean you can't be a better Christian than most."

"I would say that I *am* a better Christian than most. If we're judging on the basis of goodness and actually following the teachings of Christ."

"Yeah, unfortunately, not a lot of people use that basis."

Eleven

GAGE

I SHOULD HAVE KNOWN the kids would be too much for Cal. When it came down to it, he was pretty strait-laced. Or maybe just pretty straight.

When we walked into Drip, our group was in the back. They'd pushed some tables together, and looked like they were having a great time. I walked over with Cal. I stole a glance at him and saw that he looked terrified.

Neo stood up, so I introduced them first. "This is Neo whose pronouns are they/their."

Neo said, 'Hey.'

They were wearing a loose-fitting Taylor Swift T-shirt—which I think was meant to be ironic—close-cropped hair, jeans and a pair of Chucks.

"Neo is nonbinary," I explained. Though it seemed pretty obvious to me, I suspected Cal didn't get it.

"I prefer *enby*," Neo said.

"Okay, sure. And this is Debra, she/her. She's bisexual but homoromantic. Is that right?"

"Uh-huh. Who is this?" Debra asked. That's when I realized I wasn't leaving Cal anytime to talk nor was I telling the kids who he was.

"This is Cal, he's sort of my lawyer."

"Oh, that's right," Debra said. "You're in a lot of trouble."

"Come on guys, I said we shouldn't bring that up," Neo said.

"Why would you say that?" I asked. "You didn't think I was coming."

"Oh, we all thought you were coming," Millie Marie said. To Cal she said, "I'm Millie Marie. She/her. I'm trans." She turned back to me and said, "Don't you think it's a bit reductive to introduce us by how we identify."

"It probably is," I admitted. "But we do it at weekly rap and Cal is straight. He/him. He's less likely to say anything offensive if we give him the information he needs."

"Always having to bend over backwards for straight, cisgendered males."

"Or we can call that being polite."

"I'm fine with whatever," Cal said, rousing himself. "And it's nice to meet you, Millie Marie."

"Why don't I get us a couple of coffee drinks and some lunch. They have good paninis," I said.

"Oh, no, let me," Cal said. "You like a latte with almond milk. How about the Christmas dinner panini? Turkey, cranberry sauce and stuffing in a panini."

"Wow, that's either amazing or terrible."

"Coming right up," he said, then walked away.

I sat down at the table next to the kids. Stephen was next to me. Sixteen, he/him, gay, very gay. He was giving me the look, and said, "Mmm-hmm. He's hot."

"Straight."

"They all say that. You make an adorable couple. Let me know if and when you get an OnlyFans page."

"Don't let your parents know you watch porn."

"I didn't say I watched porn."

"You didn't have to." I leaned over to Neo and asked them, "Did you bring the gifts?"

"Of course. Do you want to give them out now?"

"Yeah, why don't we."

I stood up and said, "Thank you all for being here this year. The time I've spent at NorthStar has been amazing and that's because of all of you. I know I'm not that much older that you are, but still, I'm impressed by your bravery, your passion, your determination to be yourselves. Merry Christmas kids."

The kids began chanting "We're here, we're queer, get used to it," just as Cal came back with our drinks and sandwiches. I saw him go pale and look around the coffee shop. The place was half full, but I didn't notice any neo-Nazis. Still, he looked completely freaked out, so I stood back up and quieted the kids.

"All right, all right. Don't you want your gifts?"

That elicited a cheer. Not my intent.

While Cal spread out our lunch, I began handing out gifts. A baseball hat with an embroidered rainbow flag for Neo —they were older and living on their own, so they could bring a gift like that home. The others were a bit more challenging. I wasn't able to resist an eyeshadow kit for Millie Marie and the same for Debra. Stephen got a copy of *Tales of the City*.

"Yuck. Is this Dickens?"

"No, it's far from Dickens."

"You idiot," Debra said. "It was on Netflix."

"Oh, okay."

"And there's a gift card, so you can download the e-book if you don't want your parents to see the book itself. Just leave the paperback at NorthStar."

I had gifts for kids who weren't there: Elbert, Pearl, Tiff— and Ralph, who walked in just as I finished. Stephen jumped up from the table and ran into his arms. They'd been on-again, off-again for a year. It looked like they were on-again, at least for the holiday.

They were all busy, so I turned my attention to poor Cal.

"This is a bit much for you, isn't it?"

"It's fine. Your sandwich is getting cold."

I noticed he'd taken a couple of bites of his. "Did you get the same one?"

"I did."

"How is it?"

"Not bad. I'm probably going to get sick of turkey this week."

"Every year." I took a sip of my latte and then a bite of my sandwich. He was right, it wasn't bad.

Millie Marie popped into the chair next to me. "My grandparents are coming to dinner tomorrow and my dad says I have to be Mark for the day. He says if I don't do it, he'll throw me out."

"What does your mother say?"

"She's not saying anything, really. I mean, it's because of her that I get to be myself at all, so I can't get mad at her."

"You're sixteen and a half now, aren't you? You only have a year and a half then you can move out. It's probably best to do what you need to do to stay safe until you're eighteen."

"It's illegal for him to throw you out," Cal said, speaking into his sandwich.

"What?" Millie Marie asked.

"I said it's illegal," he looked up and explained. "If your father throws you out before you're eighteen he could be arrested."

"Really?" Millie Marie said as she thought it through. "That might just make things worse, though."

"It might," Cal said. "The other thing is that you don't

have to wait until you're eighteen. We can emancipate you. Do you think you're ready to be an adult?"

"I don't know."

"That's a good answer," Cal said. "Look, Gage is right. You have options. You need to stay safe. But sometimes it's hard to know what safe is. Exploring your options makes it easier to figure out what you should do."

I may have been gaping at Cal. What he was saying was so nice. The look on his face though, it was so dour. Or frightened. It was like it actually hurt him to help Millie Marie.

I was totally confused. It might have something to do with the things that were going on with Mary Ann, I thought. I wished I could help more with—I had an idea. I said, "Excuse me for a second" and went and sat by Neo at the far end of the table.

"Are you busy later?" I asked.

"What do you mean by later?"

"Early this evening? If you could come by while we're trimming the tree."

"That feels a bit intrusive."

"Well, I'm there so... The thing is, Cal thinks his wife might be a lesbian. Your gaydar is better than mine—at least when it comes to lesbians."

"At least when it comes to all queer people."

"Okay. Fine. You are the enby ruler of all things queer."

"Thanks. I'll be there."

When I went back to sit next to Cal, there was a middle-aged woman standing over him, saying, "What you're doing with these children is disgusting. And on Christmas Eve, too. You should be ashamed. Groomer."

The look on his face was absolute terror, so I stepped in and said, "We're not doing anything with these kids except helping them have a nice holiday no matter what they're facing at home."

"What they're facing at home? You mean, decent God-fearing parents?"

"I mean, judgement and hatred. They deserve a little time at Christmas to relax and be themselves. You're getting in the way of that."

"Hatred! You call saving a child from eternal damnation hatred!"

That's when the manager, who couldn't have been more than nineteen, came over and said, "Ma'am, I think you need to leave."

"Me?! You're throwing *me* out?! You should be throwing these pedophiles out! You should want to save these children!"

"Please don't make me call the sheriff."

"Sheriff Watkins believes in protecting the family."

"You can't harass our customers, no matter what Sheriff Watkins believes."

The look on her face suggested she wasn't so sure what Sheriff Watkins might do. "What about my freedom of speech?"

The manager, who'd probably had a recent class in U.S. government said, "If you're referring to your constitutional right, the First Amendment has to do with the government restricting your freedom of speech. A business like this one has every right to restrict your speech in any way they choose."

"Well... I can't stand here arguing with you about things you clearly do not understand. I will be posting extensively letting people know what kind of place this is. I will not be back."

The last made the kids break out in cheers and applause. She gave them a look that suggested she'd send them to hell right then and there if she could. Then she walked out of Drip.

I took a deep breath and thanked the manager for helping us out.

"You're welcome. She's done things like that before. She'll be back in about two weeks." He turned to the kids and asked, "Does anyone need anything? I'll do one round, coffees only, on the house."

The kids jumped on that. Half of them following him up to the counter. When he walked away, I looked at Cal who was visibly shaken.

"I guess you've never had to deal with someone like that."

"I'm fine," he said, though he obviously wasn't.

"Come on, you're a nice straight guy. People don't talk to you that way. Look, everyone thinks things are better for queer people—and they are, they really are. But at the same time hate crimes are up and people like that woman feel entitled to say horrible things to us."

"How do you deal with it?"

"You just do, because you have to."

Twelve

CALVIN

FUNNY STORY. I became a lawyer because my parents threw me out a couple weeks after my sixteenth birthday. I didn't even really come out. One night my mother was lecturing me about getting some hypothetical girl pregnant, even though I did not, and had not and never would have a girlfriend. I finally said, "You don't have to worry about it, okay?"

That apparently let the cat out of the proverbial bag, and the next day I was somehow, surprisingly homeless. I had a few bad months, four or five, and I got to know some bad parts of Detroit. And then my aunt found me. I've never actually figured out how. I lived with her for the next two years until I went away to college—which I paid for with student loans since, clearly, my parents weren't paying my way.

I do remember my aunt asking me if I wanted to go home shortly after she found me. We were in her kitchen. I remember thinking she must be asking because my parents missed me, but then she said, "It's illegal to throw your children out before they're eighteen. I can make them take you back—if you want me to."

No. I did not want her to do that. Going home to parents who didn't want me sounded like a terrible idea.

But the idea stayed with me. I could have my parents arrested any time I wanted. That gave me a sense of empowerment I hadn't had before. I wasn't a kid they'd just thrown away. I was a kid choosing not to have his parents prosecuted.

That's when I got interested in the law. Having the law on your side matters. I know that's not always true for queer people, but it's far from what it was fifty years ago. Yeah, they keep trying to legislate against us, but it doesn't seem to take. You can't discriminate on the basis of sex; you can try and say that in law sex only means gender, but it's impossible to separate sexuality and gender expression from the legal definition of sex.

It seems like we get closer to an even playing field every day, which is probably why some people feel it's important to make a scene in a coffee shop. A world where everyone is just like them is slipping away and they hate that. The things she was saying... struck a nerve. Dug up a bunch of stuff I didn't want to think about. Didn't want to think about it then, don't really want to think about it now.

Before we left the coffee shop, I got a text from Mary Ann saying that Douglas still had not called. I knew she probably wasn't happy about that. The next text said we might as well come back, which managed to sound defeated even though it was only six words.

It was a short drive back to the house. Before we took the tree off the roof of the car, Gage and I sat in the car for a few minutes. He had some things he wanted to say.

"I appreciate you trying to help Millie Marie. It was nice of you."

It was kind for a straight guy. If he knew I was gay, he might wonder why I didn't do more. I told him, "Don't mention it."

"Before we go in, there's something I want to talk to you about. Being with the kids made me think... well, you're guessing that Mary Ann might be a lesbian, but she hasn't actually said anything. Don't decide her identification for her. She might be bisexual or ace or, yeah, a lesbian. The point is, it's really up to her and you want to create a space where she can learn who she is."

"Thank you. I'll give that some thought."

At that moment, I was so grateful not to be Mary Ann's sex-starved heterosexual husband, since I had no idea what 'create a space where she can learn who she is' really meant. Did he think I was going to put a yurt in the yard where she could explore alternative sexualities? And why did it not occur to him—or fictional me for that matter—that I might just be bad in bed?

We got out of the car, undid the bungee cords holding down the Christmas tree, managed to slide it off the roof of my car without knocking anyone down, and then slowly carried it up to the porch. Mary Ann must have been keeping an eye out for us because she opened the door well before we got there. We brought the tree into the parlor. Mary Ann had already set up a tree stand and a skirt in front of the big window. We put the tree into the stand and then tightened the bolts that kept it in place. As we were moving the tree around, trying to make sure it was straight, Mary Ann whispered to me, "I need to talk to you."

I whispered back, "I need to talk to you."

"Is it straight?" Gage asked.

"What? Who?" I asked nervously.

"The tree. Is the tree straight?"

"It's fine," Mary Ann and I said at the same time.

"I don't know. It seems a little crooked to me."

"Look, do what you can," she said. "Cal and I have to have a talk. About the kids."

"Yes, about the kids."

Then she pulled me out of the parlor, leaving Gage alone to deal with the tree. We walked through the formal dining room into the kitchen and then went directly into the laundry room. Mary Ann shut the door behind us and then turned on the dryer.

We both spoke at the same time. She said, "My mother's here," while I said, "You're a lesbian."

Then we both said, "WHAT!?"

"But your mother never comes for Christmas. Doesn't she spend the holiday with friends?"

"Her bridge club. Unfortunately, they threw her out for cheating. She and her partner devised a way of passing information using the names of their grandchildren. What do you mean I'm a lesbian?"

"Gage picked up on our not getting along well. He thinks there's trouble in our marriage. He started asking questions and it just came out... I mean, you don't know you're a lesbian. I *think* you're a lesbian."

"You think I'm a lesbian? Why?"

"Because there's no passion in our marriage."

"Of course there's no passion in our marriage. You're gay!"

"I couldn't tell him that now, could I?"

"Why not? If you're going to tell him one of us is homosexual it should maybe be the homosexual."

"Look, he's not going to say anything to you."

"Then why did you have to tell me?"

"Because he might."

I was pretty sure she was about to hit me, so I asked, "Did you tell your mother about, you know, everything?"

"Yes, I did."

"How did it go?"

"Worse than you can possibly imagine."

And then, right on cue, Betsy Hinchmen-Jones opened

the laundry room door and walked in. Mary Ann hastily closed the door behind her.

Betsy was, by my best estimate, well over sixty. Very well over. Tall, thin and impeccably groomed, she had carefully dyed brunette hair and clear green eyes. She'd had work done, though it was hard to say how much. Mary Ann had tried to figure out what and when but had never been able to. Betsy had taken several 'trips to Europe' that probably didn't require a passport.

"Mary Ann, I told you not to leave me alone with your children for more than five minutes. You know I have a low tolerance."

"They're your grandchildren, you should want to spend time with them."

"I don't know what you're talking about. Family is the most important thing to me—in small doses." Then she looked at me and said, "Hello Cal. I'd say it's nice to see you, but it's not."

"It's not nice to see you either."

"Was that the firestarter I saw in the living room? Do you think it's safe to leave him alone with a Christmas tree?"

"He's fine, Mother. He seems like a very nice guy."

"With a mild case of pyromania."

"He says it was a rash decision and he seems to regret it. It's probably best not to talk about it," Mary Ann said.

"You know me, I'm the soul of discretion." To me she said, "So, we're all telling a bunch of lies so you can pull the wool over some nice old judge's eyes. Am I understanding this correctly?"

"He's not a *nice* old judge. I mean he's old, but he's also a homophobic, anti-Semitic, misogynistic—"

"He sounds delightful." Not giving me a chance to respond, a habit of hers, she said to Mary Ann, "The minute you told me you had a gay for a friend, I knew something like this would happen."

"You knew I'd end up pretending to be married to him?"

"Well, not that exactly, but something very much like it."

"Mother, you have to play along. It's only for three days. Can you do that? Please?"

"I just think... well, even though he's a pretend husband you could do better."

"I'm standing right here."

"If you were a good friend, you'd find her a better fake husband."

"I'll get right on that." I was starting to sweat. I knew Betsy was basically a very silly woman, but so soon after the horrible woman at the coffee shop... I felt on the verge of blowing up.

"And speaking of husbands, Mary Ann what are you doing about getting your real husband back?"

"Nothing. Our divorce is almost final. He's not coming back, and I don't want him back."

"Nonsense, of course you want him back. Douglas was an excellent husband."

"He was a cheater."

"Which is better than a homosexual you're only pretending you're married to. Now darling, you just don't understand the advantages to a cheating husband. They feel guilt, lots of guilt, or at least they pretend to. Either way, you're the one with the upper hand. You can get almost anything you want from a man who cheats."

"I am getting what I want. A divorce."

"We'd better get out there," I said. "Gage is going to get suspicious."

"Yes, by all means, let's worry about what your friend the arsonist thinks of us."

As soon as we were out of the laundry room and into the kitchen, Betsy asked, "Mary Ann, where's Shirley?"

Shirley was the woman who had been their housekeeper throughout Mary Ann's childhood. She'd been more than a housekeeper though; she'd done almost everything for Mary Ann when she was a child. They were still close, and Mary Ann visited her often at her family farm.

"I knew something was wrong the minute I walked in. I just couldn't put my finger on it. Why isn't she here?"

"Because she's eighty-two and has her own family. She called and offered, but I told her she should spend time with them."

"But she loves spending the holiday with us. I always got her out of here by three on Christmas day so she could go home and make dinner for her own two children."

"Six, Mother, Shirley has six kids."

"You're sure? Did she adopt some?"

"No, she always had six kids. Now she has more than a dozen grandchildren."

"Why don't I call her and see if she'll come over."

"No, you're not going to do that."

"But we can't spend Christmas waiting on ourselves. That sounds so depressing. Can you call a staffing service?"

"I don't think we have anything like that in Bellflower."

"We'll be fine," I said. "We'll all pitch in."

Betsy looked at me as though I was insane. "How about a women's shelter? Maybe they could send someone."

"Mother that's awful."

"I'm trying to be charitable. Are you saying I *shouldn't* hire someone who needs money? That's an absurd idea, if people didn't need money, no one would work."

Just then, Gage walked into the kitchen.

"Quick, hide the matches," Betsy said.

Mary Ann sighed heavily. "Gage, this is my mother, Betsy

Hinchmen-Jones. She's very rude and unpleasant so don't feel you have to be nice to her."

"Speaking of rude and unpleasant, it's the middle of the afternoon and you haven't offered me so much as a glass of wine."

"Fine, I'll get you a glass of wine."

"So, Gage, when you're not breaking the law, what do you do?" Betsy asked.

"I run a drop-in center for queer youth called NorthStar."

"And what kinds of things happen at this induction center?"

"Drop-in center. It's a safe space for teens and young adults to come and hang out, find support and help when they need it. The suicide rate for queer children is double that of their straight counterparts."

"And you don't think that's a reason to discourage these, as you call them, queer children? If normal children commit suicide less, then shouldn't all children be normal?"

"It's the discouragement that kills them," I hissed, my jaw tense. This caught Gage's attention and he gave me a curious look. I added, "Well isn't that obvious? *Mom.*"

"I'm just raising other possibilities," Betsy said sweetly. "You can't really be threatened by other viewpoints?"

"Some things are simply true," Gage said. "I'm sorry, but your view is wrong and it hurts people."

"Mother, here's your glass of wine. Try not to choke on it. Why don't we change the subject?"

"Everyone has to conform to society's expectations. I know I did. Do you think I set out to be a rich old lady who spends her time cheating at bridge?"

"Yes, Mother, I think that's exactly what you did."

"Well, you might be right. But I could have done other things along the way. I could have divorced your father instead of being a good wife and waiting for him to die."

"There's nothing wrong with divorce," Mary Ann said. Now it was her turn to be angry and terse. "You know what, we're going to have dinner and decorate the tree at five. I think we should all do whatever until then. Take a nap, read a book, watch TV—whatever. I know I need a break."

"Great," Gage said, ready to be done with us. "I'll be in the guest room."

"Mary Ann..." Betsy said.

"Oh, yeah, about that..." Mary Ann said. "We're a little short on beds. My mother is going to sleep with me and Cal you'll need to bunk in with Gage."

"What? No," I said, probably a little offensively.

"You know, Cal should stay with you. Your mom can have the guest room and I'll sleep on the couch," Gage said, reasonably.

"The couch in the parlor has a very narrow seat and it's also a valuable antique, so no. And the TV room has a love seat and a recliner, both of which are far too uncomfortable. Plus, it's my house and I decide who sleeps where."

Gage and I looked at each other for a moment. Then I said, "Fine. Whatever."

"Okay, well, I'm going to rest for a bit," Gage said, then he added to me, "I guess, if you want to rest, as well, too, you can—"

Quickly, I said, "That's okay. I'll go hang out in the TV room."

"The kids are in there watching a movie," Mary Ann said.

"Then that's what I'll do. I'll watch a movie with the kids. My kids. My children."

Of course, this was all a plot on Mary Ann's part. I was sure she thought if she put two gay men in a bed together they couldn't help but have sex, even if one of them was pretending not to be gay. Well, I'll show her. I will not, absolutely will not, have sex with Gage.

Thirteen

GAGE

I DID TAKE A NAP, for about an hour. Of course I was annoyed that Cal would be sleeping with me that night. Mary Ann kept her house very warm and the night before I'd had to throw off the covers and take off my gym shorts—that's how hot it was. Now, I'd have to wear the pajamas I'd brought with me, which were flannel. So, between the flannel pajamas, another body in bed, and the abundance of heat in the house, I would probably sweat like I was on a tropical island.

I took out my phone and hit the number for the burner phone my dad had used the day before. When he answered, I said, "Dad, it's Gage."

"How did you get this number?"

"You called me yesterday. It's on my phone."

"Oh, okay. Are you in a secure location?"

"I'm in the guest room, all alone."

"Is there a fan or a window air conditioner."

"No, it's December. People don't use those things in December."

"We need white noise. Are you near a tap? Could you run water?"

"Dad it's fine, I checked for bugs. Plus, you and I are not going to discuss anything criminal."

"Speak for yourself." Then he asked, "How is it going? Is it a nightmare? Are they treating you badly? They are, aren't they? Make a clicking noise if you can't talk."

"No one's treating me badly. They're really very nice. I don't think their marriage is going well, so their focus is somewhere else."

"I've been thinking. I should just confess."

"No, don't do that. This is almost over. Okay?"

"I can't stand the idea of you ending up in prison."

"I'm not going to prison. I'm getting probation. All I have to do is tell the judge what he wants to hear."

"Do you think you'll be able to do that?"

"I don't know."

"I am sorry about all this, it's just that I got so angry every time I saw that tree. And the things he was saying on his show."

"You don't listen to his show, do you?"

"You have to know what the enemy is up to."

"Oh, Dad."

"I hate that I'm missing Christmas with you. I hate that you're all alone with those people."

I might not always know where he was or even how to contact him, but he did show up for holidays. He was often the star attraction at my misfits' dinners.

"They're not that bad. They're just normal straight people."

"And you don't think that's bad?"

"I'm fine. Where are you, by the way?"

"Stop asking me that. You know I can't tell you."

"Are you warm enough? Do you have propane for your heater?"

"Yes, I'm fine. It's sweet of you to worry, but I've been

living off the grid for a long time. I know how to take care of myself."

I resisted the urge to say, "Yeah, not so much."

After the call I lay back down on the bed and worried about the statement I had to make to the judge. To be honest, I was dreading it. I was going to have to lie my head off and I hadn't ever been good at lying. Not that I didn't have practice. My father taught me to lie to the police, school officials, neighbors and anyone asking leading questions. Once he figured out how bad I was at lying, he stopped telling me things. Like where we lived.

When I went downstairs, I found Mary Ann, the kids and Betsy opening box after box of Christmas ornaments. Cal was standing on a step ladder putting lights on the tree.

Mary Ann saw me and smiled, "Hello Gage, dinner will be here in a few minutes. If you want to jump in, you can start with that box over there."

She pointed at a box of vintage glass ornaments. Opening the box, I took out one of the elaborate, indented ornaments which were all green and red and white.

"They're lovely," I said.

"They were my grandparents'. My mother would hang them on the tree when she was Gus' age." Mary Ann said. Then, "Piper, put down the phone and help Gus put ornaments on the tree."

Betsy huffed. "What she said is not true at all. I never hung ornaments on the tree. The help decorated it for us as a surprise every year. And we pretended that they were being kind and not groveling for the bonuses my father was about to give them."

"You're so sentimental," Mary Ann said dryly.

"I *am* sentimental. I often think of the woman who was my nanny. And I so wish I remembered her name."

I focused on the ornaments I was hanging on the tree. Eye

contact with Cal seemed dangerous just then. His mother-in-law was something else. If I looked at him, I'd crack up.

"Were they indentured servants?" Piper asked. She hadn't budged from the sofa.

"Oh sweetheart, I'm old but not that old. No, that ended after the Civil War; they confused it with slavery. Which is a shame. It's really just a way of buying in bulk. You pay a servant's salary for five years up front and then you work them as hard as you can to get your value. Really, if it was legal today, you'd be able to get indentured servants at Costco."

"Mother, just stop," Mary Ann said. "Piper knows exactly what indentured servitude was. She was just goading you. Which she needs to stop. Piper, if you could help your brother."

"It's okay," Gus said. "I can reach a lot."

Mary Ann went over and helped Gus herself, since he really couldn't reach much at all. To Cal, who was nearing the top of the tree, I said, "What about you? Can you reach a lot?"

"I'm doing just fine," he said, though he was beginning to totter. I stepped over just in time to steady him on the ladder. That meant grabbing him by the hips—well, okay, the ass. I could feel the muscles in his butt moving as he balanced himself. Red-faced, he looked down at me and said, "I'm fine. Really. I'm fine."

I let go but allowed my hands to hover nearby.

"Grandma, did you know that the Puritans didn't celebrate Christmas and even made it illegal?" Piper asked, a twinkle in her eye as she completely ignored her mother.

"Piper..." Cal said in a fatherly tone.

"I really don't think that's true," Betsy said. "Sounds like liberal propaganda to me. Mary Ann, hand me that box."

"No, it's true. I found multiple sources."

"Well, that could be liberal sites copying off one another,

creating an echo chamber. There's no way any Christian anywhere would ever make Christmas illegal."

Piper suppressed a smile. "It is *true*, Grandma."

"Yes, and just because something's true doesn't mean you have to believe it. You're an American and you have every right to live in your own special world."

"Piper, what you've found out is correct," Cal said. "The Puritans did not like ostentatious displays. They would hate our Christmas tree."

"Or," Betsy said, "that's what the deep state wants you to think."

"Oh, Mother," Mary Ann said.

"Why would the deep state not like Puritans?" I asked, having grown up on conspiracy theories about the deep state.

"Because they hate America and who is more American than a Puritan?" She was rooting around in the box of ornaments Mary Ann had given her. And before I could say anything about the Puritans basically being English and not really much of a thing after the revolution anyway, she exclaimed, "Oh, I love these. Mary Ann, look, I found the crystal ornaments I get every year from that little bank in the Cayman Islands. The one I like so much."

"I really don't love putting those on the tree. Their logo is so big. It's crass."

"Oh, that doesn't bother me. It reminds me that it's time to send them some money so the tax man doesn't find it."

"Mother, please don't talk about committing felonies in front of the children."

"Felonies? Don't be silly. Tax avoidance is perfectly legal."

"Tax evasion is not."

"But really, aren't they the same thing?"

"Cal, tell her they're not the same thing."

"They're not the same thing. You need a good accountant

to explain the difference. And possibly a tax lawyer." He climbed down the step ladder, then folded it up.

Betsy sighed. "You all get so caught up with the meaning of words. The one thing I know for certain is that smart people do not pay taxes and *I* am a smart person."

Cal plugged the lights in, and the tree lit up. There weren't a lot of ornaments on it yet, but with the lights on it was starting to look like a Christmas tree. A wonderful Christmas tree.

The doorbell rang. Mary Ann jumped up, saying "That must be the ChowDown driver. That was fast."

"Um. Actually, it might be my friend, Neo. I suggested they stop by for a real fast drink."

"They?" Betsy said. "How many of them are there?"

"Just one. Neo is enby."

"I'm sorry. What language are you speaking?"

"Enby means nonbinary," Piper said.

To me, Betsy said, "Oh, I get it, you're speaking Woke. Please don't do that in front of my grandchildren."

"I'm going to get the door," Mary Ann said with a sigh. She popped into the foyer.

"What's *woke*?" Gus asked.

"It's a virus, dear. Like Covid."

"Do I need a mask?" he asked.

"Oh no, masks just make it more contagious."

He looked very confused. I probably did too.

Then Mary Ann and Neo came into the parlor. Having left their coat in the foyer, Neo was wearing an oversized Christmas sweater, skinny jeans and a very elfin pair of boots. Mary Ann wore a white cable sweater, black tights and chunky red plastic jewelry. They looked cute together. I had a feeling I already knew what Neo's gaydar was going to say.

"I'm sorry to crash your holiday," Neo said.

"No, no, no, the more the merrier," Mary Ann said.

They held out a bottle of wine with a Christmas bow on it. Mary Ann took it. "Thank you. We have some open. Let me grab you a glass while Gage introduces you around."

Mary Ann scurried off to the kitchen.

I said, "Well, this is Betsy, Mary Ann's mother. You've met Cal before. And these are Mary Ann and Cal's children, Piper and Gus. Everyone, this is Neo. Neo uses the pronouns, they and them."

"Cool," Piper said.

Cal looked on edge, but then I realized he was watching Betsy's every flinch and flicker. She was going to say something, we all knew it. Well, Neo might not have.

"You know, I get it." Betsy said. "When I was young, we called people like you androgynous. Of course, I think they all died in crack houses before age thirty. Hopefully things will go better for you."

"I think they will. I don't like drugs."

"A lot of people say that, right before they overdose." She gave Neo a very big, charming smile and asked, "You're a friend of Gage's, what kind of criminal, are you?"

Neo glanced at me, basically asking with their eyes if it was all right to strangle this woman. Unfortunately, it wasn't.

"Now Betsy," Cal said.

"Yes, my dear son-in-law."

For some reason Cal didn't say anything else, so I said, "I think we need to get more ornaments on this tree." I grabbed a box that looked like it was from the eighties and handed it to Neo. "Why don't you spread these around."

I grabbed a box for Cal and one for myself. "We need to move this along."

Mary Ann was back with a glass of wine for Neo. She'd also brought the bottle and topped off everyone else, which killed it.

"Another dead soldier," Betsy said, meaning the empty

bottle. It was our second of the night. "I remember those ornaments, Neo. They're from the Reagan years. Such a wonderful man. He had the courage to take from the poor and give to the rich."

"Wow," I said. "I would have said the same thing. Except, you make it sound like a good thing."

"Oh, it was a good thing. I don't expect you to understand economics, though gay men have other valuable skills. What do you think about Mary Ann's drapes. Hideous, right?"

The drapes were a bronze-colored velvet. They seemed okay to me, but then I had a better grasp of economics than decorating.

"I love my drapes, Mother. You have to stop attacking them." Mary Ann stood up and said, "Well, I think we're almost ready for the presents."

"Do you need help?" I asked.

"That would be great."

As I followed Mary Ann out of the parlor, I grabbed Neo by the arm, so they'd come with us. The three of us went up the stairs.

"I keep the presents under my bed, so the kids are less likely to find them."

"Your house is very nice," Neo said.

"Thank you. It's a hundred and fifty years old. There are a lot of rooms, but they're all small and there are never enough electrical outlets. Electricity was installed in 1905, but there weren't a lot of things to plug in. I should rewire the whole house, but that's a huge project to take on."

"Do you do much of the upkeep yourself?" Neo asked. "Are you good with tools?"

"No, I'm not what you'd call handy. Scheduling repair services and getting the contractors to show up is a chore unto itself."

Then we were in the master bedroom. Mary Ann was

right, it wasn't a large room. Most of it was taken up by a queen-sized bed. Yeah, their separation was not going well if she wouldn't let Cal sleep with her in this large bed. You had to be pretty angry at someone to make them sleep on the floor.

"You're playing Christmas music downstairs. Can I put in a request?"

"Sure. I'm using one of those streaming services. We can find just about anything you like."

"I really like the Indigo Girls Christmas album. And, of course, Melissa Etheridge. Do you like those?"

"Um, I've heard of the Indigo Girls and Melissa Ethridge. I didn't know they had Christmas albums. But I'm sure we can find them."

As Mary Ann got on the floor and began to pull out Christmas presents, Neo looked at me with a big frown on their face. Then they mouthed, "I don't think so."

"No?" I mouthed back.

Neo shook their head.

Meanwhile, Mary Ann stacked Christmas gifts on the bed. There were a lot of them. She finished pulling gifts from under the bed and stood up. She started loading me up.

"You know what I was thinking about the other day?" Neo asked. "Field hockey. Did you play in high school, Mary Ann?"

"No, I didn't."

"Softball? Soccer?"

"I've never been sporty."

Neo raised an eyebrow at me. Then we all left the room carrying stacks of presents.

"Mary Ann, you go ahead. I need to ask Neo a couple things about business at NorthStar."

"Okay, don't be too long. The kids will think I've short-changed them."

As soon as she was out of earshot, I whispered, "You don't think she's a lesbian?"

"No, I don't get that vibe."

"Your questions were pretty stereotypical. I think there's a lot more to being a lesbian."

"What did you want me to do? Stick my tongue down her throat? I mean, speaking of stereotypical, that would be the predatory lesbian."

"I don't know what I thought you'd do. You really don't think she's a lesbian? What about bi, or pan or ace, or... I don't know."

"I think she's just a plain ordinary straight lady. Now her husband. He's definitely gay."

"What? No. He keeps freaking out about anything remotely queer. You saw him around the kids this afternoon. He was totally freaked."

"I don't know what that was about, but he's too pretty to be straight."

"Okay, that's another stereotype."

"I know, but it's a true one."

"I don't know..."

"Take my word for it. He's gay. Gay. Gay. Gay."

Fourteen

CALVIN

WHEN MARY ANN, Neo and Gage came back downstairs, Gage looked odd; like someone had just told him Santa wasn't real. I wanted to get him alone to see if I could find out what was going on, but that was a real challenge with six other people in the room.

They began putting the presents under the tree. There were certainly a lot of them. I wished for a moment that I'd had time to get something for Gage. Just to be considerate, nothing more. I could, I supposed, simply wrap one of the sweaters I had with me and give it to him in the morning. He might not notice it was slightly used. But then he probably didn't get me anything and I'd just be making him feel guilty, which wasn't at all what I wanted to do.

Mary Ann was on her knees in front of the tree arranging the gifts, when the doorbell rang again.

"That will be ChowDown," she said.

Getting up, Betsy said, "Sweetheart, let me take care of it."

"Really?" Mary Ann said. "You want to pay for dinner?"

"Is that so hard to believe?"

"Well, yes."

Betsy frowned at her and then went to the foyer. As soon as she was out of the room, I said to Mary Ann, "If at any point you decide to murder your mother, I'll take a leave of absence from the DA's office to defend you."

"Sweetheart, let's not discuss murdering grandma in front of the kids, they don't know you're joking."

When Mary Ann turned her attention to what her mother was doing in the hall, I mouthed to Piper, "No, I'm not joking."

Piper giggled. Something I didn't think she did very often.

Mary Ann got to her feet, saying, "Mother, I can hear you. What do you think you're doing? Did you just offer that man five hundred dollars to serve us dinner? And a thousand to come work for us tomorrow? He's a delivery driver."

Betsy came into the parlor with a little gray-haired man carrying three gigantic bags of food. She was saying, "Well, that's *like* a domestic."

Then to the driver she said, "Now, I'm going to call you Maria. My maid at home is Maria and if I call you anything else I'll just get confused."

"My name is Phillip."

"See? Almost the same thing." Leading him across the parlor, she asked, "Do you know any Spanish, Maria?"

"No."

"I'll kick in an extra two hundred if you can speak a little Spanish."

"Me es namo es Maria?"

"Well, I don't think that is Spanish, but it will have to do. Now, whatever you do don't tell me whether or not you have a green card.

"I don't have a green card. I was born in Detroit, so I don't need one."

"Oh, you *are* a good liar. Keep that up."

Then she pushed open the swinging door to the kitchen

and they were gone. Mary Ann looked at us for a second, and said, "How about you guys put the tinsel on the tree while I deal with this."

As soon as she was in the kitchen, I looked at Gage and said, "My family's insane."

"That's the way most families look from the inside. Trust me, yours is pretty normal."

"That's a frightening thought."

I picked up a box of tinsel, and said, "I guess we should finish this off." I took a clump of tinsel and began draping bits of tinsel here and there. Gage and Neo joined me. For some reason they kept eyeing each other.

Then Neo said, "You're kind of fastidious, aren't you?"

"I do like things neat and tidy."

Neo raised an eyebrow at Gage, which made me wonder what I'd just done. Then they asked, "You work out a lot, don't you?"

"I like to take care of myself."

"Can you use the phrase down low in a sentence?"

"All right," Gage said. "Neo, knock it off." To me he said "Sorry."

Oh God, they were figuring things out. What was I going to do? I'd told him I thought Mary Ann was a lesbian, did I need to reverse course and tell him that maybe I was gay or bi or curious or undecided? Crap, I did not want to go in that direction.

Mary Ann burst through the kitchen door carrying a stack of dinner plates. Her mother right behind her.

"What did you say?" Betsy wanted to know.

"I said, 'Stop torturing that poor man and tell him to go home.'"

"I'm not torturing him. I'm paying him five hundred dollars for a few hours of work. Seven hundred if he speaks Spanish while doing it."

Mary Ann angrily set the table.

"Darling, I thought you wanted me to support poor people."

"You don't need a servant, and you certainly don't need a servant on Christmas Eve. This is a big house and I have a cleaner, but you won't see her while you're here because she's with her family."

"Really? Or do you just not want to pay holiday rates?'

"Give the poor man five hundred dollars and tell him to go home."

"And take away his pride in having earned an honest dollar?"

Phillip came out of the kitchen with a large bowl. "This is chicken tandoori from Spirit of India. Where do you want it?"

"In the center of the table," Betsy said. "Thank you, Maria."

He set the dish in the center of the table and went back into the kitchen.

"I'm not sending her home," Betsy said.

"Fine. Could you get silverware for seven."

"I will not. You're trying to take Maria's job away from her."

"His name is Phillip."

Phillip returned with two large dishes, setting them next to the first one, and announced, "Walnut shrimp and beef fried rice from Emperor Ming's Table."

"Thank you, Maria. And could you get silverware for seven?"

"Yes, ma'am."

When he was back in the kitchen, she said, "Let's go back into the living room. The tree is almost finished." Betsy swept out of the dining room and into the parlor. With a broad, genuine smile, she said, "Oh, you've all done such a lovely job!"

Mary Ann began picking up the boxes the ornaments had been in. "Cal, step back and see if it's balanced."

"Oh, I think it's fine," Betsy said.

"You need more tinsel over there," Piper said, pointing.

I realized that Gus hadn't been saying much, so I asked, "What do you think, Gus? Does it need anything else."

"A fire extinguisher?"

Betsy cackled, while Mary Ann said, "Oh my God, Gus is that a joke? Because it's not very nice."

"It's not a joke. Last night Piper said a hundred and sixty trees catch fire every year. It might catch on fire."

Betsy yelled, "Maria!"

Phillip stuck his head out of the kitchen, saying, "Yes?"

Mary Ann answered, "There's a small fire extinguisher under the sink. Do you think you could bring it out and put it by the tree?"

"Of course."

Mary Ann turned to us and said, "I guess we should sit down and have dinner."

As we were gathered around the table, Phillip came out of the kitchen with another large bowl and the fire extinguisher. Setting the bowl on the table he said, "Classic pad thai from Star of Siam."

"Thank you, Phillip," Mary Ann said. To us, "This is very informal, so I just want everyone to dig in." With that she picked up Gus' dish and began to fill it for him.

"I just love Asian foods," Betsy announced. "It's just such a shame that we can't get Asian food without Asians. I'm sure there are actual Americans who could make Asian food if they just put their minds to it."

"Some of the kids I go to school with are Asian," Piper said. "I think they're actual Americans, too."

To Mary Ann, Betsy said, "I told you I'd pay for private school. I don't know why you won't let me."

"The public schools up here are good and we should support them. And I shouldn't have to tell you this, but there are Asian children in private schools, too."

"Yes, but they're the rich ones. You've never understood this. I'm not prejudiced. I like all sorts of rich people."

I couldn't help asking, "So, you really just hate poor people?"

"I never used the word hate. Did I use the word hate? I'm just expressing concern for my grandchildren's education. As most grandparents would. I don't see what's wrong with that."

Phillip was back with mounds of white rice and plates of naan.

I said, "Everything looks wonderful."

"Oh, it does," Neo agreed, as they reached for the orange chicken.

"Where do you live when you're not here," Gage asked Betsy.

"Palm Beach. I just love Florida. The climate is fabulous."

"You don't find the politics a little much?" Neo asked.

"They do lean liberal. I'll say that."

Gage and Neo gave each other a look but chose not to challenge that. I breathed a sigh of relief.

"Gus, do you have a girlfriend?" Betsy asked.

"Mother, he's barely seven."

"He knows I'm teasing him."

"No, he doesn't."

"What about me, Grandma, don't you want to know if I have a boyfriend?"

"You're twelve. If you have a boyfriend, I'm having him arrested."

"I've asked you not to do this," Mary Ann said.

"What? What am I doing?"

"You're re-enforcing rigid gender roles. I want my children to be free to be whoever they want to be."

"You mean like this it person?"

"Mother! That is so rude." Mary Ann stood up. "All right. You kids need to eat in the kitchen."

"Oh, Mary Ann, really."

"But we want to stay with the adults," Piper said, practically smirking.

"And I would let you if I thought there were any adults here."

"Should I leave?" Neo asked, their fork midair.

"You are not going anywhere," Mary Ann said. And then she swept into the kitchen.

"I don't know why she's so touchy. When I was her age, my mother would say things I didn't agree with and I would just ignore her. Of course, we drank more then. And I seem to remember taking a lot of Xanax. But really, is it so hard to pretend that things are fine even when they're not?"

Gage, Neo and I sat there quietly, pretending things were okay when they weren't. It was actually quite hard. Even with alcohol.

I said, "I'm really enjoying the pad thai."

And then Gage said to Betsy, "I'm sorry, I have to say this. It is very rude to call someone an *it*."

"Gage, just forget it, okay," Neo said.

"I'm not going to forget it."

"But I'm not the one who decided she was an *it*," Betsy said. "She decided that."

"No, I decided I'm a *they*," Neo said. "It's actually very different. I'm not an inanimate object."

"Kids today are just trying to be themselves," Gage said. "What is so wrong with that?"

"No one should be themselves," Betsy replied. "At least not in public."

Then she asked Neo, "How old are you, dear?"

"Twenty-two."

"There you go. You're a tomboy and that's okay. Sooner or later you'll meet the right boy, and you'll grow your hair out and put on a dress. It happens to all of us."

Mary Ann had come into the room and caught most of that.

"Oh God. Mother if you can't behave, you'll have to go to your room."

"I don't have a room; someone is in my room."

Seeming to burst, Gage turned to me and said, "Okay. You were right. There's no reason to put ourselves through this. We'll just tell the judge we spent the whole holiday together, and I'll tell him I learned all these amazing things from your family, which frankly will be easier to think up if I'm nowhere near them."

He stood up and as he did the doorbell rang.

"Maria!" Betsy screamed. "Can you get the door?"

"Si senior," he said as he flew through the dining room on his way to the foyer.

"Well, as I was saying, it's time for me to leave. I'll just pop upstairs and get my things. You can give me a ride, can't you Neo?"

They nodded.

"Cal, maybe we could meet on the 26th and go over some possible statements."

"I'm sorry this wasn't as easy as you thought it would be."

Before Gage could answer me, Judge Dudley Winthrop and a frumpy woman in her late thirties entered the room. They were nicely dressed, and he carried a Christmas gift bag. He held it out to Mary Ann.

"Merry Christmas. I hope we're not interrupting."

Fifteen

GAGE

THIS WHOLE THING was a disaster on so many levels and as soon as Judge Winthrop walked in I knew it was only going to get worse.

"Judge Winthrop, thank you so much for coming," Betsy said.

"Thank you for inviting us. This is my daughter, Imogene."

Imogene nodded timidly. She was nearly forty, had terrible bangs, wore a sack-like dress and thick glasses.

"I bring this one everywhere. Hoping to marry her off. My other daughter is with her husband and children. Barely has time to speak to me. I couldn't be prouder."

"This is my daughter, Mary Ann," Betsy said.

"Yes, of course. I have to say, it's always a pleasure to see the picture of your little family when your husband is in my courtroom."

Mary Ann smiled at Cal, a tight, grinding smile that couldn't have been good for her teeth. I wondered what that was about.

"And of course, you know Cal and the pyromaniac."

"I'm confused," I said. "How did you... Do you know each other?"

"Young man, there's an invention your generation seems to have forgotten," the judge said. "It's called a telephone book. As a public servant, I always list my number."

"Yes, I called him up and invited him to join us for Christmas Eve," Betsy said before calling out, "Maria! Bring two more settings."

The judge stared at the table for a moment saying, "Interesting meal you're having."

"Our Christmas Eve tradition is takeout and trimming the tree," Mary Ann said.

"Oh, yes, your tree is lovely," the judge said. "Just lovely."

Phillip came out of the kitchen with two more place settings. As he set the dishes in front of the Judge and Imogen, Betsy said, "Thank you, Maria."

"You're welcome. You didn't order no dessert. You got something or do you want me to run out?"

"There's a carrot cake in a white box on the second shelf in the fridge," Mary Ann said.

"Okay, I'll look around for some of them tiny plates," Phillip said.

As he left the room, Judge Winthrop looked terrified. "You said, 'Maria.' Was that a transexual person?"

"You know, I have no idea," Betsy said. "I didn't think to ask."

"Stop it," Mary Ann said. "My mother is just lazy. Her housekeeper at home is named Maria and she doesn't want to bother to learn this poor man's name. Which is Phillip, by the way."

"It's okay, you don't need to lie," Judge Winthrop said. "There's nothing illegal about being a transexual person. As long as they don't use the restroom and keep their distance from children. Which reminds me, where are Piper and Gus?"

"You know my children's names... I'm not sure how I feel about that." Mary Ann glared at Cal, cold and predatory.

"Our children, Mary Ann," Cal said, gently. "He sees their photo every time I'm in his courtroom."

"Yes. I keep trying to forget that. The kids are eating in the kitchen. Things got a bit political out here."

"That's too bad but probably wise. Have you started Gus in peewee football, yet?"

"No," Mary Ann said. "And I doubt we will. My Gus is not that kind of boy. He likes reading. Both of my children read quite a lot."

"Yes," he said as though he'd just bitten into a piece of rotten fruit. "Imogene is like that. Don't know where she gets it from. Her mother could barely get through the society page. I haven't read a book since law school. And to be honest, I don't think I read any while I was *in* law school."

"That's so clever of you to get a law degree without doing any of the work," Betsy said.

"Thank you," Judge Winthrop blushed.

"Speaking of the law," Cal said. "You don't think your being here is a little un—"

"Judge Winthrop," Betsy said. "I caught a glimpse of you on television the other day. You've really stirred people up."

"Yes, a lot of people are angry. This looks very good, is this chink food?"

"Father," Imogene whispered.

"What? No one here is Chinese."

"You know, Your Honor," Cal began again. "It may not be appropriate that you're here with us. Since you didn't sign off on the plea bargain, I still have a case in front of you."

"Oh pish-posh," Betsy said. "I invited them. How could that be inappropriate?"

"He's not wrong, though," Judge Winthrop said. "I suppose if the press got a hold of this... But, no, hold on...

When I gave my order we didn't discuss any verification process. Therefore... I've just stopped by to see that the order is being carried out. Which I see that it is." Then, with a glare at me, "I have to say I thought you'd try to cheat your way out of it. He hasn't tried that has he, Cal?"

"No. He hasn't."

"Well, you'll keep a close eye on him, won't you? I find that when you let them off easy they're back in court before you know it." With that the judge dug into his food.

"Yes, sir."

"Earlier, we were discussing people choosing their own pronouns," Betsy said. "What do you think, judge?"

He stopped chewing and just looked confused. To his daughter, he said, "Pronouns? What is she talking about?"

Imogene leaned in close to explain. She whispered into his ear for a few moments. He chewed for a moment. Swallowed. Then said, "It sounds to me like people think they can do anything they want."

"Exactly," Betsy said.

"People *can* do anything they want," I said. "It's called freedom."

"I don't know that freedom is a very good idea. It's very chaotic," the judge said.

"It's one of the founding principles of our country," Cal said. We locked eyes for a moment. We hadn't spent much time on the same side.

"I know the founding fathers gave it lip service," Betsy said. "You kind of have to if you're having a revolution. It gets people fired up. But once there's a government, you pull back on the whole freedom thing. That's where people like Judge Winthrop come in."

"Thank you, I try to do my part."

"You've been getting quite a lot of press, haven't you?"

"I have. I am getting a little tired of seeing the word 'crackpot' in front of my name."

None of us rushed to argue with that description. Then Betsy said, "You know, I think the press in this country is just awful. In my opinion, it's more important that news reporting be aspirational than accurate, don't you agree?"

"I do, I do, indeed. Anyway, we can't stay long. We've been invited to Jeff David Stickney's home for a party." He went back to shoveling orange chicken into his mouth.

"You really can't go there," Cal said. "It's even more inappropriate than coming here."

"Cal, he's a judge," Betsy said. "He can do whatever he wants. Didn't you learn that in law school?"

"No, but I've certainly learned it since."

"I *love* Jeff David Stickney," Betsy said. "I sometimes listen to his show on the streaming. I know nothing he says is true, but somehow that makes it more believable."

Mary Ann quickly refilled her plate and then stood up. "I'm going to eat in the kitchen with my children. I think the conversation will be more mature."

Then she left the room.

"Don't mind her, judge," Betsy said. "She's always been like that. I don't remember it, but I'm told I dropped her on her head."

"Well, that's nothing to worry about. As my mother always said, babies bounce."

"That's a horrifying story," Neo said. "It can't be true!"

"That's what I said," Betsy agreed. "I did my best to let the housekeeper do everything. If Mary Ann was dropped on her head, it wasn't me. I barely touched her."

Neo leaned into me and whispered, "Where are we? Did I stumble through some kind of portal to hell and not notice?"

"That's as good an explanation as any."

"Do you think, I know this is a lot to ask, but do you think

I could come with you to Jeff David Stickney's party?" Betsy asked.

"Of course, you can," the judge said.

"Wonderful. I'm just going to run upstairs and change my top. Don't leave without me." She stood up, but before she ran upstairs, she stuck her head in the kitchen and said, "Maria, I think everyone's done. You can clear the dishes." Then she ran through the dining room and parlor to get to the stairs. That left, me and Neo, Cal, the judge and his daughter.

It was very awkward for a moment, and then Phillip came out of the kitchen to clear our plates. Judge Winthrop took it on himself to ask, "Did a psychiatrist help you become what you are?"

"How d'you know that?"

"It's common. Now, if you feel the psychiatrist pressured you to become what you are in any way, you might be eligible for a settlement."

"You mean sue?"

"Yes, particularly if you did anything irreversible." Then he made a motion with sound, "Snip-snip."

Phillip stopped. "How do you know all this? It's supposed to be HIPPA-d."

"It's the same pattern of deception over and over again. I think with the right settlement you could have a lot of this reversed. Probably not the snip-snip—"

"I don't want the snip-snip reversed. Best thing to happen to my marriage in years. My wife loves it. I mean, three kids is enough and she's already got so much to worry about. Yeah, I had to see Dr. Williamson for six months, but he made me understand that just because you have the snip-snip doesn't mean you're not a man. I'm grateful to him. Anyhow, I took a peek at the carrot cake and you definitely wanna stick around for that."

Phillip carried out dinner plates into the kitchen. Judge

Winthrop, whose mouth had dropped open, said, "That poor man. He's completely deluded."

We sat there for an awkward moment. Then Neo asked, "Imogene, what do you like to do?"

"Softball," Judge Winthrop answered for her. "She likes to play softball. And in the winter, she trains to play softball."

"What's your favorite Christmas music, Imogene?"

"What was that you were listening to the other day when you were fixing the sink?" Her father asked.

"Indigo Girls. Classic."

Cal said, "You know, I think I should check on my wife and kids. Gage, why don't you come with me."

"I'll stay here and chat with Imogene," Neo said.

"Will there be cake soon?" Judge Winthrop asked, but we were already going through the kitchen door.

In the kitchen, Phillip was rinsing the dinner plates and putting them into the dishwasher. Mary Ann and the kids were sitting in the breakfast nook. The kids doing their thing with phones and books, not paying any attention to their mother. At some point, Cal had boxed up his case and the bankers' boxes sat waiting for him.

"The judge is asking about cake," I said.

"I found them tiny plates," Phillip said. "I'll take them out in a minute."

"Thank you, Phillip. Let me make some coffee first."

"I can do it," Phillip said.

"It's no bother," Mary Ann said. Then she asked Cal, "How is the judge's being here not an ex parte communication?"

"We didn't exactly discuss the case, so you could say it doesn't qualify."

"He did say he was surprised Gage complied with his order. Isn't that bias?" she said. "And what about going to Jeff

David Stickney's party? I mean, shouldn't he recuse himself? Either from court or the party?"

"Bad news," I said. "Your mother invited herself to Stickney's party."

"She would."

"I imagine we have grounds to ask for a new judge, but that wouldn't necessarily help Gage," Cal said.

"Wait a minute," I said. "Aren't you supposed to be trying to convict me?"

"Just because I'm trying to convict you, doesn't mean I'm not on your side."

"Oh, well thank you, that's very—" Sweet? Sexy? Romantic? Not making that mistake again. "—*kind* of you."

Oh God, this was getting difficult. I was starting to crush on this guy, which would be stupid, even if Neo was right and he was secretly and/or just realizing he was gay. Destroying a marriage seemed like the kind of disaster I wouldn't really want a featured role in. Well, I wouldn't be destroying a marriage, his sexuality was his sexuality and certainly not my fault—however if I did ever have sex with him, I'd rather that was all in the rearview mirror.

The tension must have been showing on my face, because Mary Ann said, "Don't worry. We're going to have cake and the kids are going to open one present, then my mother and the judge will go away. Then we can relax and watch a movie —my tradition is *Little Women*. The one with Christian Bale back when he was a swoony twenty-year-old."

She was so sweet and kind and suddenly I felt just awful for her. Her marriage might be, could be falling apart and she had no idea. Eventually, Cal would come to terms with who he was and that would be it. Poor Mary Ann would be a single mom. Well, single-ish. I'm sure Cal would step up and do his share. Although... now that I was thinking about it, he didn't really interact with the kids a lot. They didn't touch each other much. Maybe I was wrong, maybe I hadn't paid enough attention. Or Cal just wasn't very demonstrative. Or they just didn't matter to him.

Piper said, "I found something funny on Wikipedia. Hurricane Betsy, August 1965. An intense, deadly and destructive tropical storm that brought widespread damage. The storm's erratic nature, coupled with a lack of preparation, made it the first hurricane to cause more than a billion dollars in damage. Sound like anyone we know?"

"She gets that snarky sense of humor from her father," Mary Ann said, then seemed to regret it.

"I beg your pardon?" Cal said, pointedly.

I have to say, I agreed. I hadn't noticed that he had a snarky sense of humor. Come to think of it, the kids didn't really look much like him. He had gray eyes. The kids both had had brown eyes. Mary Ann's eyes were blue. I didn't remember my biology at all. I know we learned about what kinds of genes produced which colors. I couldn't remember, though, if you could get brown eyes from parents who both had light eyes. Somebody, somewhere had to have the gene for brown eyes.

On the other hand, both kids were smart and a little awkward and that was exactly like Cal. Not to mention, Mary Ann and her mother didn't look much like each other, and they certainly weren't alike in temperament. So it was entirely possible that the apples in this family fell very far from the tree.

Then we heard the judge in the other room saying, "Oh my word! You look lovely, just lovely."

Mary Ann told the kids to stay there and the rest of us went out into the dining room. Betsy stood in the arch between the parlor and the dining room, perfectly framed. She wore a pair of black slacks that draped like flowing oil and a shimmering silver sequined top. Over her arm, she'd slung a mink coat.

"Really Mother? That's what you packed for Christmas with your grandchildren?"

"I always travel with a sparkly top. I mean, you never know, right?"

"Yeah, typically I know what's going to happen in my life," Mary Ann said.

"How did I raise such a dull child?"

"Is that real fur?" Neo asked.

"Relax, dear. It's vintage. It's been dead longer than you've been alive."

"Don't be out too late, Mother. They're predicting several inches of snow."

"Did you want to give me a curfew?"

From her clutch, Betsy took a wad of cash and offered it to Mary Ann. "Could you pay Maria when she finishes? And remind her that I do want her to come back tomorrow. You decide what time since she'll be helping you."

Mary Ann took the cash saying, "Hold on for just a moment, Piper and Gus get to open a gift. Don't you want to watch?"

"Must I?"

"Yes, Mother, you must."

Mary Ann called out for the kids and, knowing what was coming, they rushed through the kitchen door, past their grandmother and into the parlor.

"Just pick one," Mary Ann said. "You'll get all the rest in the morning."

"Doesn't the little boy still believe in S-A-N-T-A?" the judge asked Mary Ann.

"Gus reads at a sixth-grade level, so he knows how to spell Santa. He also saw through all of that when he was four."

"I pick this one," Gus said. "It's from my mom."

It was clearly a book. He ripped at the snowflake patterned

paper and exposed that it was *Beowulf*. The graphic novel version.

"Wow, this is cool!" he said. "Thanks Mom."

Then it was Piper's turn. "This one's from my dad."

"Ah, you're welcome," Cal said.

"What is it?" she asked him.

"You're going to have to open it to find out."

"That's okay, you can tell me."

"Piper, open the gift from your father and then tell him thank you," Mary Ann said.

The box was flat and large, Piper got through the Santa-themed paper in a jiff. Inside was a white box. She took off the lid to expose a black T-shirt with the logo for Buffalo Wild Wings on the front. On top of that was a gift card for the same restaurant.

Everyone was silent for a long moment.

"I'm not understanding. You're all so quiet. Is the child a vegetarian or some such?" The judge asked.

Honestly, I didn't understand either. "You don't like chicken wings, Piper?"

"I hate them!" she exclaimed before she ran out of the room.

"Well, that was dramatic," Betsy said.

"I'm missing something," I said. "What just happened?"

"Yes, Daddy," Betsy said. "You need to let us in on the joke."

"Cal, you should go talk to her," Mary Ann said.

"You're right. I should."

Sixteen

CALVIN

PIPER'S ROOM was in the attic. At some point, someone had put up sheetrock, so the beams weren't exposed. That saved a lot of money on heating. The room felt large but wasn't. There were storage cupboards along both sides. In the middle under a window was Piper's antique metal bed. There was a desk next to the stairs and a tiny love seat at the foot of the bed. There wasn't much else.

"Piper—"

"What do you want?"

"Your mom said I should come and talk to you because that's what I would do if I really was your dad."

"But you're not really my dad so you can go away."

"I will. In a minute. I just want to say that... you know, your dad might not have picked that present out himself. He might have asked his girlfriend to take care of your gift and, well, she's nineteen which is not very mature—"

"You're not helping."

"No, I suppose I'm not. You know, sometimes parents aren't very nice and that doesn't have a lot to do with you. They do thoughtless things, mean things, not because that's what you deserve but because that's who they are. And I'm sorry about that."

She was silent.

I waited. If this were a TV show, she'd totally thank me for my incredible wisdom. It wasn't though and I'm not sure what I said was all that wise. But I did, at least, make an effort.

"You can go now."

"Okay. Sure." I said, then went down the stairs.

In the parlor, the judge, Imogene and Betsy were gone. Neo was beaming. Since it didn't seem to be the kind of evening to be happy about, I asked Gage, "Why is Neo so happy?"

"They got Imogene's number."

"Oh, great," I said, unenthusiastically. "You might want to be careful. You wouldn't want Judge Winthrop as a father-in-law."

Neo's smile turned to a frown. "You're a total buzzkill."

"How is Piper?" Mary Ann asked.

Not wanting to say too much in front of Gage, I said, "She's going to be fine."

"I'll check on her later. It's started snowing so my mother dragged the judge and Imogene out before cake. She was terrified she might miss the party. Their loss. I'll take carrot cake over Jeff David Stickney any day. Let's go into the kitchen."

Mary Ann and Neo led the way. Gage and I followed. Somehow, they managed to get through the kitchen door easily, but Cal and I almost collided. I stepped back and said, "After you."

"You're the guest so, really, it should be after you."

And then for a moment, just a moment, he looked at me, really looked, and I looked back. And it was that thing that happens when someone is into you and you're into them, except it wasn't. It couldn't be. I didn't want it to be. And he was still...

"One of us needs to walk through the door," I said.

"Oh, okay, fine," he said, sounding a little grumpy. He walked into the kitchen.

I stood there a moment wondering what had just happened. Had something happened? I mean, he might be nearsighted. Maybe he was just trying to focus. Or maybe my eyes were the color of a Naugahyde sofa he had in college, and he was trying to figure out why the color seemed familiar. I decided to stop trying to figure it out and walked into the kitchen.

Mary Ann was saying, "Phillip, you don't have to do anything else. You can go home to your family. Oh, and I have your money." She held out the cash her mother had given her.

He took the money. "It's okay. I'll stay until I'm finished."

"It's up to you," Mary Ann said. Then she took the cake out of the refrigerator.

It was a gorgeous three-layer carrot cake from Minnow Farms just outside Masons Bay. They had a bakery in addition to the farm and made the most incredible bread and desserts. In the winter, I was lucky enough to get their day-old bread a couple of times a month.

Mary Ann pulled a knife out of one of the drawers and started cutting slices. "Would you like a slice of cake, Phillip?"

"No thanks... my wife makes a devil's food chocolate cake every Christmas Eve. My kids are chocoholics."

"I hate that we're taking you away from your family."

"My wife is thrilled. Our oldest needs braces. We have dental insurance but that only covers half. We've been trying to figure out where we'd get an extra two grand. Because of your mom we're almost there."

"Ah, well, don't tell her that. She'll think she's Mother Teresa."

By that time, Mary Ann had set out slices for Cal, Neo and

me. She told us to help ourselves to coffee. "Should we go into the TV room to watch *Little Women*?"

Neo, who was already halfway through their slice, said, "I don't think I can do *Little Women*; way too heteronormative."

"We can watch the movie later," Mary Ann said.

"Oh no, it's your tradition. I have friends who are expecting me anyway."

"All right then. I really am sorry about my mother."

"Don't worry. I'm spending Christmas with my family tomorrow. They're going to spend the day calling me Nancy and forgetting my pronouns and then apologizing and then getting mad that they have to apologize. It'll be awkward and a little sad, but I'll get at least one frilly blouse I'll never wear."

"I guess you deal with people like my mother all the time."

"I do. Honestly, she's kind of an amateur. Don't tell her that though, she seemed impressed with herself."

We finished the delicious cake and then all walked Neo to the door. They wrapped up in their coat and scarf, and Mary Ann opened the front door. The snow was coming down hard.

"Are you sure you can get home all right, Neo?"

"Absolutely. I've got a Jeep with chains. "Thank you for your hospitality. You have a lovely family." Then they glanced at me as if to say, except him.

"Merry Christmas," we called after them as they walked down the walkway leaving deep footprints.

Gus was in the living room reading *Beowulf* for what might have been the second time. It was all pictures after all. "Come on Gus, we're going to watch a movie."

"Can I read my book at the same time?"

"You sure can. And I have a piece of cake for you."

"Okay."

We went into the other parlor, which was a sort of a TV room or a family room. There was a nice reclining chair and a small love seat. Across from them was a large flat screen TV, at least 50 inches. Mary Ann set up the movie and started it.

She got back into the recliner and pulled Gus onto her lap, he ate a few bites of cake but mostly he nestled against her half-reading *Beowulf*, half-watching *Little Women*. A very odd mix if you ask me.

I sat on the loveseat with Gage. It was an old loveseat. I was with Mary Ann when she picked it out. She'd just had Gus, Piper was around five. We went everywhere looking for the smallest loveseat available. Yes, the room was small, but she could have gotten something a little bigger. But this was what she wanted, something just big enough for her, a five-year-old and a newborn. I never asked but have always suspected that Buffalo Wild Wings was not the first restaurant where Douglas ordered off the menu, so-to-speak.

The loveseat was jamming me and Gage together. It was nearly impossible to find a position where I wasn't touching him in some way. Our thighs were pressed together, our elbows clanked. I held tight to the arm of the loveseat, attempting to keep from sliding into him.

It was Christmas and the March sisters were giving away their special holiday breakfast. "Teenage girls have changed a lot in the last hundred and sixty years," I said.

"Shhh," Mary Ann said.

Feeling the heat of Gage next to me, I began to worry about how I'd get through an entire night of sleeping next to him. Maybe I should suggest that he go home? Of course, that wasn't a good idea. Betsy was with the judge. Presumably, he'd be driving her home. What if he wanted to come in and check that Gage was still here? He'd certainly think he had that right.

No, he needed to stay here. I would get through it. Somehow. It would have helped if he wasn't so attractive. He wasn't my usual type. His buzzcut was extreme. He was so political... but when he looked at me neither of those things mattered.

He was just... Why couldn't he have been ugly, or at least a gay guy who *I* wasn't attracted to. That would make this a lot easier.

Oh God, between thinking about Gage being so close to me and worrying about how to get rid of him, I'd completely lost the thread of the movie. There were four sisters and an attractive boy next door. Jo was a tomboy, which means today she'd be enby, but because there was no Internet she can't figure that out, which sort of throws Neo's comment about the movie being too heteronormative out the window.

Jo wants to be a writer but only wants to write about pirates. She burns her sister's hair off. Why did she do that? Did she secretly hate her sister? It would be so much easier to follow this movie if someone got kidnapped. And then, suddenly, we were in the woods and the boy next door, Laurie, was proposing to Jo.

Gage said, "This is where the movie would end if I were Jo. I would absolutely have said yes to him, and we'd have started making babies right there in the woods."

"Oh, but I love the German professor," Mary Ann said.

I had no idea who she was talking about. I didn't remember a German professor. And yes, I'd seen the movie before. Or at least parts of it. Mary Ann played it every year, so I'd seen it just last year... or, no, I hadn't. I'd gone to Grand Rapids to see a guy on Christmas Eve's eve, which meant I was pretty tired by the time I reached Mary Ann's and had fallen asleep before the end of the first scene.

"I mean, I don't want to see the German professor naked in a calendar," she said. "But he talks to Jo about things that matter. And he's so sweet and kind, and he tells her she should write what she knows."

"What about you, Cal?" Gage asked. "Are you team Laurie or team German professor?"

Since I, a) didn't remember the movie at all and b) was

supposed to be straight, I said, "Neither. I'd go for one of the sisters. Probably the quiet one. She's hot."

"You mean the one who's dying?"

"Well, not that part."

"You're no fun," Mary Ann said. "It's not like we'd make you sleep with one of them. You're such a straight dude."

The way she said it told me I would be paying for the last two days for a very long time. Certainly, it wasn't the first indication that I was in a lot of trouble. It was simply the latest.

Gus had fallen asleep, so Mary Ann said, "I think we should put this one to bed."

She tried to get out of the recliner holding onto a seven-year-old, which honestly could have been an Olympic event. After a moment, she looked at me and said, "Could you help?" Which, as her husband, I should have figured out on my own.

"Yes, of course."

I jumped off the love seat and took Gus out of her arms. Once she was standing, I was ready to give him back. But she said, "You can take him." Then she led the way over to the stairs. We climbed the stairs and went into Gus' bedroom.

I put Gus onto the bed while his mother got a pair of PJs out of his dresser. I whispered, "Don't you think he should just sleep in his clothes?"

"I've tried that before. He'll wake up in the middle of the night and want to get into his pajamas."

"Can't he do that himself?"

"Can and will are different things."

"I guess he's pretty tired."

"It was a long day."

"I'll just... wait out here."

I stepped into the hallway to find Gage standing there. "Oh, hello," I said.

"Hi. I, uh, I think I'm going to say good night. I mean, obviously not to you, but to Mary Ann."

"She's just tucking Gus in."

"Yeah, I know. You were both doing that."

"She's better at it than I am."

"Okay. I'm probably going to read for a few minutes but maybe we should talk about how we're going to do this."

"How we're going to do what?"

"Sleep together. I mean, sleep in the same bed. Together."

"What's to talk about?'

"For example, what if I fall asleep before you come to bed and what if I'm on the wrong side or I fall asleep in the middle?"

"Don't fall asleep in the middle. Yeah, okay, let's go." I followed Gage into the bedroom, saying, "I know this is not what the judge had in mind when he said you had to spend the holiday here."

"I can sleep on the floor if you want," Gage said.

"No, you're the guest. I'll sleep on the floor."

"We both could sleep on the floor. Then we'd both be miserable."

"I think the point is to avoid sleeping together. Misery is a secondary question," I said. "We could use pillows, put them down the middle.

"That wouldn't leave a lot of room for us. It's a full-sized bed."

"I guess it wouldn't."

"We could also act like adults and just share the bed."

"Nothing's going to happen. I have a wife."

"And I know you have a wife."

"And I'm a heterosexual."

"Yes, you've mentioned that."

Mary Ann stuck her head in the room and asked, "What are you boys doing?"

"Trying to figure out the sleeping arrangements."

"What's to figure out? You get in the bed and fall asleep."

I rolled my eyes at her then reminded myself not to roll my eyes, very gay. I glanced at Gage; he hadn't noticed. I asked, "Gage, which side of the bed do you want to sleep on?"

"The side near the window.

"So, I have to sleep against the wall?"

"We could pull it out. The bed, I mean."

"I know you mean the bed."

"No, don't do that," Mary Ann said. "I have a lot of stuff under there. You remember, Cal, the photos from the first few years of our marriage. They never got into a photo album. It's kind of a mess."

I translated that to mean, after her breakup she'd hidden most of her photographs of Douglas under the bed. It would not be good to show any of that to Gage.

"Fine, I'll sleep against the wall," I said.

"I guess I'll say good night. Sleep tight boys."

Seventeen

GAGE

AWKWARD. I'm sure there were situations more awkward than this one, I just couldn't think of one. And to be honest, the idea of getting into bed with Cal wouldn't be any problem at all... if he wasn't Cal. But he was Cal. He was my prosecutor. And Mary Ann's husband. And maybe someone on the verge of coming out... and not one of those things made for good bedfellows.

I grabbed my bag and went to the bathroom to get ready for bed. I put on a pair of pajamas and brushed my teeth. I gave my underarms a sniff and decided I was okay. Then I took a very deep breath and went back to the guest room.

Cal stood next to the bed wearing a pair of plaid pajamas and a thick red sweater. I stopped and stared at him.

"Um, did you iron your pajamas?" I asked, noticing the crease in his bottoms.

"Just... very casually."

"You're wearing more clothing than when I left the room."

"It's chilly in here."

"No, it's not. In fact, last night it was very hot. That's why I wasn't wearing anything but a pair of shorts."

"Now you've got on pajamas, so it must be cooler in here."

"It's not, actually. I just, I thought it would be more polite. You know, since we're sharing a bed."

"Wear what you want. I'm straight. I could look at dicks all day and it wouldn't affect me in the least."

"Do you do that a lot?"

"What?"

"Look at dicks all day."

"I never look at dicks. Why would I look at dicks?"

"I don't know, you're the one who brought it up."

"I was just making an example of how completely comfortable I am with you wearing almost nothing to bed. Hell, wear nothing if you want to. I will not react at all."

I took off my pajamas, stripping down to boxer briefs.

"Happy?"

"No, not at all."

"Good. Do you need to go to the bathroom and brush your teeth?"

"Are you my mother?"

"No, but I'm not getting into bed until you do."

"Oh, fine. I'll be right back." He stormed out of the bedroom. I grabbed my phone and called Neo.

"I have to sleep with this guy."

"That's one way to find out if he's gay."

"That's not what I mean. I mean I have to *sleep* with him. There aren't enough beds."

"I think my way is better. Speaking of which, Imogene called me. She said the Jeff David Stickney party was a real bore. So she Uber-ed over here."

"She's there right now?"

"She is."

"And you're on the phone with me?"

"Good, you see the problem. Good-bye. Sweet dreams."

They clicked off.

I sat down on the bed then immediately got up. I was fidgety. I began worrying about where I should be when he came back. I shouldn't be on the bed, that was for certain. I'd look predatory. I could sit at the desk, but why? I could stand there looking at my phone... Would he think I was looking at a pickup app?

The door opened and he came into the room. I probably looked ridiculous. I cleared my throat and said, "After you." I couldn't help adding. "You might want to take off the sweater."

I think he was about to try the, 'I'm chilly' thing again, but a droplet of sweat trickled down his forehead. He pulled the sweater over his head and was about to fold it, when he stopped and carelessly tossed it onto the chair. He climbed into the bed and I climbed in after him. Both lying on our backs, we were almost immediately thigh to thigh.

"Could you scooch over?" he asked.

"Not really, I'll fall out of bed."

"How did people ever sleep in a full-sized bed?"

"People used to be smaller. And one of them was generally a woman. Women are smaller. Generally."

He turned onto his side facing the wall. I reached out and turned off the light. "Good night."

"Good night."

The moon was nearly full, so a lot of light came in through the window. I lay there, squeezing my eyes shut, attempting to will myself to sleep. Of course, I'm not sure that ever worked for anyone in the entire history of mankind. Why would Cal tell me his wife was a lesbian if she wasn't? He wanted to cover something up. Was it his own sexuality?

"Are you asleep?" I asked.

"Um, no."

Then I didn't say anything. Couldn't. Finally, he asked, "Are you going to say something or were you just curious."

"The reason I asked Neo to come tonight was that their gaydar is really good. I asked her to get a sense of Mary Ann... Anyway, she doesn't think Mary Ann is anything but your basic heterosexual cisgendered female."

"Oh. Okay. I guess I was wrong," he said, tersely. "Thank you for consulting an expert."

"They do have really good gaydar."

"Is gaydar really a thing? I mean, you don't get to decide about other people, nobody does."

"I know that. It's just, well, sometimes you can tell. Most of the time you can tell."

"And sometimes you can't. And sometimes you shouldn't."

"Wait a minute. You're the one who told me. You said you thought Mary Ann was a lesbian. And I'm saying I don't think so. Now, if you're saying I have no right to an opinion about someone else's sexuality, then neither do you. You should never have told me something like that in the first place."

"Fine, turn it around on the straight guy. Make it all my fault. It always is."

He was acting in the same dickish way straight guys always acted. Neo had to be wrong, he couldn't be gay. Still, that didn't stop me from saying, "You on the other hand."

"What about me."

"You pinged Neo's gaydar."

"I did, did I? Why do gays always think everyone is gay?"

"We don't think everyone is gay."

"Don't you? Isn't that what this is about? You want me to be gay?"

"Why would I want you to be gay?"

"I think the answer to that is fairly obvious."

"Is it?"

"You want me."

"Oh, yeah, sure... that's what straight guys always think. Every gay guy is out to get them."

"Have you looked at me?"

"Wow. Arrogant much?"

"So, you don't want me?"

"I don't."

"Great."

And then we were silent. I had no idea what to think of that exchange. Did I secretly want to have sex with him? Okay, not so secretly, but it *was* out of the question. I certainly wasn't about to chase after a straight guy. And if he wasn't a straight—

Hold on. Stick to the facts. Cal was a married man with two children. There was something wrong with his marriage, something which had to do with sex. They probably hadn't had sex in a very long time—which had made him doubt her sexuality. Or his.

"Are you asleep?" I asked.

"No."

"How long has it been since you lived in this house?"

"What?"

"I know you don't live here. I heard you and Mary Ann talking about you sleeping on the floor."

"It's been a few months."

"You don't want Judge Winthrop to find out?"

"You've probably never heard him on the destruction of the nuclear family."

"I can imagine. So where do you live? In your aunt's house?"

"Yeah, that's where I live."

"Where is your aunt? Is she coming to dinner tomorrow?"

"She's a snowbird. New Mexico."

"Do you miss being here?"

"You have no idea."

"So, what prompted your moving out?"

"I'd rather not talk about it."

"You say that a lot."

"Also something I'd rather not talk about."

"What was the thing with the chicken wings T-shirt? Why did that upset Piper so much?"

"She's a vegetarian."

"No, she's not. I watched her eat a half a pound of orange chicken."

"You're right she's not a vegetarian. Um, I used to take her to Buffalo Wild Wings all the time when she was younger. It was kind of our place, so I thought she'd like the T-Shirt. But with her mom and I being separated, she took it the wrong way, I guess."

"She'll get over it. Just give her time."

After that, we didn't say anything for a while. I stopped thinking about Cal, and tried not to worry about what I would say when we went back to court. Assuming that we weren't going to trial, I had a job to worry about.

While we received nothing like the money Jeff David Stickney got, our contributions had risen significantly. When all was said and done, we should have between twenty-five and thirty-thousand additional dollars to invest in the group. Since we were a not-for-profit, I'd have to call a meeting of the board and discuss it with them. I should have a plan though, an idea to pitch to them. The decent thing to do would be to start paying Neo for their work or at least some of their work. The board was unlikely to approve a full-time salary even if it hovered around poverty level.

We could try to buy our space. I'd have to figure out how much of a down payment we'd need and how much mortgage payments might be. Would they be less than rent? That was what I needed to know.

On the other hand, what we really needed was a hotline. A local phone number that kids could call and talk about their sexuality or gender issues with someone sympathetic. A place where they could get solid information—including the kind of legal advice Cal had talked about at Drip. Hold on, maybe we could pay Neo to run that? That would be two birds with one...

Around that point, I drifted off to sleep only to be woken a while later when Cal landed on top of me. My eyes popped open. There we were nose to nose. Lips hovering close. Again.

"Can I help you?" I asked.

"Sorry, I need a glass of water, so I was trying to get out of bed without waking you and my knee slipped off the mattress. And I kind of..."

"Yeah, I don't think there was any *kind of* about it. Do you think you might get off me now?"

Cal jumped off the bed. He grabbed a half-full glass of water from the nightstand and drained it. Then he turned to leave the room but then stopped, "Do you need anything... from the bathroom?"

"No, I'm fine. Thanks."

As soon as he left the room, it hit me. He could be one of those straight guys who liked to flirt with gay guys, liked to make it seem like they might be available and then, bang, nothing. That's what all this accidental pressing up against me was about. That's what the occasional locked eyes were about, too. He wanted me to want him so he could reject me.

Well, that was infuriating. It made me want to slap him or at the very least come on to him really strong. Okay, now I was completely awake. When Cal came back from the bathroom, I jumped out of bed so he wouldn't have to climb over me. He set the now full glass of water on the nightstand and climbed back into bed.

I almost climbed in after him, but I was bored with lying

there staring at the ceiling. "I'm going to sit up for a bit. If that's okay."

"Yeah sure."

I left the guest room, quietly closing the door behind me. The hallway was darker than the bedroom, but I managed to feel my way over to the stairs. I went downstairs, where there was a lot more moonlight coming through the windows. I was about to turn into the TV room—to be honest, I was thinking about the reclining chair and spending the rest of the night there—when I heard something move behind me.

Turning, I walked into the parlor. There at the foot of the Christmas tree wrapped in a blanket was Gus.

"What are you doing down here? Aren't you supposed to be in bed?"

"I just wanted to make sure the tree was okay."

That hit me like a sledgehammer.

"You're protecting it? From me?"

He nodded.

"Oh Buddy, I'm not going to burn down your Christmas tree."

"But you did burn down a Christmas tree."

"I guess I did, but the tree was owned by a man who's not very nice and he was using it to say things that hurt other people."

"Christmas trees say things? You mean they talk?"

"In a way, they do. For instance, your Christmas tree says that even though your grandmother can be a little challenging, your mom had a lot of nice Christmases when she was a kid, and it also says that she wants you to have a lot of really, really, really nice Christmases."

He seemed to think about that for a moment, and then said, "My mom and dad don't like each other."

That brought me up short. It shouldn't have. I knew they

were separated. What I didn't know was what a little kid like Gus would think about that.

"You know that doesn't mean they don't love you."

"I know. My mom told me that."

His dad should have told him that, too. I said as brightly as I could, "See, you don't have anything to worry about."

"They used to like each other, but then they stopped. I don't know why."

I could see where this was going. "They're not going to stop loving you. No matter what. Okay buddy?"

"But how do you know?"

"Because you're a nice kid. People don't stop loving nice kids." Okay, that was a complete lie, but telling someone else's seven-year-old the truth about the way the world worked was not even a possibility.

"Do you want to go back to your bed?" I asked.

"No. I think I like it here."

Eighteen

CALVIN

I **WOKE** up Christmas morning wrapped in Gage's arms. I don't know how or when that happened. I knew I had to extradite myself, but I took a few seconds to enjoy his soft rumbling breath, his sexy warmth, and the incredible feel of his body stretched along mine. And then I noticed—oh, well... a particular part of Gage had sprung to attention along the back of my thigh.

Yes, I needed to slip out from his embrace. Immediately. Of course, that was easier said than done. I was very nearly pinned to the wall. My only choice seemed to be to scrunch downward, which meant I was rubbing my ass against his hard... Oh God, just do it quickly. Otherwise, I'd be tempted to do it more than once. Did I do it more than once?

I disentangled my shoulders, then my head. I managed to sit up, which meant I was squeezed at the foot of the bed by the footboard. Then I crawled over his legs. As I did, he rolled over, knocking my hand out from under me and I tumbled onto the floor with a loud thump.

Gage sat up in bed, his sleepy eyes staring down at me. "What are you doing now?"

"Trying to get out of bed."

He lay back down. Then, before I could get off the floor, he popped back up. "Were we spooning?"

"Nope. Not even close."

"You're sure?"

"Of course, I'm sure. I don't cuddle with other men."

"If you say so."

I grabbed my bag and went to the bathroom where I took a quick shower (cold, very cold), shaved, brushed my teeth, put on deodorant (scentless) and cologne (heavy notes of cinnamon, leather and woody trails), then dressed in what I hoped was a dad-watching-his-kids-opening-gifts-Christmas-morning outfit. Khakis, a white T-shirt under a baby blue Oxford shirt, and a scuffed pair of moccasins. I looked casual and curated at the same time.

When I put my bag in the guest room, Gage had fallen back to sleep. Just as well, I thought, I could use a break from him. I just stood there, though. I didn't want to take a break from him. I wanted to get back into bed. But that would be a very, very bad idea.

Forcing myself from the room, I went downstairs and found Mary Ann, still wearing her pajamas, in the kitchen. She was lifting a turkey out of a giant pot and putting it into a large roasting pan.

"What are you doing?"

"I brined the turkey. Helps keep it moist."

"Oh, okay. Sounds great."

"I made blueberry muffins. If you want something else for breakfast, you'll have to make it yourself. I'm in Christmas dinner mode."

"Muffins are fine. Is there coffee?"

"Help yourself."

As I poured myself a cup of coffee, Mary Ann asked, "So... how was it? Sleeping with Gage?"

"Awful. I barely got any sleep."

"Oh, my."

"Not for *that* reason. It's a very small bed and neither of us is tiny, so we were crammed up against each other all night." I grabbed a plate and put two muffins on it.

"Oh, you poor thing," she said, dramatically.

"Yes, I understand, there are many situations where that might have been a lot of fun. This wasn't one of them."

"That's not my fault."

"Actually, I think you had a lot to do with getting us into that bed together."

"Whatever do you mean?"

"Oh, and by the way, you're not a lesbian, we're secretly separated, and I might be a closet case."

"Well, at least we're getting closer to reality."

"Why aren't the kids up? Why aren't they opening their presents?"

"I put that craziness to rest years ago. They don't get to open their presents until after breakfast. And breakfast is never before nine. Of course, you always sleep through that."

"That seems cruel to make them wait."

"Really? You think so? I give my kids everything they want. Making them wait an extra hour for gifts is hardly abuse."

"I don't know that you see it that way when you're seven."

"Well, you'll probably want to call child protective services after I tell you this. I make them pick two toys they don't want any more to give them to charity."

"Protective services isn't open on Christmas Day." Then I asked, "Have you heard from Douglas? Do you know when he's going to call the kids?"

"Not a word. If I wasn't so angry at you, I'd be furious with him."

"Go ahead, be furious with Douglas. Don't let *me* hold you back."

"Easier said than done. You see, Douglas has always been an ass. This is a new look for you."

One thing I've learned, when you're not coming off well in a conversation bring up someone worse. "Is your mother still sleeping?"

"She didn't come home."

"Oh, well, she's definitely grounded."

"It was probably a good idea that she stayed wherever she did. They're saying we had eleven inches of snow. You're going to need to shovel the driveway, hubby dear."

"I will, let me wake up."

"You know it's shocking how much like a real husband you are."

"That's not a compliment, is it?"

"Absolutely not."

Having wrestled the turkey into a roasting pan, Mary Ann tucked it into the lower of her two ovens. "There. I'm going to go take a shower."

"Okay," I said. Then I took my coffee and muffins and slipped into the breakfast nook. My boxes were still there. I opened one and took out a file. There were color copies of photos depicting Van Husen's bruises. They were a problem. A jury would want them explained.

I wondered if they could be self-inflicted. One photo showed bruises on his upper arms, another a bruise under his eye, and one that showed bruises all across the top of his chest as though someone had been beating against it.

My cell phone rang and I picked it up. Danny.

"Merry Christmas," I said.

"I want to know how things are going?"

I pulled my phone back to check the time. 8:07. Danny was in Colorado so that meant it was six in the morning.

"Shouldn't you be with your kids?"

"My kids are seventeen and nineteen. They spent most of last night drinking Coors and vaping. They won't be up for hours. Have you had time to work on the Van Husen case?"

"I'm working on it right now."

"Anything?"

"I did some research. Apparently abused men are unlikely to tell anyone about the abuse. So it's very unlikely he told his workout buddy, or if he did, he may have done so to set up his defense."

"Which would move this to first degree."

"Exactly. I'm probably going to need to find an expert witness. A psychologist who deals with abuse."

"That sounds pricey."

"It probably will be, but the jury can't believe for a minute that Van Husen was a battered husband."

"You'll need to find a way to do it without the expert," he said. "We don't really have the money."

How exactly would I do that? They had an expert; I'd have to wade through everything they've ever published on male abuse victims. Which would be a waste of time since the defense would have already vetted their expert witness. It would be almost impossible to score points off them.

"Is that it?" Danny asked.

I knew I should tell him about Judge Winthrop coming to Christmas Eve dinner, but if I did Danny would want the judge removed and then the case would get bounced right into the middle of the Van Husen trial and I was getting the distinct feeling Danny wanted an excuse to take that case away from me. Any excuse.

"Yup, that's it. For now."

"Oh, and I spoke to Sheriff Watkins. That video... well, two of those young men were Tony Watkins and Bart Watkins so there was no riot. Just some high-spirited young men horsing around. Do you think you can remember that?"

"Yes, I think I can."

Particularly since I'd told him there was no riot in the first place. He clicked off. I sipped my coffee for a moment and nibbled on a blueberry muffin.

Normal people called their families on Christmas. I could call my aunt in New Mexico. Well, it was too early. I could call her later, but I probably wouldn't. As much as I appreciated what she'd done for me, I was not close to my aunt. She was still tight with my mother and by extension my father. From time to time, she'd attempt to bring about a reconciliation. But it would always come with some kind of caveat.

When I was eighteen, the caveat was reparative therapy, which my parents offered to pay for. I passed on that. Later attempts were less obvious but typically came with suggestions to not say anything controversial. I passed on those, too. Given that it was Christmas, I assumed there might be another attempt, so I decided to call my aunt sometime in January.

I could call a friend but, other than Mary Ann, there weren't many. Most of the names in my contact book were men without last names and far away area codes. While I remembered a number of them fondly, it wasn't the type of fondly that made you want to wish them Merry Christmas.

I dug back into the Van Husen files. Since Van Husen wanted to rely on his medical records, they'd become part of discovery. I dug them out and began to scan through them. His doctor was on the witness list, so he'd be introducing whatever it was that the defense wanted the records to show.

Van Husen seemed to be basically healthy except for moderate to severe asthma, and some intestinal issues that the doctor suggested might be related to his use of weight-lifting supplements. I began looking for references to bruising. We already knew the doctor didn't suspect abuse, since he'd have had to report it. So, what did Van Husen tell the doctor? Did the doctor even notice the bruising? And if he didn't, wasn't that in itself significant?

Then I remembered that the photos Van Husen had taken had dates. I spread them out in date order then dug through the medical records to see if I could match them up. Most of them did not match up to any appointment. Except one.

Several months before Van Husen killed his wife, he visited his doctor regarding several severe asthma attacks he'd had. The doctor *did* note bruises on his patient's arms, knees and back. When questioned, the patient said he'd taken a fall down a short flight of stairs. Several thoughts popped into my head: 1.Van Husen would likely accuse his wife of pushing him. 2. How did the doctor even see the bruises? The notes didn't indicate that Van Husen asked to have them looked at, and an exam for asthma would not include taking one's clothes off. The visit was late spring. It's possible that Van Husen simply went everywhere in his workout gear. Those were all questions I'd need to consider when the doctor was on the stand. 3. How might this make first-degree murder more likely? a) If Van Husen deliberately fell down the stairs all by himself. b) If he deliberately wore revealing clothing—a tank top?—so his doctor would see the bruises. So how could I prove any of that?

I'd find a way. I knew I would. All I had to do was stay on the case. All I had to do was keep Danny from stealing it from me.

Nineteen

GAGE

OF COURSE, we woke up spooning. Did he really think I
didn't know that? I woke up as he was backing his butt into
me. More than once. That's the kind of thing I notice. So that
was settled. He was gay. Or bi. Or curious. Or heteroflexible.
Why did there have to be so many choices? For whatever
reason, it seemed that he was interested in, or at least consider-
ing, having sex with me. Which was not going to happen. I
liked his wife too much. Which didn't mean I wasn't going to
think about it. A lot.

After I took a shower, I decided to call my mother. I was
not as close to my mom as I was my dad. That was partly
because when they broke up she moved out West and I stayed
with my dad. I didn't see her a whole lot. When they were
married, she was every bit the left wing radical my father was,
but then she simply stopped talking about political things. She
claimed she didn't even watch the news. Her second husband,
Willard, was a retired golf pro, ten years her senior with a bad
case of emphysema. Most of her time was taken up caring
for him.

Even though it was only around eight—meaning it was

sixish in Arizona—it was all right to call, since I knew she'd be up to give Willard his medication.

When she answered the Facetime, I said, "Merry Christmas, Mom. How are you?"

"Merry Christmas to you sweetheart. I'm just fine." Her hair was closer to white than gray and the fluorescent lighting in her kitchen wasn't doing her wrinkles any favors.

"How's Willard?"

"Oh, well, he won't be bothering us. I hooked him up to his oxygen tank and gave him two gummies. He won't be able to talk for at least three hours."

"Mom, that's awful."

"It's not what it sounds like. The gummies really help with his arthritis. The pills the doctor gave him zonked him out twenty-four/seven. He'll come down about the time we call his kids in California. Then he'll be fine for most of the day."

"How's Rebecca?" My sister, the Republican.

"Amusing. She's still living her life as some kind of reproach to the way your father and I brought you kids up. She's raising her kids exactly the way my parents' generation raised your father and me. I'm already seeing signs that those kids are going to be radicalized libtards—as she calls me, to my face by the way. I call it the circle of life."

"I'm probably not going to call her then."

"No, I suggest you don't. I doubt you'll find her as amusing as I do. How is your father?"

"He's… well, you know, he's Dad."

"Is he talking about Area 51 or is it all about corporate greed poisoning America's food supply?"

"It's generalized at the moment. Mom, I never asked this question. When I was a kid, you were right there with him. You believed all the same things. What happened?"

"Exhaustion. As crazy as he might sound, your father is right about most things. I mean he's probably not being followed, but the rest of it... he's got his eyes open. He knows who the bad guys are and he knows what they're up to. And he's like that all the time, you know that. I couldn't live that way. I have to close my eyes some of the time, actually most of the time these days. I have to pretend things will be okay even when I'm pretty sure they won't be. I do love your father—there's no one like him. I've never been sorry I was with him. I'm also not sorry I'm without him. Other than his medical problems, Willard is the blandest man alive. And I enjoy that about him."

She took a deep breath and said, "I've been following your case. You should never have done it, Gage."

"It was a spur of the moment decision. Every time I drove by that tree—"

"Oh please, that's not what I mean. I know you're just covering for your father. You should never have done *that*."

"Oh."

"Yes, oh."

"The thing is... I can't imagine him doing well with any of this."

"And it's going well for you?"

It wasn't, clearly.

"It's almost over."

"If it takes a wrong turn, you need to let your father take responsibility."

"How did you know—"

"I just do."

She wished me Merry Christmas again and then clicked off. How did she know my dad wanted to confess? Did she just know him that well? Or were they in contact?

I went downstairs looking for breakfast. Peeking out the windows I saw that it must have snowed most of the night.

The entire world seemed to have turned white. A white Christmas. We were lucky this year.

In the kitchen, everything was warm and cozy. Mary Ann still in her bathrobe, fresh out of the shower with towel wrapped around her head, was chopping potatoes while Cal sat at the breakfast nook with his nose deep in his case files. Maybe Piper did take after him.

"Help yourself to coffee and a muffin or two. If you want eggs or something you're going to need to make it yourself. I'm deep in Christmas dinner prep."

"You really don't have to take care of me," I said. "I know I'm a weird kind of guest."

"I don't think of it that way," she said, then to her husband, "Cal, I asked you once to shovel the driveway. Could you go do that? My mother's going to show up at some point and I wouldn't want to lose her in a snow drift."

"Mmm," Cal said barely looking up.

"Do you have two shovels?" I asked. "I'll lend a hand."

"We do have two shovels. Cal?"

"What?"

"Shovel the driveway. Gage is going to help."

He stood up, the look on his face that of someone who'd just woken up. Obviously, he was trying hard to convict this guy.

"Okay, let's do it," he said.

I grabbed a muffin, and we went out to the foyer to put on our outside gear. He started to walk out of the house without buttoning his overcoat.

"Button your coat," I told him, through a mouthful of muffin.

"Excuse me?"

"You have to button your coat."

"No, I don't. Don't talk with your mouth full."

I swallowed hard and said, "People die shoveling snow."

"Old people."

"No, people who let their cores cool down to dangerous temperatures. Didn't you hear about that eighteen-year-old pregnant girl who died last year? It was national news."

"I'm not pregnant."

"Okay, that's not the point."

With a huff, he buttoned his coat and walked out onto the porch. I shoved the rest of the muffin into my mouth and followed him. Silently, we began to push the snow off the porch and its steps. When we got down the walk to the driveway, I said, "Why don't you push down the walk in a kind of rough draft and then I'll come by and neaten up the sides."

He shrugged. This was not particularly important to him. Not that it was to me. I was just trying to figure out the fastest way to get it done. The snow was deep, but we managed to get clear to the driveway in about five minutes.

"Why doesn't Mary Ann park in the garage?" I asked when we took a break. The garage was a wooden structure set back behind the house.

"It's full of junk," Cal said. "Mary Ann has a secret case of 'maybe-someday'."

"What does that mean?"

"It means we have a garage full of things she might want someday and so we're keeping them."

"Are any of those things a snow blower?"

"I think there's a broken one in there."

"Ah, okay." Then I pointed at the driveway and asked, "Shall we?"

We started digging out the driveway. It wasn't particularly long, but there were two snow covered cars to clean off. As soon as we got it cleaned off, we were going to have to push the snow off the cars and then clean that up. We'd basically cleaned up the driveway around Mary Ann's minivan and were about to start on Cal's Prius when we took another break.

"So, I was wondering about something," I said. "You said you lost your parents? When did they die?"

"They're not dead. I lost them in another sense."

"What happened?"

He took a moment before he said, "They're religious. I told them I didn't believe the same things they did. They tried getting me to repent for a while before they finally threw me out."

"Wow. I'm sorry. I get so focused on my own community that I forget that people throw their kids out for all sorts of reasons, not just because they're queer. How old were you?"

"Just sixteen."

"That's why it was hard for you being with the kids yesterday. You identified with them."

"I did. Kind of."

That seemed like a dangerous road to go down again, so I said, "It must have been a struggle getting through college, going to law school."

"It was. No one paid my way. No one gave me a used car to drive."

"Sorry about that. It's impressive though. It shows a lot of grit."

"It's just—I mean, I did it. It's not a big deal. I got a lot of financial aid and I have a giant student loan to pay off. Everybody's got something."

"And not everyone handles it as well as you have."

"I don't know that I'd say that."

At just that moment, a large, black SUV pulled up in front of the house. Betsy stepped out of the passenger side. Her hair was a fuzzy mess, the fur floated around her elbows, her slacks were creased in all the wrong places. She stumbled forward and then turned around. With a Herculean effort she slammed the door of the giant vehicle. Then she walked unsteadily up the driveway.

"Walk of shame Betsy?" Cal asked.

"Cal, she's your mother-in-law."

"Fair point. Walk of shame, Mommy dearest?"

"Now you just get your mind out of the gutter. We were snowed in. That's all. Not that I didn't have offers..."

To me she said, "You sir, had best watch your step. Judge Winthrop is itching for you to go to trial. He assumes you'll fail at finding a suitable meaning of Christmas. And he's thrilled. He's planning to throw the plea deal out and find a jury that hates you."

Twenty

CALVIN

I **FELT** horrible about lying to him. I mean, I've been lying to him every single second since I met him at Drip, but this particular lie seemed worse somehow. The thing about my parents was all true, except I'd left out one important detail—which happened to be the most important detail. Yeah, my parents threw me out because I didn't believe in their religion. And I didn't believe in their religion because it didn't believe in me. I was gay and that was that.

Of course, the news about Judge Winthrop was equally distressing. I was going to have to figure out what to do about that. His behavior was incredibly inappropriate. Not surprising, though, inappropriate seemed to be his middle name.

As soon as Betsy walked away, I said, "Don't worry. It's going to be fine."

"It's going to be fine? How is it going to be fine? There's nothing I can say to that judge that he'll find acceptable. Which means he won't accept the plea deal and I'll be going to trial."

"His behavior has been unacceptable enough that we can

have him removed, and once he's gone we can submit the plea deal to a different judge."

Of course, that would be happening during the Van Husen trial, and even though it would only take a half a day and Danny could actually do it for me, I knew he wouldn't. He'd be using it as an excuse to snag the Van Husen trial away from me. And not just the trial, my work on the case, my prep, my strategy, my win. He'd swoop in and snatch it all away.

"Are you okay?" Gage asked.

My thoughts must have been showing on my face.

"Trust me. I'll fix it."

"You know, I think you just might."

Shortly after Betsy went into the house, Phillip got there. We'd finished the driveway and were nearly done brushing off the cars when he tucked his aging SUV into the driveway. Once the SUV was parked, he, a small woman about his age and three children ranging from eight to fourteen spilled out. They were carrying roasting pans, casseroles and bags of food.

"Good morning, Phillip," I said.

"Good morning. I've brought my wife, Maria, and my children Allan, Paige and Max. I hope that's okay."

"I'm sure Mary Ann will be fine with it. She'll be happy you're spending the holiday with your family."

Maria was holding a roasting pan. "We brought our dinner to share with you. Ham, yams, peas, potatoes, pumpkin bread pudding. The bread pudding is to die for. I make it every year."

"Sounds wonderful," I said.

"It does," Gage agreed.

They went into the house while we finished brushing off the cars. When we were done, I said to Gage, "I feel like I should apologize in advance for anything that happens today."

"I feel like I'm supposed to say it won't be that bad, but I'm afraid if I do it definitely will be."

"Good call. Shall we go in?"

We went inside the house, took off our outer gear, and then walked through the parlor and dining room to the kitchen. Inside it was already a little chaotic. Phillip was washing pots in the sink.

On the stove, a couple of large pots were boiling, potatoes, I think. A smaller pot held boiling cranberries.

"Your kitchen is fabulous," Maria said to Mary Ann as she rolled out biscuits. "Phil told me about the two ovens. I was so excited."

"They come in handy," Mary Ann said as she studiously read a cookbook.

"Don't pay too much attention to that," Maria said. "They always leave something out so yours is never as good as it's supposed to be."

"Oh, I know. I made notes last year, but I can't read my own handwriting."

"Probably too much eggnog," I said.

"I heard that."

At some point, Gus and Piper had come down, they were now sitting in the breakfast nook with Phillip and Maria's three kids. None of the kids seemed to be interacting but were comfortable enough sitting together. The files for the Van Husen case were still spread around. I went over and began boxing them up again.

Betsy walked into the room wearing a bathrobe and a towel around her head. One hand shielded her eyes from the light, she was struggling to focus.

"Are there a lot of people in this room or am I still seeing double?"

"Phillip brought his family," Mary Ann said. "Which I'm very happy about."

"Phillip?"

"Maria."

"Oh. Fine. But I'm only paying Maria. The rest of them are out of luck." Maria brought over a cup of coffee. Betsy took it. "Thank you, who are you?"

"I'm Maria."

"No, you're not."

"I am, do you want cream and sugar in your coffee?"

"Absolutely not." Pointing at Phillip she said, "That's Maria over there. Are you saying you're also called Maria?"

"Mother, you need to stop calling Phillip, Maria."

"What? Why?"

"Because this is his wife, Maria, and it will be too confusing if you call them both Maria."

"Nonsense. It will be easier if everyone is called Maria."

"Oh dear."

To Gage, Betsy said, "I met Sheriff Watkins last night. Charming man. He wants to arrest you. I negotiated your surrender. On the front lawn in two days."

"I won't be here in two days."

"Yes, I know. Say thank you."

"Why would you do that?"

"I did it for Mary Ann. I didn't want anyone ruining her Christmas."

"Anyone other than you," Mary Ann said.

"Well, I *am* your mother."

"Don't worry," I whispered to Gage. "The sheriff can't do anything."

"I've made a list," Mary Ann said, taking a piece of paper out from under the cookbook and holding it out to Betsy.

"What is this?"

"It's a list of topics you can talk about during dinner."

"You can't be serious."

"Very."

Betsy snatched the list away from her. She took a moment to glance at it. "Gardening? I can talk about gardening? I don't even talk to my gardener about gardening. Bridge?"

"Don't mention the cheating scandal."

"Well then there's nothing to say."

"Then don't say anything."

Betsy scowled at the list. Maria whispered, "Turn the potatoes down a little" while she stirred the cranberries.

Reading, Betsy said, "I can talk about the food. The weather. The children. It's like you don't want me here at all."

"Well, you did invite yourself." Mary Ann had stopped cooking and crossed her arms across her chest.

With a sniff, Betsy continued, "Gratitude? I don't even understand what that means."

"What are you grateful for, Mother?"

"I'm rich. I don't have to be grateful for anything. Poor people have to be grateful. Can I talk about how ungrateful poor people are?"

"No. You may not."

Taking a long sip of her coffee, Betsy asked, "What about my freedom of speech?"

"Last time I looked, the Constitution did not say Betsy Hinchmen-Jones gets to say any hurtful and offensive thing that comes into her head." Mary Ann said. I had the feeling she'd had that one ready for a long time.

"I don't think I said anything yesterday that people aren't saying on television."

"Fine, get your own television show. But this is my house and you are going to behave today."

"But I gave you this house."

"And that got you in the door."

"It's very unkind of you to do this while I have a hangover."

"Oh, I have a hangover remedy," Maria said. "Phil used to

drink. Now he never has more than one. Or two. I should make it for you."

"Of course, please, yes, as long as it doesn't have a raw egg in it."

"Oh."

"Also Mother, you're going to need to apologize to Gage."

"Good God, why?"

"You were very rude to him and his friend."

"It's fine," Gage said. "We both have very thick skins."

"Mother."

With great panache, Betsy turned to Gage. "Apparently, despite the fact that you're a criminal and a homosexual, I'm the one who's in the wrong. So, I'm sorry. And please tell your friend, Neo, that I'm sorry if I hurt *their* feelings."

"They'll appreciate that."

"I'm sure *they* will. Now, have I used the correct pronoun enough times to prove sincerity?"

"Sure," Gage said. I think he just said that to be nice.

"You know, I was the belle of the ball at Jeff David Stickney's. And I was saying the same kind of things I was saying here. In fact, I probably said some of the *same* things." To Gage she pointedly said, "Not everyone thinks like you and your ilk."

"People have been making that clear to me since I was a small child," he replied.

I think the last thing she expected was agreement. "I suppose that would be unpleasant," she admitted. Then she struggled very hard not to say whatever hateful thing she wanted to add. "This is going to be a difficult day. I can tell already."

"Then let's go ahead and get it started," Mary Ann said. "Time to open presents!"

She led us out of the kitchen and into the parlor area. Gus and Piper were on the floor. Mary Ann and her mother sat on the settee. There was an empty chair, that Gage or I could have sat in, but neither of us moved toward it. We remained standing, a little closer than strictly necessary, behind the sofa.

"All right, kids first. Now, I want you two to take turns. Gus, you go first."

He grabbed a box with his name on it and began to rip off the paper. His mother stopped him, "Who's it from?"

Gus read the label, "It's from grandma." He continued pulling off the wrapping to expose the latest iPad. "Wow!"

Under her breath, Mary Ann said to her mother, "I thought I said no screens until he's eight."

"The young man at the store said they should start at two."

"He was trying to sell you something."

"Well, I chose not to get the mobile plan so he can only use it here at the house and there's an application-thingie that shuts it off after two or three or four hours whatever you decide."

"Wow, you actually thought that through."

"I listen to you." And then after a moment, she added, "Your voice can be grating, it's hard *not* to listen to you."

"Can I go?" Piper asked.

"Yes, you can."

Piper pulled a big box out of the pile and read the card. "This is from my mom." After ripping the paper off, she exposed that her gift was a pink overnight bag.

I realized I should be more involved watching my kids get presents, so I said, "Wow, that's a great gift for sleepovers."

Now it was Gus's turn again, he pulled out a medium-sized box and said, "This is from my dad." Ripping into the box he exposed a baseball mitt. The look on his face said he wasn't excited about the gift. I was thinking, *Douglas is such a dick*, when I remembered certain people standing within inches of me thought I was the dad who'd bought him the wrong gift.

"Hey Buddy, if you don't like it, we can take it back and get you something else."

Gus didn't say anything, he just pushed the gift to the side.

"My turn," Piper said, grabbing a giant box. "From Grandma," she read and then destroyed the packaging. It was a giant make-up set featuring all kinds of make-up in a rainbow of colors. She didn't seem to know what to make of it.

"Mother, she's a twelve-year-old girl, not a drag queen."

"And you think we're *not* living in a world where twelve-year-old girls have to compete with drag queens?"

"That isn't the sort of competition I want my daughter involved in."

"You're preaching to the choir. Why do you think we're trying to keep drag queens away from children?"

"Thank you, Grandma," Piper said, trying to keep the peace.

"You can't wear any of that to school," her mother said.

"Whatever," Piper said, which even as her not-really-Dad I knew meant she was going to do whatever she wanted.

Gus brought a small box over to his mother. She took and checked out the tag. "Well, this is from Cal. Thank you, dear."

"Our daughter picked it out," I said, knowing it was about to become relevant.

"Oh. All right." She got the wrapping off and read the name of the perfume, Fucking Fabulous. "You picked this out, Piper?"

"It smells really good."

"I'm sure it does."

Around that time, I stopped paying as much attention. The kids gave Mary Ann her chocolates and she acted much more excited than she needed to. Meanwhile, all I could think of was how good Gage smelled next to me. I don't think he was wearing a lot of cologne. If any. He smelled clean, of soap and healthy, warm, touchable skin. I wanted to get very close and bury my face in that wonderful smell. Fortunately, I was smart enough to actually take a step away from him.

Mary Ann had said I should date him after this was all over. I was beginning to think, want, wonder... could I? Could I date him after this was over? I'd have to tell him I'd been lying to him. He'd hate me for that. He seemed like the kind of guy who hated being lied to. Which was a little odd since he was also the kind of guy who committed arson. Could I negotiate this? I'll ignore that you committed arson if you'll ignore the fact that I lied? And I'd only been lying to him for about forty-eight hours. To be truly egregious a lie should last at least a week. Under a week and it wasn't even really a lie, it was more a tiny lie, a lie-let, an itty-bitty teeny-weeny lie-let. Completely understandable. As much as I wanted to, I didn't believe a word of that.

Then it was Betsy's turn and I tried to focus on the room around me. My fake family. The kids each brought over their gift, then Mary Ann handed her a package, with Mary Ann saying, "It's from Cal and me."

"Of course, it is."

Betsy opened the first package. "Pickles." She patted Gus on the head. "Thank you, Gus, that's so... dill of you."

Picking up the next gift she said, "This one is from Piper, thank you sweetheart." Ripping the paper off she stops and stares at the gift for a moment. "Well, jam."

There were six jars in the oblong box.

"They're funny flavors," Piper said. "Pineapple, watermelon, basil—"

"Yes, I see that."

She set the jams down on the floor. The largest package was the one from Mary Ann and me. It was a rather large box.

Betsy's smile brightened. Happily, she peeled the paper off. Inside was a box of six, individually wrapped pears.

Betsy's face fell. A tear appeared in one eye.

"Mother, is something wrong?"

Betsy shook her head but didn't speak.

"Something is wrong. What is it?"

"Food? Really? I'm too young for food."

"I don't know what that means."

"When I was a child, my mother would buy gifts for our older relatives. She always said that there was an age when you stopped buying *things* and started buying *food*. Since you weren't sure how long they were going to be around you bought them something you were sure they'd live long enough to enjoy."

"Well, that's not what—Mother, you have everything. There's nothing left to buy you."

"No woman ever has enough jewelry. A scarf is always nice, particularly if it's Hermes. For that matter, virtually anything with a designer label on it."

"We'll do better next year. I promise."

Twenty-One

GAGE

I KNEW PERFECTLY well I should not be trusting my prosecutor as much as I'd begun to. I mean, that was Breaking the Law 101. But weirdly, I did trust him. Hopefully there was some shred of logic, like we had mutual interests, or he believed what I did (well, what my dad did) did not deserve to be punished.

And, yes, I was perfectly aware that I might just be trusting him because I was developing a crush. Sex requires trust and most of us have deluded ourselves into thinking someone was trustworthy just to have sex with them. That was probably all that was going on here so I should watch my step. At some point, I should call Lonny and tell him what Betsy said about Judge Winthrop. I mean, he was my lawyer, and it was his job to make sure I didn't get screwed over.

Finally, all the presents were dispersed. Betsy stood up and said, "I have one more present for my wonderful grandchildren. I've put ten thousand dollars each into your brokerage accounts. I picked out a very stable mutual fund with an average nine percent return. If you each hold onto the investment until you're my age, no one will be able to tell you what to do... well, unless you have children. Which I don't recommend."

"Thank you, Mother. It's very sweet of you to think of their futures."

Neither child seemed particularly impressed, but they both said thank you.

"Let's get this cleaned up," Mary Ann said, as she began to pick up the wrapping paper, cleaning up most of it herself.

I asked Betsy, "So, you don't believe in motherhood?"

"Of course I believe in motherhood. It's the most important thing a woman can do in life."

"But you only have one child."

"Do you have any idea what happens during childbirth? There's no way I was doing that more than once."

Mary Ann looked up from the floor and raised an eyebrow.

"What? I'm saying nice things."

Cal got a little too close to me, and said, "Sorry I didn't get you anything."

"That would be a little outrageous, given that we've known each other two whole days. And I didn't get you anything, either."

"It might have been interesting picking out a gift for you," he said, right before he walked away. He headed out to the kitchen, presumably to rejoin his murder files. *What did that mean?* I wondered. There was a kind of purr in his voice that suggested obscene underwear. Or worse.

Shaking that off, I decided it might be a good time to call Lonny. He'd given me his cell number in case of emergency, and he wasn't celebrating Christmas so it seemed okay. My phone was upstairs, so I went up to the guestroom.

"Lonny, sorry to bother you. I mean, I know you don't celebrate Christmas but it's still a day off."

"It's all right. What's happening? Are you having an awful time with the Cutlers?"

"They're very nice, actually. The thing is... the judge stopped by last night for dinner."

"You're kidding? That's inappropriate. Did he talk about your case?"

"Not exactly, but it gets worse. After dinner, he went to a party at Jeff David Stickney's house. He took Mary Ann's mother with him."

"Okay. That's inappropriate. Do you know if anything was said about your case at this party?"

"Yes. Mary Ann's mother told me the judge wants to throw out the plea deal completely so we can go to trial, and he wants to find a jury that hates me."

"Okay, that's beyond inappropriate." He thought for a moment. "There's really nothing to do except ask him to recuse himself. I'll ask for a sidebar so as not to publicly humiliate him. It will drag things on, but if we get a new judge we can resubmit the plea deal. Provided the DA is still offering it."

"The thing is, Cal says he's going to handle it."

"Do you know what that means?"

"No, I don't."

"I don't either. I know the DA wants this to go away, that's why we got the deal in the first place. But I can't imagine he'd ask the judge to recuse himself. Judges are predisposed to the prosecution. I wouldn't want to risk that."

"You think he's going to throw me under the bus?"

"I wouldn't think of it like that. It's his job to put you in prison. 'Throwing you under the bus' implies that you have some kind of relationship, which you don't."

That was sobering. And he was right. We didn't have a relationship. The number one thing I knew about Cal was that he was supposed to punish me. There was no amount of staring or flirting or spooning that would change that.

"Thanks Lonny."

"Have you decided what you want to say to the judge?"

"Does it matter? It sounds like he won't accept it no matter what I say."

"You should still make a good faith effort. I'll have a draft of something ready for you. In the meantime, take a stab at it yourself. We'll figure out a time when we can mix and match."

I thanked him and clicked off.

The conversation had made me feel uncomfortable in the Cutler home, possibly even unsafe. But that was silly. I was a grown up. I could take care of myself. I had a signed document. Nothing I said could be used against me. Even if Cal is lying when he says he'll take care of the situation with Judge Winthrop, I have Lonny and we'll be ready for our next court date.

I'm fine. Everything's fine.

I took a few deep breaths and went downstairs. I made my way through the parlor and into the dining room. Betsy, who'd gone upstairs and changed while I was on the phone with Lonny, was starting a game of Monopoly with all the kids. Piper sat next to her, reading from her phone. "Monopoly was created by Elizabeth Magie to demonstrate the negative aspects of concentrated ownership in private monopolies."

"Hmmm," Betsy said. "I'd say that didn't go very well. Instead, she taught millions of Americans the sheer joy of destroying your neighbors."

Philip and Maria's three kids seemed to be chomping at the bit to do exactly that.

I made my way into the kitchen. Cal was exactly where I thought he'd be, deep in his murder files. Phillip and Maria were chopping vegetables. Mary Ann was mixing stuffing.

"You don't put stuffing in the bird?" Maria asked.

"No, I've read that you shouldn't because it's easy to not

cook the bird enough, so you end up with raw turkey goo all over your stuffing."

"Okay, that's gross," Maria said. "I'll never do that again."

There was something I was curious about, particularly after Betsy mentioned putting money in the kid's investment accounts. "Mary Ann, you don't have to answer this if you don't want to, but why does your family have so much money?"

She blushed a little. "Basic plunder. On my mother's side, my great-great grandfather owned an iron mine in the upper peninsula. His son, my great grandfather, bought up huge swaths of land after the timber companies clear-cut them. The iron mine petered out in the forties, so my grandfather started judiciously selling parcels of land as it became valuable. Most of that money he invested in stock. IBM in the late fifties."

"Oh, wow," I said.

"My dad's side goes back to the beginning of the automotive industry. Rivets."

"Oh, Phil's family was in the auto industry. Real union types."

Phillip said, "My great-grandfather got his head cracked by Pinkerton strike breakers."

"Cal, tell them about your family history," Mary Ann said.

"Ministers. Lots of ministers."

In the other room, the kids were chattering as the game began. Piper was giving Gus and Max a refresher course in the game. Including strategies she found online.

I went over and slid into the breakfast nook, sitting directly across from Cal. He looked up and stared at me. It felt like there was an electrical current dancing around inside of me. As casually as possible, I asked, "Find anything?"

"I shouldn't talk about it."

"Oh, come on Cal," Mary Ann said. "You can talk about it. Use hypotheticals if you have to."

"I shouldn't."

"He always talks to me about his cases. This is one of the most fascinating."

Cal gave his wife a look that bordered on domestic violence.

"Fine," he said. "I feel like the key to this is his doctor. But there's something I'm not seeing, or that I don't know."

"Go on," I said.

"Well, his defense is that his wife was abusing him. His proof is that he's got pictures of himself covered in bruises and that he told his friend about the abuse. We've talked about him possibly setting up his defense by telling his friend before he killed his wife. I'm going to try and get an expert witness to talk about how likely that might be. But I feel like the jury will still want to know where the bruises came from."

"You have his complete medical record?" I asked. "Is he on any medications?"

"He's a pretty healthy guy... well, that's not true, he has asthma. He sees his doctor about that."

"Prednisone?"

"Yes, he's taking that when he has a flair up."

"That's probably your answer, right there," I said. "When I was in college, I did an internship with Child Protective Services. We were called into a preschool because a four-year-old kept showing up with bruising. The teacher was quite worried but by the time we got there she'd figured it out. The girl had asthma pretty badly. They kept an inhaler at school. So she knew that, she just didn't know prednisone could cause bruising. She didn't put it all together until one day she picked the child up putting her hand onto the girl's thigh. Two days later she noticed bruising and realized she was the one who'd put it there."

"He's the bodybuilder, right?" Phillip asked.

"He is."

"If he's taking other steroids, you know the kind you don't tell your doctor about, that would probably just make the bruising worse."

"I need to find a doctor to call."

The kids erupted in the dining room. One of them was being sent to jail. I couldn't hear which one, I was just glad it wasn't me.

"Why not just call his doctor to the stand?" Mary Ann suggested.

"Get to him first? Tempting. But it could blow up in my face. Even if I get the doctor to admit that the bruises might be the result of prednisone, they have cross and then their own direct to rebut. And... if they do a good job on cross, they might not call the doctor at all, cutting me off."

"I guess there's a lot to think about."

Mary Ann still had a landline, a wall phone in the kitchen. I noticed it because it was ringing. She and Cal glanced at each other nervously. Mary Ann picked up the phone and said, "Hello." After a moment, "Yes, Merry Christmas to you, too. We're having a lovely day. And you?"

She listened, then said, "Let me get them." Walking over to the kitchen door she said, "Piper, Gus, it's your aunt Elaine."

"Can you bring the phone here?" Piper asked.

"She's on the landline. You have to come in here."

There was some shuffling as they left the dining room table. Betsy said, "Break. If you have to go to the bathroom, go now."

Piper and Gus came into the kitchen. Piper took the phone first. "Hello? Aunt Elaine? Merry Christmas."

She listened a moment and said, "I got a make-up set, and an overnight bag. Gus got an iPad. I really need a new one," the last bit was directed at her mother. "Okay, yeah, Merry Christmas."

She handed the phone to her brother, who took it and

said, "Hello? Okay. I got a baseball mitt. No, I don't like baseball. I don't know. I just don't. I got *Beowulf*. I like that. What? No, it's not about a wolf. It's about a king who slays monsters and dragons. Uh, huh. Okay. Goodbye."

Gus holds the phone out to Mary Ann who says into the receiver, "Thank you for calling Elaine. No, I haven't. I'm sure he'll call. Eventually. You have a wonderful Christmas."

I tried to figure out whose aunt that was on the phone. Mary Ann just called her Elaine. Was she Cal's sister? Did he have a sister? And why didn't she want to talk to him? Weird. Very weird. I almost asked about it, but I'd already done too much fishing around in their personal lives. I let it go.

Then Betsy popped her head into the kitchen, saying, "Mary Ann, the Beverly Hillbillies have just pulled up in front of your house."

"I don't know what that means," Mary Ann said.

I did, though. I got out of the breakfast nook and hurried through the house to the front door. Opening it, I saw my father walking up the driveway. He was wearing his Sunday Best: a red Christmas sweater under a vintage Army jacket and a pair of frayed bellbottom jeans. He'd combed his gray hair back and looked almost stylish in a retro way. He carried a nicely wrapped Christmas gift.

"What are you doing here?" I asked.

"I wanted to see my boy on Christmas. Is that so wrong?"

"That's nice, but you shouldn't be here. And how did you find me anyway?"

"I put a tracker on your duffle bag."

"You what?"

"I need to make sure you're safe. You know they'll try to get to me through you. Did you check your room for bugs?"

"Yes, I did. And there was nothing there."

"Well, you couldn't have done a very good job if you didn't find the tracker."

"I really wasn't worried about you spying on me. Although now I guess I'll have to."

"Who's this?" Mary Ann said behind me.

"Mary Ann, this is my father, Nate Hammond."

He smiled while I explained to him, "Mary Ann is Cal Cutler's wife. Cal is my prosecutor."

"I'm so sorry to intrude, I just wanted to wish my boy a Merry Christmas."

"Please come in. You have to stay for dinner, there's plenty believe me. You'd be doing us a favor. I have no idea what I'm going to do with all the leftovers."

We stepped into the foyer and my dad handed me the gift and took his coat off. Mary Ann had stepped back into the parlor to try and get the kids under control; they'd become quite unruly.

Behind us, Betsy said, "Nineteen seventy called, they want those jeans back."

My dad looked her up and down before he said, "I didn't know Nancy Reagan was still alive."

"I can't tell if I've just been insulted or complimented."

"A little of both."

My stomach flipped. The two of them in the same room really did not seem like a good idea. Out of necessity, I said, "Dad this is Mary Ann's mom, Betsy Hinchmen-Jones. Betsy, my dad, Nate Hammond."

"It's lovely to meet you Mrs. Hinchmen-Jones."

"I see where Gage gets his good looks from, not to mention his politics."

"Politics? I don't believe in politics. I believe in justice. If you're always talking about politics, you'll never get justice."

"Clever turn of phrase. Wrong, but clever. Don't let us stop you from opening your gift, Gage."

I glanced at my dad who very subtly shook his head. "I'll open it later. Let's put it under the tree for now." I led my dad over to the tree, before he put the present under the tree, I whispered, "What is it?"

"Tear gas. In case things go sideways."

"Nate, what on earth is that thing you drove up in?" Betsy asked.

"My home."

"You live in that contraption?"

"I do. I live wherever I want to, whenever I want to."

"Are you on the lam?"

"Mother, really." Then to the kids, "Piper help Max take his turn." That set off a conflict over who should help Max, Piper or his brother.

"No, no, it's a legitimate question," my dad said. "Of course, I'm on the lam. I'm sure there are warrants out for my arrest in a dozen states."

"There actually aren't," I explained. "We had a private detective check on that last year. Dad, why do you keep saying that? You give people the wrong idea."

"Or the right one."

"Another criminal for Christmas," Betsy said to Mary Ann. "Santa must be very unhappy with you."

"Christ was a criminal," my dad pointed out. "You wouldn't invite him to dinner?"

"Christ was not a criminal."

"They had to have convicted him of something or they wouldn't have crucified him."

"The Jews wanted to get rid of him, that's why he was crucified."

"The Jews were occupied by the Romans. I really doubt they told them who to crucify."

"Okay," I said, "Sunday school is over."

"Why is it we can never discuss the weather in this house?" Mary Ann asked.

Twenty-Two

CALVIN

THANKS TO GAGE I had the answer in the Van Husen case. I had everything I needed to destroy his defense. Because of Gage. I never would have believed that two days ago. Part of me wanted to forget about Christmas entirely and start writing out my cross-examination questions for Van Husen's friend and his doctor. I was pretty sure that the defense would come to me after I questioned them and ask for a deal. We wouldn't go for one though, too late in the trial. Giving him a sweetheart deal wouldn't save the state any money. No, I was sure I had first-degree murder in the bag.

Once I won the Van Husen case, I should ask Gage out. A casual dinner, as a thank-you for his help. Over our appetizers, I would begin talking about the various pressures involved in being a prosecutor. The politics—acknowledging he'd just had a front seat view of that. I'd go on to explain that you needed to win against those people whatever it took. No, I couldn't do it that way. Coming out would take until our fifth or sixth date. I should do it quickly, rip off the Band-Aid...

There was a commotion coming from the front of the

house. I looked over at Phillip and Maria who'd been quietly working on a couple of relish trays. They'd heard it too.

A moment later Betsy, a weathered but attractive man in his sixties, and Mary Ann came through the door. The man was mid-sentence, "...I'm just saying that telling a woman to shut up is misogynistic."

"She's my daughter, she can tell me to shut up any time she wants. I mean it, darling, you tell me to shut up any time you feel like it."

"But... you never shut up when I ask you to," Mary Ann said.

"As your mother, it's my right to ignore everything you say."

"Ignoring misogyny won't make it go away."

"Dad, give it a rest," Gage said as he squeezed through the door and into the kitchen. "Cal, this is my dad, Nate Hammond."

"Hello, it's nice to meet—"

"You're the man trying to put my son in prison."

"Actually, I'm the man trying to get your son probation and having a lot of trouble doing it."

"How's the turkey doing, Maria?" Mary Ann, attempting to divert the conversation.

"I just put the thermometer in, and it's got another five degrees to go."

Piper stuck her head through the door, "Grandma, it's your turn."

"Oh, dear... if I form a shell corporation and appoint you CEO will you roll for me."

"That's corruption," Nate said. "You're teaching—"

"I don't think you can do those things in this game," Piper said. "But I can roll for you."

"Yes dear, do that – and no rent discounts while I'm away."

Piper left and Nate followed, saying, "Excuse me, these children need a lesson in the value of anti-trust regulation in a free market."

As soon as they left, Mary Ann asked Maria, "How much longer will the turkey be, do you think?"

"Twenty minutes. But then we should rest it."

"Mother, can you and the kids finish the game in half an hour."

"I doubt it, not with certain people trying to turn those children into little socialists. If they lose the desire to destroy each other the game will take forever."

"Well, then you might need to move the game to the coffee table while we eat."

"I hate doing that. It opens up opportunities for cheating."

"Really? You know, you're the only one who cheats."

"That's not true," Maria said. "Paige cheats. We have great hopes for her."

"I knew there was a reason she's winning," Betsy said as she flew through, the door.

Gage looked apoplectic for a moment, then said, "Cal, Mary Ann, I apologize for my dad showing up. I did not invite him."

"It's fine," Mary Ann said. "You should get to spend Christmas with your dad. I do think, though... Cal can you put away your little murder case. I think the kids should eat in here, while the adults are in the dining room. That will limit any collateral damage."

"Fine," I said. I had my strategy so I could reasonably leave it alone for the rest of the holiday. I thought I might as well put the boxes in my car.

"Can I help?" Gage asked.

"Sure, thanks."

We each grabbed a box and walked out of the kitchen. In

the dining room, the game of Monopoly seemed to have reached an impasse.

"I suppose you regret the revolution," Nate asked Betsy. "Are you a loyalist? Should we go back to being part of England? Long live the king?"

"For heaven's sake," Betsy replied. "The English monarchy is a joke. They haven't cut anyone's head off in centuries. I mean, what are they even there for?"

I ducked my head and hurried through the room; Gage close behind me. In the foyer, we stopped and put on our coats and boots. We were outside in a jiff, and I opened the back of my Prius.

"So, this is over tomorrow," I said. "It hasn't been that bad, has it?"

"You and Mary Ann have been very gracious, and I appreciate that. I did want to suggest—and please don't take this the wrong way—but the two of you might like to see a couple's therapist. I think... well, I'm fairly sure, you have some issues to work out."

I stood there a moment, trying to decide how I should respond to that. Yesterday, I would have been angry and rejected the idea completely. But today, this morning, what should I—

"You're right. That sounds like a good idea. There are things I really ought to tell Mary Ann."

I closed the back of the Prius. I took a step toward him and leaned—

"What are you doing?"

"Um, I thought—"

"It's broad daylight. We're standing in front of your house and those things you ought to tell Mary Ann haven't been told yet." He turned and stomped off.

I suppose he had a point.

Walking back into the house, I just wanted to hide. I

thought about going up to the guest room and hanging out there until dinnertime, but I didn't know where Gage had gone. He might be up there, which would completely defeat the purpose of my being up there since he was now the person I wanted most to avoid.

Even before I got to the dining room, I could hear Betsy and Nate going at it.

"It really seems like you don't understand English," Betsy was saying. Then, "Oh my God—you went to a state university, didn't you?"

"As a matter of fact, I did."

"Facts. That's the difference between private school and public school. I went to Vassar where I learned that facts were simply not important."

As I tried to slip by, I heard Piper say, "Daddy? Daddy—"

"What class did you learn that bit of nonsense in?" Nate demanded.

"Daddy—"

"It wasn't in any class," Betsy said. "All the real learning took place outside of class. That's what the whole Greek system is for."

I realized Piper was talking to me. "Uh, yes, sweetheart?"

"Help!"

It was then that I noticed all five children had panicked looks on their faces. The thing Mary Ann was trying to avoid by having the kids eat in the kitchen was already happening. But I was the dad, so I could do something about it, should do something, would be a total dick if I didn't do something—

"All right kids, the game's over. You're going to be eating in the kitchen, so you need to set the table for yourselves." The kids were out of there in a matter of seconds.

"Cal, they don't need to set the table. That's what Maria's here for."

"It's good for them to set the table. They need to take care of themselves."

"What right do you—"

"I'm their father."

With a deep frown, Betsy said, "I suppose that's true."

"Do the two of you think you could put away the game without killing each other?"

"We're not going to kill each other," Nate said. "We're just having a friendly disagreement—"

"About everything," Betsy said.

"Except that, we agree that we disagree."

Before I went into the kitchen, I braced myself. Gage might be in there. I opened the door and there was Phillip, Maria, Mary Ann and the kids setting the breakfast nook for dinner. No Gage.

I stood as close as I could to Mary Ann and whispered, "Why hasn't Douglas called?"

"I don't know."

"Who's Douglas?" Maria asked.

"Nobody," Mary Ann and I said at the same time.

And then, in a moment of perfect timing her phone rang.

Mary Ann looked at me and said, "Creepy." Then she picked up the wall phone. "Hello." A moment later her face fell, "Oh hi Rachel. You're welcome, I hope you enjoyed them. Uh-huh. All right, that's fine. Merry Christmas."

When she clicked off, I grabbed her wrist and pulled her into the laundry room. I turned on the dryer and said, "I tried to kiss him."

"Tried?"

"He didn't go for it."

"Oh, he doesn't like you?" She frowned. She might have been a little over-invested in our having sex.

"I don't think that's it. I think he likes *you*. He doesn't want you to get hurt."

"Oh, isn't that sweet of him?"

"He thinks we need couples therapy."

She rested her hand on my arm and very seriously said, "Cal, we do."

"You don't need a therapist to let me know I'm a jerk. You're doing a good job all by yourself."

"I'd stop thinking you're a jerk if you told Gage the truth."

I couldn't do that. I knew I couldn't do that. Why I couldn't do that was starting to get a bit fuzzy.

The door to the pantry flung open and in came Betsy. "That man is infuriating. Do you think he likes me? He is straight, isn't he? So many libtards aren't."

"Gage hasn't said he's not."

"Mother, if you want to make a disaster of your life, could you at least wait until tomorrow?"

"I'm sure I could sleep with him and then cast him aside. Isn't that what women's lib is all about?" Betsy said.

"No. And you're not a feminist, you never have been," Mary Ann said.

"That doesn't mean I can't take advantage of the strides they've made whenever it suits me."

"I wouldn't call treating men badly feminism."

"Well, no wonder it hasn't caught on."

The door to the laundry room opened and in came Maria. "What's going on? Phillip said I should ignore this, but I just couldn't. You're all obviously up to something. I just wish I knew what!"

"Wait, if we're all in here, who's supervising Maria?" Betsy asked.

"I'm Maria," Maria said.

"The other Maria. The one who was here last night."

"Phillip."

"Yes, that Maria."

"That's not a Maria," Maria pointed out. "That's a Phillip.

And he's watching the kids and cleaning things up. Dinner is pretty much ready Mary Ann."

"Thank you, Maria," Mary Ann said, and pointedly rolled her eyes at her mother. She swanned out of the laundry room. Maria trailed behind.

Betsy stood there a moment, then seemed to realize she and I were alone. "Well, I'm not staying here alone with you."

That left me standing there, listening to the dryer. Mary Ann was probably right. I should tell Gage the truth. Obviously, I should wait until the holiday was over. It could go badly. It probably would go badly.

I would drive him home in the morning and tell him in the car. In the meantime, maybe I could say some things to soften him up. Like, I could remind him that Elton John was once in the closet. That was kind of stupid, pretty much every gay man was once in the closet. That was the wrong direction.

I could mention that lying was sometimes a good thing. The people who protected Ann Frank lied to the Germans. That was a good thing. Although, in that analogy I was comparing him to a Nazi. That could be offensive.

I was going to have to think about this. I turned off the dryer and left the laundry room. All the adults, except Phillip, had left the kitchen and were arguing in the dining room. As I walked through the kitchen, Phillip said, "You might not want to go in there."

I said, "Oh God," and walked into the dining room.

Betsy was clutching a place setting while Mary Ann tried to pull it away from her.

"No, no, no," Betsy said. "We are not eating with the servants."

"They're not servants," Mary Ann replied. "They're very kind people you lured here with the promise of a lot of money."

"Isn't that the definition of a servant?"

"It's all right, Mary Ann," Maria said. "We're fine in the kitchen."

"No, you're not."

"The one percent are a blight on this country, parasites feeding on the very soul of this nation," Nate said.

"Did you just call me a parasite?" Betsy asked.

"A very, very, attractive parasite."

"Oh... thank you," she said, giggling like a schoolgirl. That allowed Mary Ann to get a better grip on the place setting and she pulled it away from her mother.

As she put the setting back onto the table, she said, "Mother, sit there."

Nate pulled out the chair and went to sit next to Betsy, but Mary Ann said, "No, absolutely not. You can sit there, Nate. Cal, sit between them?"

"Do I have to?"

"Yes, you have to. I'm sitting here at the head."

"Maria you can sit next to me."

"After I bring out the food."

"Of course."

"Where do I sit?" Gage asked. I turned and he was standing in the archway between the dining room and the parlor.

"You can sit across from Cal." Which meant I'd be staring at him all through dinner.

"Lovely," he said, meaning anything but.

Twenty-Three

GAGE

HE TRIED TO KISS ME. And I should really calm down. People who are just coming out often make mistakes, they misunderstand things, they act on what they think it means to be gay rather than what being gay actually means. People on the cusp of coming out can be like puppies, impulsive and pissing on everything.

And I did feel pissed on. Yes, I may have had sex with a married man here or there. If you're single, there are many sexual situations where you simply don't ask. But that's different. If you don't know someone's name, it's all on them.

This was not one of those situations. I'd spent two days with Cal's wife, I'd met his children. It wouldn't be all on him. I had to approach this situation differently. I wasn't in some dark back room trying to remember a guy's name, barely having time to wonder about other relationships. We couldn't just start making out behind his car, in his driveway, with his wife and kids in the house.

After he tried to kiss me, I went upstairs to the guest room. I didn't think he'd have the nerve to follow me. After a few minutes of pacing, I began to wonder, was I hoping he'd follow me there? What did I think I could say to him? Did I want to say anything to him? Or did I just want to be in a room with him where no one could see us? Oh crap, I'd gone there hoping he'd follow me. What was wrong with me?

There was no way I could stay there that night and sleep with him in that bed again. I packed up my things and left my bag in the middle of the bed. I'd have dinner and afterwards I'd say my goodbyes and leave with my dad. If the judge was going to send me to trial no matter what I said, then there was no reason for me to stay. I was risking nothing by leaving. And if I stayed, I risked a lot.

When I arrived in the dining room, they were haggling over who would sit where. I asked, "Where do I sit?"

"You can sit across from Cal," Mary Ann said. She seemed completely oblivious to the things going on with her husband. I hadn't done anything, but I still felt guilty. I felt like a homewrecker. I hated feeling like a homewrecker.

To Maria, Mary Ann said, "Can Phillip carve a turkey?"

"Well, yes, but shouldn't Mr. Cutler do it?"

"Cal? Every piece would be perfect, but it would take until New Year's." Then she walked into the kitchen calling for Phillip.

Reluctantly, I sat down across from Cal. We stared at each other for a long moment. It was a look that was like holding your hand over a flame. It wasn't so bad at first, but then it began to hurt more and more. I couldn't sit there. I got up and moved to the seat at the end of the table, next to my dad.

Mary Ann came back into the dining room with a basket full of rolls. "We're going to get the kids set up then we'll bring everything in. In the meantime, here are some rolls so you don't starve to death."

As she put the rolls down, she noted that I'd moved.

I said, "I really want to sit next to my dad, if that's okay."

"Of course, it's all right. Sorry, if I got a little bossy."

"It's your house."

"It is. But I'm not a dictator."

And then she went back into the kitchen. Betsy immediately said, "When I was talking to Jeff David Stickney last night at his party—"

"You know that walking biohazard?" My dad asked.

"He's really very charming."

"He's more dangerous than climate change."

"That's a meaningless statement," Betsy said lightly. "Climate change isn't real."

"Ninety-seven percent of scientists believe it's happening right now, as we speak."

"Yes, but *thousands* don't," Betsy said smugly.

A large smile appeared on my dad's face. He was going in for the kill. I'd seen it happen before. "I knew you'd say that."

"Oh, are you psychic?"

"No, I just knew you'd repeat the propaganda you've heard. This is how that breaks down, there are roughly eight billion people in the world. Millions of them are scientists. Three percent of millions is thousands. You see, you simply repeated back what I'd said to you. It's just that when you say thousands it *sounds* like a big number. But it's not. It's a tiny number."

"Could you people please stop doing math," Betsy complained. "It's confusing me."

"Betsy," Cal said. "Didn't Mary Ann give you a list of topics to stick to?"

"Yes, of course, I haven't forgotten. In fact, I think one of the approved topics was the weather. Which we were just discussing."

Maria came through the door with two bowls: one

mashed potatoes the other sweet potatoes. Betsy asked, "Maria, do you know if Mary Ann is planning to serve wine?"

"She hasn't mentioned it. Did you want me to get a bottle of wine?"

"That's all right. Cal will get it." Then to Cal she said, "Something fruity." The way she said fruity was almost a slur. Did she know something?

Cal got up and went into the kitchen right behind Maria. Which left me with my dad and Betsy. I tried to think of a neutral subject. "Dad, Betsy is an avid bridge player. Have you ever played?"

He shook his head. "Isn't that a rich man's game."

"I cheat," Betsy said. "We play for money, so I cheat."

"And do you give your winnings to the poor? Are you the Robin Hood of bridge players?"

"Don't be ridiculous. Why would I give to the poor when I can buy myself a new purse?"

"And this is why trickle-down economics never works," my dad said.

"That's not true," Betsy said. "Somewhere in some random East Asian country a ten-year-old earned a dollar fifty and got to eat because I bought the two thousand dollar purse they made. Why do I never get credit for that?"

"A ten-year-old child should not be working in a sweatshop."

"Well, I certainly can't control the politics of third world countries. That's the CIA's job."

My dad was about to say something, but Mary Ann came back into the room carrying bowls, with her were Maria and Phillip. She apparently overheard the last of what was said.

"Mother, what were—"

"You can stop right there. I've been very good. While you're flitting about, we've discussed the weather, bridge and fashion. All topics on the list you gave me."

Mary Ann looked at her suspiciously. Cal came through the door with wine and began to pour it for people. Betsy said, "Thank God," as he poured hers.

As everyone settled into their seats, Maria asked, "Do you say grace?"

Mary Ann said, "No." Just as her mother said, "Of course."

"Mother, we never say grace."

"I think we should start."

"But you're not religious."

"I am so."

"I can't remember the last time you went to church."

"I don't go to church. I find that the more I think about God the less I believe in him. So, I don't think about him."

"Does your family say grace, Maria?"

"We do."

"Then why don't you go ahead."

We bowed our heads while Maria said a brief, inoffensive prayer over our meal. I watched Cal out of the corner of my eye. He was being quiet. And I guess I was too. He had a lot to think about, of course. I wondered if he'd ever loved Mary Ann. Had he known he was gay when he married her? What did that say about him that he'd do something like that now, in the twenty-first century? Did it make him a terrible person? Was he a terrible person? Or should I feel bad for him?

How much of it was really his fault? Closets were a construct of a heterosexual world. A world that wanted you to stay in that closet and pretend to be one of them. They didn't care if you actually were one of them, they just wanted you to pretend to be. Even with super liberal parents, I still felt that pressure from the world around us. I still felt the hatred from Christians, almost always dressed up as kindness. Coming from a religious family, it must have been particularly hard for Cal.

"You know, Betsy, you're a perfect example of a contemporary Christian," my father said after the amens.

"Thank you," she said.

"Oh God," I said under my breath.

"It's not a compliment, Mother," Mary Ann said. "Everyone pick up a dish, serve yourself and pass it around. Clockwise."

I grabbed the mashed potatoes, which were nearest to me, and served myself. Meanwhile, my father was saying, "'If you want to be perfect, sell your possessions and give to the poor, and you will have treasures in heaven.'"

"Oh my God," Betsy said. "What kind of liberal tripe is that?"

I passed the potatoes to Phillip and asked my father, "Dad, could you pass the cranberry sauce?"

He did as he was saying, "Those are the words of Jesus."

"Atheists get so hung up on what the Bible says. It's simple, my friends in Florida show their love of God by building gigantic churches and making sure their preacher has a private jet. I'm sure there's scripture which says that they should do that."

"What do you think, Phillip?" Mary Ann asked, attempting to be a good hostess.

"I think we're too busy working and taking care of our kids to worry much about all that."

"I think God just wants us to be kind," Maria said. "It's difficult sometimes, but it's really pretty simple."

Mary Ann turned to her mother and said, "See, you just have to be kind. Take the green bean casserole."

"I can't stand green beans," Betsy said.

"Then pass it along."

"We'll have a log jam if I do. Cal is dawdling with the dressing."

"I am not."

"Take the green beans and wait patiently."

Betsy did. While she was holding them, she said, "Last night, at his party, Jeff David Stickney was talking about how America is a Christian country and it's about time we amended the Constitution to say so."

"That would be a disaster," my dad said. "The different denominations would be at each other's throats in no time."

"You have no basis for that whatsoever," Betsy said.

"Four centuries of European history."

"Exactly. We're not European."

"All right, that's quite enough," Mary Ann said. Turning to Betsy she said, "Is Jeff David Stickney on your list?"

"No."

"Are constitutional amendments?"

"Mary Ann, you wrote the list. You know what's on it."

"How about European history?"

Betsy didn't answer.

"Stick to the list."

There was an awkward silence while we all ate. From the kitchen, the sound of the kids giggling and chattering drifted into the dining room.

Then Mary Ann said, "Maria the ham is wonderful."

"Thank you. You said you brined the turkey. What exactly is that?"

"You put the bird into a very large pot of salt water and soak it overnight."

"You're not being fair, Mary Ann," Betsy said.

"To the turkey?"

"To me."

"Your politics are unkind, Mother. And it's Christmas. The whole point is for us to be kind."

"But I don't think my politics are unkind. My most fundamental belief is that we shouldn't go around handing money to people. People should be allowed to pull themselves up by their bootstraps."

"Not everyone has bootstraps," my dad pointed out.

"Nonsense. everyone has bootstraps."

"What are bootstraps?" Maria asked.

"Something very old-fashioned," Mary Ann explained. "People don't have them anymore."

"And even if people did, it's actually physically impossible to pull yourself up by your bootstraps," I said.

"It's a metaphor," Betsy said. "Really, do you all have to be so literal?"

"We understand it's a metaphor," I said. "It's just that your metaphor means the opposite of what you want it to mean. If you think about it, what you're really saying is that it's impossible for people to lift themselves out of poverty."

My dad patted me on the shoulder and said, "That's my boy."

"This is so tiresome," Betsy said. "Why is it that the rich always have to help the poor? Can't someone else help them?"

"The rich are the ones with the money."

"Don't be ridiculous. The government has money."

"But, Mother, you don't want the government giving it to the poor."

"I don't want the government giving them *my* money... Why don't they just tax the poor, keep it in a separate account, and then give the money back to them."

"Well, that wouldn't help anyone, would it?"

"Yes, it would. I'm always happy to get a check in the mail no matter how small. I think everyone is."

"Would anyone mind if I change the subject?" Maria asked.

"Please do," Mary Ann said.

Maria turned to me and my father. "I don't mean to be

rude but, well, Phillip and I have been wondering, who are you? Are you a cousin? Or brother? Or?"

Mary Ann said, "He's our guest. Can we just leave it at that?"

"Oh, well, sure. Of course, we can."

"Gage is here by court order and I'm his dad," my father said. A very succinct explanation that explained almost nothing. He added, "A perfect example of government overreach."

Cal stepped in and explained. "I'm prosecuting Gage. He's admitted to burning down a Christmas tree—"

"Not just any Christmas tree," my dad said. "A Christmas tree mixing church and state in a particularly offensive way."

"Ah! I get it now," Maria said. "You're the Christmas tree guy. And the judge... Oh, my, we're in the middle of that?"

"Clearly, they should have eaten in the kitchen," Betsy said.

"The judge wants Gage to learn the meaning of Christmas," Cal said.

"Well, Mary Ann just said it. The point of Christmas is to be kind." To me she asked, "Did you not understand that already?"

"I understand kindness," I said. "I try to practice it every day, not just on Christmas."

"Idolatry," my father said. "That's what's wrong with the tree. Idolatry mixed with jingoism. And hypocrisy. And—"

"Dad, I'm the one who burned down the tree. I should probably be the one explaining it."

Without warning, my father stood up and said, "I can't stand it any longer. There's something I have to say."

I grabbed his sleeve and pulled him back into his chair. "No, there isn't."

"Yes, there is," he said, trying to get up again.

"No, there isn't."

"But I have to."

"No, you don't. Come with me." I pulled him out of the dining room, saying, "Excuse us."

I couldn't drag him into the kitchen, so I pulled him through the parlor to the foyer, but that wasn't good either, people could still hear us. I dragged my father into the TV room and shut the pocket door.

Twenty-Four

CALVIN

I WAS SUPPOSED to spend another night in bed with Gage. How was I going to do that? Of course, it wouldn't be in broad daylight, or in front of my house. That just left the things that ought to be told to Mary Ann to be told. Things which she already knew. Should I have her tell Gage that she knew I was gay? Could I have my wife give her approval?

That was a very interesting idea. If I wanted to have sex with him once. After his case ended, he was bound to find out I'd lied to him about who I really am. In which case, he'd probably hate me. He'd hate me more if we had sex. Not to mention having sex with the defendant was completely unethical. Not that very much of this holiday had been ethical.

"...can't do this, Dad, you really..."

"...keep taking care of me... have to take care of..."

"We can hear what they're saying," I said.

"It's an old, drafty house," Mary Ann said. "Why do you think we keep going into the laundry room and turning on the dryer?"

Betsy got up and stepped into the parlor where she could hear better.

"Mother, sit back down."

Then Nate's voice drifted through the house, "I'm the one who…"

"He's the one who burned down the tree!" Betsy said.

"I should be the one taking the blame."

"Oh, God," Betsy said. "This is better than anything I've seen on HBO in the last year."

We could hear Nate saying, "I should be the one explaining… what Christmas… believe me, I've got a few ideas on that score."

"We really shouldn't be listening," Mary Ann said. "Mother, sit back down and let's have a conversation."

"Now you want me to talk? You've been trying to shut me up all night."

To provoke her mother, Mary Ann said, "I think immigrants should have all the same opportunities our families had. I mean, we're all immigrants after all."

Betsy turned and walked back over to the table. "I am *not* an immigrant. My family has always been in this country."

"Really? I didn't know we were First Peoples," Mary Ann said.

"You mean Indian? Of course, we're not."

Gage's voice, saying "You wouldn't do well in prison, Dad," wafted through the dining room.

"They were here first, Mother. That's why they're called First Peoples.

"Oh please, they were here, big deal. The country wasn't here. My ancestors came on the boat right after the Mayflower. They were given land grants by the British Crown."

"For land that didn't belong to them."

"I'm sure they did an extensive title search."

"That's ridiculous," I said, trying to drown out the argument in the other room. "The indigenous people didn't have written language, so they would not have had documents."

"Good. You see the problem. Trust me, I've owned many properties in my life and the amount of paperwork, not to mention, does anyone really own anything without a notary public?"

"You do understand that they were already living here when the colonists arrived."

"I do. And without a shred of documentation. That's called squatting."

We all heard the pocket door slide open. Gage and Nate came back to the table. "Sorry about that," Gage said. "What did we miss?"

"Indians," Betsy said. "We're talking about Indians.

"Terrible what we did to those poor people," Nate said.

"I was just about to tell Mary Ann that scads of our ancestors were killed by Indians."

"I'm sure we killed them as well," Mary Ann said.

"Yes, of course, but that's not the point."

"What is the point?"

"Your ancestors were scalped."

"So."

"Ugh."

At that point I got up and grabbed Gage by the arm. "Come with me."

I dragged him through the kitchen and into the laundry room. I turned on the dryer.

"Why are we in here?"

"This is the only room in the house where people can't hear what you say."

"Really? Wait. What? No."

"I heard your father confess. Well, Betsy heard and relayed the information."

"Oh God. He didn't mean—he *wishes* he burnt the tree down. That's all."

"You lied. To protect your father."

"I feel like it's a good time to remind you that you signed a legal document that says you can't use anything I say against me in court."

"Technically, I wouldn't be using it against you."

"You can't."

"I didn't say I would, but I could. This is why there's no physical evidence against you, isn't it?"

"There's no physical evidence against my dad, either."

"Because you've had plenty of time to destroy it."

"No comment."

"You almost went to prison. You could *still* go to prison."

"I've been paying attention so I'm very aware of that."

"This changes everything, you know."

"It does? Why? Why can't you just leave it alone."

"I can't prosecute you."

"Even if I want you to?"

"I'm going to have to think about this," I said, then walked out of the laundry room.

When I got back to the dining room, Nate was saying, "The way you know what conservatives are up to is to look at what they're accusing liberals of, it's usually exactly what they're doing. If they're attempting to destroy democracy, they accuse the liberals of trying to do it."

"Oh my God," Betsy said. "I was going to say the exact same thing. Except in reverse. Liberals do what you're talking about all the time. Jeff David Stickney was talking about it last night.

Nate, "That's my point. Stickney is telling you that's what liberals do. But that's what conservatives do. He's trying to hide their bad deeds in plain sight.

"Or, that's what liberals do and he's just caught on."

"Well, I guess we have a chicken and egg situation. Which came first, the conservative asshole or the conservative asshole's lie."

"That's really quite rude."

The doorbell rang. Mary Ann stood up, "I'll get it. Can someone think of a topic they won't fight about while I'm gone?"

She walked out of the dining room.

"Baby formula," Maria said quickly.

"Baby formula should be provided free to any mother who needs it," Nate said.

"That's a foolish idea," Betsy said. "Women will start having babies just to get more baby formula."

"I don't think—" Maria said.

"Mother's milk is free. Baby formula should be too."

"That's the point. Women will nurse their babies but take the baby formula anyway. Before you know it there will be an entire black market."

"Go away! Just go away!" Mary Ann was yelling. I got up and ran to the front door. When I got there, I saw Mary Ann standing just outside the door. Douglas was on the steps to the porch. "Leave Douglas, leave now."

Everyone was standing just behind me. In my ear, Gage whispered, "Who's that?"

"My wife's husband."

"Wait. Your wife—You're not married to Mary Ann, are you?"

"She's my best friend."

"So, you really are gay?"

"Very."

I glanced back into his face. It was rock hard.

Douglas was saying, "I was in Aruba and suddenly I thought, 'What am I doing here with this girl? This isn't who I am.'"

"She broke up with you, didn't she?" Mary Ann guessed.

"No, no, no... I let her think that's what was happening. It seemed kinder."

"Wow. I guess that makes you a hero."

A look of doubt passed over his attractive face. "Why is it important who broke up with who? We broke up. And I want to come home."

"You've been here thirty seconds and you've told at least two lies. That's why it's important. Not to mention, I don't want to be second place. And this feels like second place."

"Mary Ann, we can work this out."

"No, we can't. Do you want to see your children? Technically, it's still your holiday with them. I could pack a couple of overnight bags and you could take them home with you."

"I'm not really in a great place. Emotionally."

"Okay, why don't you come in and wish them a Merry Christmas and then go."

"I can't even get a cup of coffee and a piece of your famous apple pie?"

"You have five minutes. Take it or leave it."

"Mary Ann, be reasonable."

"Douglas, I've known you for fourteen years. 'Mary Ann be reasonable' means 'do it my way,' and that's never going to happen again. Five minutes."

Shoulders slumped, wearing a hangdog expression, Douglas pushed by us to get into the house. I felt like I should go support Mary Ann, but Gage grabbed me and pulled me into the TV room.

"Explain all this."

"Okay," I said, keeping my voice low. "Remember that we can be heard in here."

He folded his arms and glared at me. "I don't care."

After a very deep breath, I said, "It's simple really. Judge Winthrop. You have to play his game or you don't win in his courtroom."

"So, you're a closet case."

"I really don't like that phrase. I prefer professionally discreet."

"What about giant asshole? That's a good description."

"That's a little harsh. Doesn't everyone deserve to come out in their own time?"

"Yes, children who are at risk, young people with emotional issues, people in danger of losing housing or jobs or important relationships... but lawyers who want to get ahead in the world? Not so much."

"Um, once again. People can hear us."

"Okay, let me make sure I understand this. You're a gay guy pretending to be a straight guy who's secretly a gay guy."

"That wasn't the plan, exactly. You were just very good at figuring out that Mary Ann and I weren't a loving couple. I had to do something."

"Because the truth was entirely out of the question."

"I've known you for approximately two whole days. And don't take this the wrong way, but until twenty minutes ago I thought you were a criminal. Criminals are not the most trustworthy people in the world."

"Did your parents even throw you out? Or did you make that up too?"

"They threw me out. Because I'm gay."

"I'm sorry about that. But it doesn't give you a pass. You don't get to lie to people because you've been treated badly."

"I know that. And I do know right from wrong. I just... I want to succeed. I want to find my place in the world."

"Yeah, you know what... you need to stop changing yourself to fit the world and start changing the world to fit you."

Twenty-Five

GAGE

NORTHSTAR OCCUPIES A SMALL, brick, one-story, flat-roofed building with a large parking lot. It was the kind of building that looked decent if there were half a dozen in a row. Alone it looked, well, orphaned. It did have a nice big parking lot, though. The day after Christmas I called Neo and asked if they thought it was safe to open.

"I drove by earlier and it was pretty quiet," they said.

"I think I'll chance it."

"Great. I'll meet you there."

I opened the doors two hours later than normal, but that didn't seem to bother anyone. There were three kids waiting when we got there: Debra, Stephen and Ralph. Stephen was deep into his phone watching videos even though Ralph was right there. I wondered if they'd slipped back into the off phase of their on again/off again relationship.

"How was everyone's Christmas?" I asked.

That earned me a couple of shrugs and a pair of rolled eyes.

"That good, huh?"

"How was *your* Christmas?" Stephen asked. "That's the more interesting question, don't you think?"

"It had its moments, but overall, it kind of sucked."

I really didn't want to go into it. Didn't want to explain that I'd been caught in my lie about burning down the tree. And I certainly didn't want to talk about Cal's being a closet case. The kids weren't supposed to be there for me, I was supposed to be there for them.

"Come on guys, we're here so you talk about things. If you had a rough Christmas you should talk about it."

Just then, Neo walked through the door. Without even a greeting, they grabbed me and pulled me into the office. "So, he's gay, right?"

"How do you—"

"You were there twenty-four hours after I left. I was pretty sure you'd find out."

"He tried to kiss me."

They gasped. "Ha! The bastard."

"But that's not the worst of it."

"I should hope not."

"He's not married to Mary Ann. And those aren't his kids."

"Oh. Well, that's unexpected. Did you bone him?"

I shook my head. "He's a closet case. He pretends to be a married man to win his cases."

Neo considered that. "He'd lose if the judges knew he was gay?"

"Probably."

"Then good for him."

"Neo. That's not going to help anyone."

"It's going to help put bad guys in jail. Present company excepted."

"You're not helping."

"Am I supposed to be?"

"Yeah, if you're my friend."

"Naw, friends tell the truth. I don't think it's such a big deal. I mean, people get to be in the closet if they think they've got a good reason. And, you know, it sounds like he had a good reason."

"At thirty-four or thirty-five, or however old he is? You really think it's okay?"

"People come out in their seventies."

"It's just—"

"You know, being in the closet isn't the same as lying. I mean, yeah, a lot more people are out these days, but that doesn't mean the pressure isn't still there to hide. Particularly for people from religious families. Is he from a religious family?"

"Um, yeah, he said he was."

"It's hard to shake that. In fact, I'm not sure it ever goes away."

None of that mattered, I told myself. Cal was exactly the kind of gay guy I'd have nothing to do with if I met him tomorrow. He was basically an assimilationist. He prided himself on being just like your average heterosexual with the exceptions of what dating apps he was on and what kind of porn he watched. I was sure that he dreamed of having a three-bedroom, suburban home and 2.5 children to share with his gorgeously vanilla husband. I mean, what was the point of being gay if you were just going to be some alt version of a straight guy?

But was that all there was to him? No, the thing with his parents sounded real. I didn't want to be thinking about this. I was at work, and I should be thinking about that. I tried flipping the script on Neo.

"So how are things with Imogene?"

"You know the thing I love about bad relationships?"

"What?"

"When they last less than twenty-four hours."

"You processed that fast."

Stephen stuck his head into the office. "I found a video online you should probably watch." *Oh God,* I thought. Stephen was always doing this. Giggling maniacally, he'd shown me videos of condoms being put on bananas, rugby players with their pants down, and straight porn.

"I'm not up for this right now, Stephen."

"I think you will be," he said, as he held up his phone so I could see the video he was playing. It was taken in Drip, and it only took me a second to recognize the woman who berated Cal. She was saying, "What you're doing with these children is disgusting. And on Christmas eve, too. You should be ashamed. Groomer."

"Could you turn the sound down. I don't want to listen to that again."

"I can turn it off, if you don't want to see it."

"I want to see it; I just don't want to listen to it."

"Okay. Weird. But fine." He turned off the sound and then ran the video back to the beginning. I took the phone from him and held it in front of me. As it played, I watched Cal's face. As the woman yelled at him, he looked terrorized. I'd noticed it when it happened, but it seemed to me then that it was the look of a straight man who'd never dealt with anything like that. But now, now I saw all the trauma he'd suffered growing up with religious parents who didn't approve of him. All the trauma of living on his own as a teenager.

I'd been lucky. Even with the craziness of my dad's paranoia, I never felt unsafe as a child. I never felt that either of my parents were a danger to me. But I knew the kids I dealt with had to face that, and now, looking at Cal in the video, I saw that he'd faced it too. And had never fully gotten over it.

He didn't need my anger. He didn't need me to hate him. He needed to be forgiven, taken care of, helped. People had been spending a lot of time telling me I needed to take care of myself. But isn't the best way to take care of yourself to care for those around you? Isn't taking care of each other the whole point?

I stopped watching the video and gave it back to Stephen. "Thank you."

Okay, I'm not a saint. I didn't run out of there to go find Cal and say, "Hey dude, it's all okay." I knew I had to think this through. Settle with it. Make sure I really was okay with it.

That didn't mean anything was going to happen between us. At some point tomorrow, after court, I needed to let him know I didn't hate him. And that was it. We could go our separate ways and never think about this Christmas again.

"We have a lot of work to do," Neo said.

"What do you mean?"

"We have about ten thousand emails to look at and two bags of snail mail, not to mention the donations. We really should send thank-you emails. Could you write one up?"

Our website had a donate button on it. I knew that we'd been getting donations, but I hadn't checked since the twenty-third and I certainly hadn't had time to send out thank-you emails. We could have set up an automatic thank you on our website, but we hadn't been getting a lot of donations. It seemed nicer to send personalized thank you's. Obviously, that was a goof.

"Thanks, Neo."

We spent the rest of the day opening emails and putting them into folders depending on what kind of answer they required. Obviously, the website donations required an email. When we agreed on a basic response, I set Neo to thanking them.

That left me with the ten thousand emails and the snail

mail. I decided to break the emails up by date. My goal was to get through emails from the 21st and 22nd. I created three folders: positive, negative, further thought.

After about two hours, I'd gotten through more than a hundred negative emails—which ranged from garden variety slurs to outright threats of violence. Some of them, a lot of them, should be reported to the—well, not our local sheriff, probably the FBI. Or maybe the state police. I would have to ask Lonny about that.

I had nearly an equal number of positive emails, some of which offered me money for my legal defense—hopefully, I'd be saying thanks not necessary in about twenty-four hours, otherwise I'd have to set up a GoFundMe account or something—while others tried to get romantic with me. I got at least twenty dick pics.

There wasn't time to get to the snail mail, although another smaller bag of it arrived that afternoon. I suppose I could have asked the kids to get involved, but some of the emails had been hard to read and I didn't want to be responsible for exposing the kids to that kind of hatred, whether it came digitally or on paper.

About an hour before it was time to call it a day, my dad called.

"I'm not going to be in court tomorrow," he said.

"Yes, I know how you are about government buildings."

"Have you decided what you're going to say to the judge?

"I'm going to say what I want to say. I don't think it matters one way or the other. This judge wants to fry me, and I don't think anyone's going to stop him."

"I'm not so sure about that. Cal seemed like a decent guy."

"I don't know where you get that. He's just a closet case driven by blind ambition." And that would be why I hadn't rushed out to forgive him. I still had resentment bubbling up.

"I guess you'll find out if that's true tomorrow. Meanwhile, I'll be taking off for a while. I'm thinking I might head South."

"Not Florida," I said. He couldn't be thinking of hooking up with Betsy. That would be—

"Possibly Florida. They could use a few extra liberals there to help tip the balance."

"Dad. That's a really, really bad idea."

"I know. But it's the best bad idea I've had in a long time."

Twenty-Six

CALVIN

AFTER GAGE LEFT, I had a little too much to drink and ended up spending another night at Mary Ann's. She insisted. Which made me a little teary and I said, "You like me, you really, really like me."

Even her response, "I like you better silent," didn't dampen the warmth in my belly. All right, it might have been all the wine I drank. But really, deep down, Mary Ann was a great friend, and she deserved better than me.

It was after nine the next morning when I stumbled into the kitchen. Mary Ann sat in the breakfast nook enjoying a cup of coffee. I grabbed a cup, sat down across from her and asked, "What are you doing?"

"Enjoying the quiet."

"Where are the kids?"

"Douglas took them out for breakfast. Gus has a play date this afternoon with Phil and Maria's boy, Max. And Piper is texting back and forth with one of the older two, I don't remember which. Maybe both."

"That's great," I said. "You wanted them to find friends."

"It is great. I'm happy about it." She watched me for a moment then asked, "What are you going to do about Gage?"

"What do you mean? I don't think there's anything to do."

"You can't prosecute him. He didn't do it."

"He confessed; I think he wants to be prosecuted."

"I doubt that. He was just protecting his dad."

"Or at least that's what he wants us to think."

"Oh Cal, he's a decent guy. You couldn't see that in the last few days?"

"I can't think that way. I have to put that aside. Here are the possibilities. Number one, he did it and they wanted us to hear his dad confess so that I'd drop the charges. Number two, he didn't do it, and they didn't know they could be heard, and his father legitimately confessed. Number three, they did it together and this is their way of getting away with it."

Mary Ann frowned at me. "You listened to his dad. His dad is exactly the kind of person who'd burn down a Christmas tree because of its ridiculously patriotic ornaments, and Gage is exactly the kind of person who'd take the blame."

"Two days. You can fake who you are for two days."

She opened her mouth to speak but stopped. I'm sure it was something to do with my faking who I was for two days, but then she'd done that too.

After a moment, she said, "He didn't know he was coming here until four days before Christmas. Gage was all set to take the deal. There's no reason for him to concoct some grand plan."

"Okay, you have a point. I'll accept that one. If they're trying to put one over on us, they'd have to have put it together Christmas morning after your mother said the judge was out to get Gage."

"Oh my God. Cal, stop thinking like a lawyer and think like a gay man."

"I don't know what you mean by that."

"No, you don't. And that's a problem."

"Are you saying I should let Gage off because he's cute?"

"I'm saying you should go see him and apologize."

"Apologize? For what—okay I know for what. But he lied to me, too."

"He lied to protect his dad. You lied to protect yourself."

"I lied to win a case, it's not the same."

"Yeah, if you were lying to put a rapist behind bars, I'd be all for it. But that's not what you did."

Betsy floated into the room. "I had the loveliest dreams last night. Holidays are so cathartic." She poured herself a cup of coffee and slid into the breakfast nook beside Mary Ann.

She studied her daughter carefully until Mary Ann asked, "What?"

"You can't really let Douglas get away?"

"I think I'm fine with that."

"You'll be hard pressed to find another like him."

"That's a good thing. I don't want another man like Douglas."

"Well, what *are* you going to do?"

"Actually, I think I'm going to take the bar."

"What?"

"I should have done it a long time ago."

"You're going to practice?" I asked.

"Divorcing Douglas has made me realize something."

"That he's an asshole," I suggested.

"Kettle, black," Betsy said to me.

"Well, that, yes," Mary Ann said. "But also, that I have it pretty easy. A lot of women struggle through a divorce. They don't know how they'll take care of themselves no less their kids. I'd like to help them."

"Really, Mary Ann, a do-gooder?" Betsy said. "I tried to teach you better than that."

"Don't worry, Mother. I'll take on some big juicy rich people divorces, just so I can pay for the others."

"Promise? Oh! You know the Martinson girl's marriage is on the rocks. If you hurry up and take the bar, I can talk to her mother about you handling her divorce. And then there are the Smiths. Married forty years, thirty-nine of them a living hell. If I gave Jeanine just the tiniest push, I think she'd show up in your office. Oh, you need an office. Do I still own that building on Lakeshore and Keswick?"

"Yes, Mother, you do."

"Oh good. If I'm remembering correctly there's an office on the third floor, lovely view."

"It's probably rented."

"Don't worry, dear, I'll throw them out."

"No. You won't. We'll talk about this later. After I've passed the bar.

"Well, if you insist," Betsy said, before standing up. "I have to go buy a burner phone."

"You what?"

"Nate said he wants to call and ask me out. He doesn't want to use my regular phone because... you never know who's listening." She mouthed the words, "Deep state."

"I really don't think the deep state wants to listen to the two of you scheduling a sex date," Mary Ann said.

"Mary Ann, I'm your mother. You know I demand dinner first."

"Don't try to tell me you want to get to know him?"

Betsy shrugged. "It is true, he'd be more interesting with a sock in his mouth. But you could say that about most men."

"Please, just pretend I'm not here," I said, sarcastically.

"Always, dear," Betsy said to me. Then, "Well, I'm off. I'll be back later and then it's home to Florida tomorrow evening. There's a New Year's Eve party at a certain resort that I'm thinking of attending."

I'm sure she wanted us to ask for more information on that, but we didn't. When I heard the front door close, I said to Mary Ann, "It must have been difficult being raised by Betsy Hinchmen-Jones."

"You have no idea."

"Now I see why you're such a good mother."

"I'm not following."

"It's the best way to get revenge on her."

"She really doesn't notice."

"But you do."

"That's a very sweet thing to say. Don't be sweet until New Years. I'm not sure I'll be able to forgive you before then."

A bit later, I went upstairs to pack up my things to go home. Packing only takes a minute or two, my habit of folding everything as soon as I take it off comes in handy. I was just about to go back downstairs and say goodbye when my phone rang. It was Danny.

I should have begun the conversation with the information I'd found out about prednisone, but something told me he was about to step in for the kill.

"Listen Danny, the Hammond case is going away tomorrow, so I'm all clear for the Van Husen trial."

"About that... I think it's best if I take over." And there it was. Exactly what I thought he'd do.

"And why is that?" I said, grinding my teeth.

"I just feel like it's the right thing to do. If you could write up your thoughts on the case, any ideas you have for strategy, any additional information you've dug up."

"No. I won't have time to do that. Since you're taking over the Van Husen case, I'm going to put in for vacation. I have almost four weeks accrued. I'm going to take them now."

"You can't do that."

"I'm afraid I can."

"You have to give me the work you've done on the Van Husen case."

"That was the plan all along, wasn't it? You wanted me to do all the work and then you'd take the glory. Well screw you, Danny. I'm going on vacation and I'm not giving you my strategy notes."

"Strategy? There's more, isn't there? What is it? You have to tell me."

"It's right there in discovery."

"I don't have time to go through fourteen boxes."

"You would have if you hadn't gone skiing with your family."

"You have to tell me what you found."

"I'll tell you all about it when I come back from vacation."

"The trial will be over by then."

"Well, that's unfortunate, isn't it?"

I clicked off. I stood there a moment. There was another call I'd been thinking about making. It was time to make it.

Twenty-Seven

GAGE

JUDGE WINTHROP'S court looked decidedly different. The Christmas decorations were gone, though there were traces of them left on the walls. It looked as though someone had pulled them down in a hurry. There were already people there when I walked in. Mary Ann and her kids. Betsy. Jeff David Stickney. Phillip and his family. Neo and several kids from NorthStar. There were also a couple of people I didn't know, in particular a severe-looking woman sitting just behind Cal. She had a note pad on her lap and a pencil in hand.

Cal. I tried not to look at him but failed. He looked sad, but also determined. I had no idea what he might do. I pulled my eyes away and sat down next to Lonny.

"How were your days off?" I asked.

He shrugged and said, "Days off. Did you get the statement I emailed you?"

"I did, thank you."

"Are you going to read it?"

"I know what I want to say."

"That's not an answer. Gage—"

"Who's the woman sitting behind Cal?"

"Her name is Miss Robb. She's from Judicial Tenure Review. Someone filed a complaint."

"You didn't?"

"No. I couldn't decide if it would be good or bad for you."

"Who do you think complained?"

"Given the publicity the case has gotten it could have been anyone. Usually, you need to have been before a judge to complain, but this is a unique situation."

Abruptly, the bailiff said, "Court is in session. Honorable Judge Dudley Winthrop presiding."

The judge entered the courtroom and sat behind the bench. He glanced around the room, noting the disappearance of the decorations. From the look on his face, he hadn't been expecting that. A lot of people left their decorations up until New Year's.

"Bailiff, could you approach?"

They spoke too softly for the rest of us to hear. At one point, the judge looked up and picked out Miss Robb behind Cal. He frowned deeply. His eyes darted around for a moment like a trapped rat. Then he said, "Good morning. I hope you all had a... Happy Holiday." He looked like he might choke on the phrase, "Happy Holiday."

Then he put on his glasses so he could see who was in the gallery. He perked up and gave them what passed as a smile.

"I see we have some familiar faces in the gallery. Jeff David. Betsy Hinchmen-Jones. Lovely to see you here."

Miss Robb began to take notes on her pad. The judge noticed and frowned for a moment.

"And Mary Ann Cutler, with your children."

Cal stood up. "Your honor, there's something important I need to tell you. Mary Ann's last name is not Cutler."

"I understand. Women today are like that. Disrespectful if you ask me."

"No, sir. She doesn't use my name because we're not married. We've never been married. She's my friend, my very, very good friend. And the kids, as much as I love them, they're not mine either."

"But I was in your home on Christmas Eve. Your lovely home."

"Mary Ann's lovely home."

"You lied to me. You all lied to me. Why would you do something like that?"

It took Cal a moment to work up this final bit of courage. "I'm gay your honor."

"Oh. I guess that explains it. Complete lack of morals, anti-Christian, anti-American, and a lying liar to boot. I hope this situation amuses you."

"Your Honor, I only lied to you because you're a well-known homophobe and I didn't want you ruling against the state for that reason."

"I'm *not* a homophobe. I'm not afraid of homosexuals. I just don't like them.

"That would be my point," Cal said.

"Well, your point has been made. Sit down."

"I have more—"

"No, you don't. Sit down."

The courtroom was completely quiet but for the sound of Miss Robb's pencil on her pad.

"So, Mr. Hammond. The meaning of Christmas. What did you learn spending the holiday with Mr. Cutler and his, well someone's family?"

"I learned that Christmas is about kindness."

"And...?"

"Why does there have to be more to it than that?"

"I'd say there's a lot more to it. God for one. Christ for another. And America. A country full of the world's best

Christians. You should have learned about that. Though I can certainly see why you didn't."

"I don't think you understand me, your honor."

"I beg your pardon."

"When I say kindness, I don't mean be kind to your friends and family and people like you. I mean be kind to all people, be kind to strangers, to people you'll never meet, be kind to the poor, the troubled, the people others reject. And be kind with how you vote. Don't vote for people who inflame hatred to get themselves elected."

The judge was glaring at me angrily. He seemed to calm himself. Then put on a deliberative face—though honestly, I doubt that he actually deliberated. Then he said, "It's not enough. I'm afraid we're going to have to hold you over for trial."

"Your Honor," Cal said.

"I thought I told you to sit down and shut up?"

"As the assistant district attorney, I think I'm allowed to speak."

"Very well, what is it? And by the way, I'm voting against your boss in the next election."

"I'm sure he expects nothing less. In the meantime, the state is dropping all charges against Mr. Hammond."

"On what grounds?

"On the grounds that he didn't do it."

"But he confessed."

"Yes, but I personally overheard someone else confess to burning down the tree."

I stood up and said, "Your Honor, I did it. And I'm prepared to go to trial."

"Sit down and shut up," Lonny hissed.

Cal looked at me and said, "Too late. The charges are dropped."

"If Mr. Hammond confessed to a crime he didn't commit,

that would be obstruction of justice. Bailiff, take Mr. Hammond into custody."

"Your Honor, what I heard is hearsay and therefore inadmissible. And Mr. Hammond has not recanted his confession, so we can't prosecute him for obstruction of justice."

"But you can prosecute him for arson."

"Except we know he didn't do it."

"Well, you have to prosecute him for something."

"Why?"

"Because that's what we do here!"

The judge noticed Miss Robb making extensive notes again. "I mean, obviously a courtroom is also a place for... mercy. Now and then."

Then Jeff David Stickney stood up in the gallery. "Am I understanding this correctly? Are you saying no one is going to be prosecuted for this vile act of anti-Christian terrorism? This treasonous attack on the very core of our nation?"

"Oh, for heavens' sake Jeff David, it was a damn Christmas tree," the judge said, close to the breaking point.

"Your Honor," Cal said. "Mr. Stickney has raised substantial amounts of money and received an invaluable amount of publicity from this event—"

Piper stood up, and reading from her smartphone said, "Two-hundred-thirty-five thousand six-hundred and fifty-five dollars."

"Thank you, Piper," Cal said. "Your honor, Mr. Stickney has the option of pursuing this matter in civil court, though since he has to show that he's been damaged he may not get far."

Then Piper said, "There's a conspiracy theory on Reddit that Jeff David Stickney burned the tree down himself to get the publicity."

"That's completely not true!" Stickney whined.

"You did do a show about conspiracy theories, Jeff David. You said they were always true," the judge pointed out.

"I meant conspiracy theories about libtards. Not about me!"

Cal said, "Your Honor, we have no reason to believe that Mr. Stickney burned down his own tree. Though if you feel there's a need for us to investigate..."

"All right! Enough! This is dismissed. Thrown out. Vacated. Get out of my courtroom! All of you! Now!"

Before anyone could leave the courtroom, the judge ran out of it himself. The bailiff hastily stepped forward and said, "Court is adjourned."

I looked at Lonny. "Is that it? I'm free."

"Charges have been dropped. You're free."

Turning, I found people gathering behind me. Neo and the kids mostly, but then Mary Ann broke through saying, "I'm glad you're not going to jail. And I never got to say this, but we enjoyed having you in our home for the holiday. We hope you'll consider coming next year."

"Really? Wow. I mean, I guess we'll have to see." I didn't want to say it, but I'd probably go back to having a misfits dinner. I'd missed that part of my holiday this year.

"The offer is always there."

"Thank you."

Betsy stepped forward, saying "I want to give you a little Christmas gift."

"Um, okay." I mean, it was pretty weird, right?

She took a folded piece of paper out of her purse and pressed it into my hand. I opened it and saw it was a check for five thousand dollars made out to NorthStar.

"I don't understand. I *really* don't understand."

"It's for your little group."

"You liked what I said?"

"Goodness no. You really don't understand the way the

world works, do you? People like me need people like you. Without you I have nothing to talk about at parties."

She patted me on the shoulder like I was some kind of mental patient. Was she serious? And then she winked at me. Which didn't help at all. All I knew for certain was that she was a very strange lady who'd just done something very kind in the rudest way possible.

I glanced over to the prosecution table. Cal was already gone. Looking around the courtroom, he wasn't anywhere to be seen. Miss Robb was gone too. He must have been the one to call her. I accepted hugs from Neo and the kids. Said a quick thank you to Lonny. And finally walked out of the courtroom.

CALVIN

WHEN I GOT to the lobby outside the courtroom, I noticed two things very quickly. First, Jeff David Stickney was speaking to a reporter. A single reporter. One. Christmas was over and the media interest with it. That was a relief.

The other thing I noticed was my boss, Danny Shepard, having a few words with Miss Robb. He was a tall, wolfish man, and if I hadn't known he had fits of ethical behavior I might have been worried for her. They finished their conversation and Danny walked over to me.

"I thought I saw you in the gallery," I said.

"Well, you promised it would be over today, and you were right. Good job."

"Good enough to get the Van Husen trial back?"

Danny just smiled at me. "I've decided not to run next year. I have the feeling there's a judgeship opening up. If you win the Van Husen case, you ought to think of running."

"*If* I win the Van Husen case? Oh, I'm going to win."

"Then I guess you'll be running for DA"

Then Mary Ann and the kids were in front of me, she was saying, "Good job in there. I'm proud of you."

"Thank you."

"Come for dinner on New Year's."

"Are you sure? You're forgiving me?"

"We need to talk bar exam. I said I was going to take it, so now I have to."

"You'll do great."

"I know I will. You'll be studying with me twice a week for the next few months."

I opened my mouth to object, but instead said, "I will indeed." I mean, I did owe her, didn't I? Mary Ann noticed Gage coming out of the courtroom.

"Go talk to him," she said.

"I don't know."

"Yes, you do."

I took a deep breath and walked over to him. "Hi."

"Hi," he said back to me. "You didn't have to do that."

"Actually, I did. I know you're innocent. I don't prosecute people when I know they're innocent. It takes all the fun out of the job."

"Are you really not going to prosecute my dad?"

"The confession I overheard was not admissible. And there is no other evidence. As long as no one finds any evidence, my hands are tied. Not to mention he's probably already left the area, hasn't he?"

Gage shrugged, unwilling to commit either way.

"So, if I hadn't confessed?" he asked.

"We probably wouldn't have met. And that would have been an injustice."

"Or at least very disappointing."

I glanced around, the crowd was thinning out. To our right was the exit to the parking lot. To our left a short hallway with half a dozen doors. Having worked there for years, I knew what was behind each door.

"Come on," I said to Gage. I hurried down the hall. He

kept up with me. When I reached a particular door, I opened it, stepped inside and pulled him in with me. It was a utility room. I pushed him against the door and pressed myself to him.

"Feel familiar?" I asked.

"Very. Except this time I think it's deliberate."

"Very deliberate."

He looked deep into my eyes which somehow made all the breath leave my body. And then I kissed him.

IN THE DOM REILLY SERIES

Year of the Rat

A Mean Season

The Happy Month

A Week Away

IN THE WYANDOT COUNTY SERIES

The Less Than Spectacular Times of Henry Milch

A Fabulously Unfabulous Summer for Henry Milch

The Fall and Rise of Henry Milch

A Winter of Discontent for Henry Milch

OTHER BOOKS

The Perils of Praline

Desert Run

Full Release

The Ghost Slept Over

My Favorite Uncle

Femme

Praline Goes to Washington

Aunt Belle's Time Travel & Collectibles

Masc

Never Rest

Code Name: Liberty

Fathers of the Bride

Sentenced to Christmas

Marshall Thornton writes several popular mystery series, most notably the *Boystown Mysteries* and the *Pinx Video Mysteries*. He has won the Lambda Award for Gay Mystery three times. His books *Femme* and *Code Name Liberty* were Lambda finalists for Best Gay Romance. Other books include *My Favorite Uncle*, *The Ghost Slept Over* and *Fathers of the Bride.* He holds an MFA in Screenwriting from UCLA.

www.ingramcontent.com/pod-product-compliance
Lightning Source LLC
Chambersburg PA
CBHW022126310726
48972CB00007B/2215